From the Other Side

by

Julia Harrison

Cover Art by *Lisa Dawn MacDonald*

The Wild Rose Press, Inc.
PO Box 708
Adams Basin, NY 14410-0708
Visit us at www.thewildrosepress.com

Publishing History
First Edition, 2025
Trade Paperback ISBN 978-1-5092-6256-4
Digital ISBN 978-1-5092-6257-1

Published in the United States of America

Dedication

For Simon

Chapter 1

The microwave would not work. It had power, the numbers on the display were illuminated, but the dot refused to blink. I stabbed at the buttons, opened and closed the door, but 5:27 continued to stare back at me, the same number reflected on the oven beneath.

I staggered over to the sink, fumbled with the faucet, and shakily filled a glass with water. I was experiencing the world's worst hangover, yet I had no recollection of drinking. I had no recollection of anything. A thick hazy fog filled the space between my ears. The appliances weren't the only things not working.

I took a breath and willed my brain to engage. I needed to concentrate, but something pulled at my attention. A constant hum sat just in the background, low enough not to cause immediate alarm but loud enough to distract and irritate me. A hum that changed in speed and pitch, a hum that metamorphosized the more I focused on it, that shifted from just noise to voices, specifically a low murmur of voices. I scanned the kitchen quickly, fear-induced adrenaline snatching me out of my disassociated stupor.

No one was there, and everything stood still.

The house felt empty and, aside from the murmuring voices, eerily silent.

I clutched at the sink as a wave of nausea made the room sway. As I looked out of the window, my eyes stung as I attempted to adjust. I scanned the front yard trying to piece together the fragmented shards of my memory. There were many things missing, voices and people and household noises. Strands of inexplicable threads danced around me; I needed my most recent recollections to tie them together. I massaged my temples. The voices murmured, pulling my attention from where it needed to be.

As I stood and stared out of the window, something across the street caught my eye. I shuffled from the kitchen, every muscle and bone aching like I'd run a marathon. I had to pull strenuously to open the front door before I stumbled outside. Although my limbs remained heavy, I quickened my steps as I reached the sidewalk, the voices becoming louder with each step I took.

I looked across the street. The glint of a single tiny stud earring sat partially obscured by pieces of gravel that lined the opposite side of the road. I stepped tentatively closer, crossed the quiet street, and crouched down to inspect the small crystal embedded in its silver claw. It reflected a multitude of prisms, far brighter than they should have been. I turned my head slowly toward the house. How could I have seen something so tiny from so far away?

I blinked.

The shrill alarm of panic rattled my delicate brain. Something was very wrong with this picture. My eyes were not working the way they should. I rose slowly to my feet and turned my head to the side. Two figures stood at the end of the street. No, that wasn't right. Hastily I blinked again. They were still there at the end of the street! There had to be at least three hundred feet between where I stood and where they stood, yet I saw them as clearly as if they were standing right before me.

Dumbfounded, I looked down at my feet, then round at my house, like there was a possibility I'd somehow used astral projection to travel unaware to the end of the street.

*Wait, what the…*Rooted to the spot, I scanned slowly from one side to the other, my brain scrambling to make sense of what I saw. Everything was different. Subtle at first, but the longer I stared at something, the more I saw. I was surrounded by colors that were vibrant—not just vivid but a multifaceted network of shades. The petals on the violas that dotted the edge of the neighbor's driveway were an intricate blend of lilac and blue hues, their leaves consisting of three shades of green woven tightly and covered in fine white hairs. The gentle thud of beating wings shifted my attention upward as a swallow swooped down from the high branches of the backyard cedar tree, its tall limbs visible above the single-level garage. The dense clusters of evergreen foliage trembled at its departure. The bird's feathers, iridescent indigo and cobalt blue, glimmered in the morning's rays.

The voices, relentless and infuriating, snapped me out of my trance. *God damn it, would you just shut up!* In disbelief, I realized that the voices belonged to the couple at the end of the street.

Did I bang my head? Am I under the influence of something?

I didn't feel high.

It was impossible, an entirely ridiculous notion, and yet I could hear them, the movement of their mouths synchronized perfectly with the words I could now so clearly hear. The irritating humming morphed seamlessly into their dialogue. "I could hear you in the kitchen," I whispered in their general direction. But there was something else, something I couldn't quite put my finger on. It wasn't something I could see, nor hear. It was a feeling, so powerful and oppressive I could almost visualize it, resonating like a dark cloud from the gossiping couple at the end of the street, but even more so from behind me, from my home. A desperate sadness so deep, so raw, that when I turned to face the house, it caused me pain, a deep agonizing pressure that radiated from the center of my chest. I winced.

The words traveled like notes through the air, not just a jumble of syllables this time. Actual decipherable words. Words that demonstrated shock and sadness, sympathy, and condolences for the residents of 1074, the house just down the street, for the shocking incident that had robbed someone of their life just days before.

1074.

My house. Our house.

Someone died?

I laughed, producing a hollow sound that startled me. I lived at 1074. The blood in my veins turned to ice. Sucked into a permafrost, the once-warm liquid transformed and solidified. I was left frozen from the inside out as every muscle and fiber was pulled into a glacial state.

What the fuck is happening?

My feet started to walk backward before my brain was fully engaged. The flight response hit me hard—I turned and fled. There were no thoughts of an intended destination, just the need to escape.

Out of the quiet suburban street with neatly trimmed lawns and white picket fences, past the park and children's play area, across the busy freeway, on and on, my feet pounded the concrete, sidewalks, grassy verges, and roads. I had no idea where I was going until I got there. And when I did, it made sense.

The hospital loomed ahead of me, familiar and comforting. I had every intention of dashing inside, of heading to the ER or the ICU, to search for a sign, a memory, anything. But I didn't. It felt so loud. The air around it charged and heavy, so much energy, so many emotions pulsating from every doorway and window, seeping through the brick and cement walls. Too formidable for my fragile state, so instead, I allowed my legs to carry me around the exterior of the building and in through a rear entrance, close to the kitchens. As I rounded the final corner, I knew where I was going. Silently I drifted along the deserted corridor, through the emergency exit door, and down the cold concrete stairs. A ship on autopilot, navigating the narrow stairwell.

The seed of dread I had felt as I maneuvered around the hospital grounds had grown and blossomed into a thick web. It enveloped my internal organs, wrapped tightly around my nerve endings, inhibited my breath, and restricted my heartbeat. My feet padded gently, a sharp contrast to the beating they had given the sidewalk outside of the hospital grounds.

I cried before I got there.

Tears streamed down my flushed cheeks before I pushed open the cold metal doors. Before I crept silently across the frigid tiled floor. Before I approached the ice-cold metal gurney. Before I reached out and tentatively grasped the corner of the crisp white sheet. Because I knew.

I carefully lifted the sheet. I recognized the strands

of long blonde hair immediately. I had fought with those locks my entire life. A need for finality or morbid curiosity pressed me to continue. I looked at the face. My face. My body. A body I had treated harshly, been overly critical of, a body I realized too late that I loved, that I longed for, because those arms were the arms that had held the ones I loved, that provided comforting hugs to my friends, that embraced lovers no matter how fleeting, that nursed patients and sometimes, just sometimes, did really good things in the world. Or so I thought.

Maybe not.

I'm dead.

No majestic heavenly gateway had opened when I died, no beam of light appeared to guide me to eternity. Whatever sins and transgressions I had committed must have been of greater consequence than I ever could have imagined. Although to be fair, I wasn't burning in a fiery hell either. The eternal optimist, every cloud and all that.

Well, isn't that just...leave it to me to screw up dying.

I stood there for some time, unaware of the minutes as they turned into hours. I cried, I trembled, I apologized to some otherworldly entity for whatever it was I had done wrong, and I begged for help until the smell of ammonia and formaldehyde started to make me nauseous.

With weighted feet, I trudged back home and sat down heavily on the curb at the front of my house. And then I started to think. Nothing made sense. I was dead. My body was dead, and yet here I was. I held out my hands, clapped them together, tapped the ball of my foot on the ground. Yup, I definitely still had a body. I reached over and picked up one of the maple leaves that littered the sidewalk. Held it up in the air, then dropped it. Watched as it floated delicately to the ground.

I could hold things; I could move things. I nervously chewed on my lip as I stood and walked to the front door. I reached out and touched it, my hand pushed again the solid wooden structure. I pulled my hand back and thrust it forward quickly. "Ouch! Fuck!"

My hand most definitely did not pass Casper style through the damn door, and if it was at all possible to break dead bones, I might just have. I quickly retreated, praying the thud of me punching the front door hadn't alarmed anyone who may be inside. *Idiot!*

Over the next couple of hours, I paced up and down the street, holding my throbbing hand, talking to myself, having bouts of hysterical crying, and in between emotional meltdowns, being mesmerized by the power of my new eyes. The only thing I was able to ascertain during that time was that I could not be seen by others. Unfortunately this discovery was only made after I had, in a panicked state, dove headfirst into Mr. Williams' hedge when he unexpectedly appeared to retrieve his mail while I was in mid-breakdown mode on his driveway.

With no questions answered and no clarity gained, I admitted a desperate defeat, returned to the curbside, and sat down. Numb and cold, with the chill filling me from the inside out. There I stayed, through the dark and lonely night, watching the suburban wildlife go about their nightly business, unperturbed by my presence. Hours passed as I peered upward, transfixed by the silver-white aura from the moon as it cast a river of muted light through the black shades of the evening, exhaustion robbing me of all sensation and soothing me into a dazed calm.

The darkness slowly transformed into a sky of cotton candy pink with dove gray edging upon a canvas of pale blue. Another day dawned. I remained on the curb. Rooted to my spot, my eyes staring dead ahead, falling somewhere within the easement between two of the houses opposite. Unfocused, uncaring, dead, just not as dead as they should have been.

That was the first time I saw it. That was the first time I experienced terror.

Chapter 2

I assumed the shadow that started to emerge from between the dense thicket and the wooded area between the two houses across the street, was simply a visual disturbance, a byproduct of the tears I had shed, or the lack of moisture caused by hours of motionless staring. Until, that is, blinking did nothing to alleviate it. It moved steadily, taking form the closer it got. Two piercing eyes stared straight at me. An ugly menacing smile snaked across its face and the feeling, oh God, the feeling, the manifestation of a fear so absolute, so intense, so powerful that it became almost palpable.

The fear was so strong it triggered an internal alarm that seared my brain and cast icy particles into my blood as it pulsated through my veins. The anticipation of extreme danger reverberated around me. I wanted to break free of its gaze, but it had me locked in. Without making a conscious decision to do so, my body rose from the curbside and, as if retreating from a wild animal, I backed away, but it continued steadily and stealthily, moving toward me with intent.

Oh God, is this it? Am I going to hell?

I ran. I couldn't do anything but flee. I didn't look back. I didn't need to. I could feel it, whooshing through the air like a disembodied plume of spiritual smoke.

Out of my street, spurred by the most basic survival instincts, I sprinted wildly into town, driven by a desire to be around people, driven by a desire not to be alone, applying flawed human logic. Being in a public place doesn't act as a deterrent when you're dead. But even a false sense of security was better than nothing.

The world around me hurtled at dizzying speeds. My footsteps and heartbeat synchronized perfectly as I sped through the town and beyond.

I ran until I could no longer feel the prickly sensation on the back of my neck. Until my breathing became almost impossible and my parched lungs felt like they were bleeding. I was supposed to be dead, but no one told my body that. My muscles ached and my stomach had coiled into a knot that sat heavy in my abdomen. I had traveled an impossible distance. I had to be at least fifteen miles from home, close to the bustling port district of New York and New Jersey.

I ducked around the side of an apartment building that overlooked the containerized cargo port and propped myself against the wall until my breathing slowed, until I was sure it was no longer there. Like a scared child, there was only one place I wanted to be, whether it was still lurking there or not, and that was home. Whatever it was that was pulling me back was powerful and controlling and despite my fear, I adhered to its demand without a second thought.

The walk home was painfully slow. Every new street had to be assessed from a concealed spot, a constant dart across open spaces, ducking and diving between buildings, cars, and trees, eyes searching for the shadow creature, body on high alert ready to bolt in the opposite direction should it reappear.

It was dusk by the time I returned. Again, I found myself on the curbside. Again, the night slid silently by.

Again, daybreak brought little comfort.

The hours drifted by, but I remained, seemingly as lifeless as I should have been, silently poised, watching and waiting to see if it appeared again.

It did.

This time I sensed it before I saw it, slithering out from underneath the neighbor's car. It moved steadily, unrushed, eyes riveted as they held me in place. The energy hung around it like a vile shroud of darkness, odious and detestable, igniting a primordial fear that triggered an instantaneous fight-or-flight response, or at least a flight response, a response now ingrained within my muscle memory. Just as I had done previously, I bolted. Adrenaline driven, I bounded over walls, around buildings, across intersections until I reached the town center.

The scent of a smoky residue, like burnt incense and embers, alerted me to its continued ominous presence as my pace was slowed by the busy sidewalks crammed with people. I was hoping a sprint into town would have lost it. It had, however, seemingly acquired a new level of determination. I weaved between humans through the crowded streets, heading in the direction of the train station, carried along by an ocean of evening commuters rushing to make the next train. I prayed I would become lost within the sea of bodies as I dodged and darted, moving with the masses, not wanting to deviate from the herd, not wanting to do anything to draw its attention. I made it onto the platform, but a quick glance at the overhead screen told me I had four minutes to wait. It might have well said four days, shit!

The air instantly felt heavy. I was out of time, it was close, and this time I had nowhere to run. I felt like if I extended my arm, I could touch it. The thought made my skin crawl. The crowd thinned out. Was it, *he* doing that? The bodies that were packed so tightly seconds ago suddenly spread apart, exposing my meager attempt to evade it. I saw it out of the corner of my eye and instinctively turned away. The muscles in my legs were tense. My body was poised to run, but I didn't. As much as every instinct within was urging me to bolt, I stopped. I stood still. It felt like volts of electricity zipped sharply through my body, every nerve ending screamed, and the wave of dread that washed over me was so cold that I was consumed by an uncontrollable shudder.

I knew I should run. The voice in my head was furious at my stupidity. And yet I remained, rooted to the spot. Empowered by extreme stubbornness that refused to lie dormant, that seized my fear with an iron grip as I fought manically to escape.

I turned, willing my eyes to stay open and stare, obstinate and foolish. Dark eyes snared me, but its step faltered, a shadow of uncertainty swept swiftly across its face. It was clearly as confused as I, momentarily at least. Its smile spread like a nasty gash, slithering slowly across its face. "Bravery, or defeat?" it mused, as it took slow purposeful steps toward me.

Still, I stood.

I could barely hear anything beyond the thunderous beating of my heart, which had clearly developed a mind of its own and decided its survival chances would be far higher if it broke free from the idiotic vessel carrying it. The thought of such a ridiculous notion caused a semihysterical laugh to explode with a splutter from my mouth. Again, a brief shadow of confusion passed over its face, quickly replaced with angry indignation.

It stopped a mere three feet from me. It was only then I noticed the woman that stood between us, barely twenty, dressed in navy slacks and a white cotton shirt. With long dark hair and big brown eyes that stared passively at the tracks, patiently awaiting her means of getting home. So carefully, it leaned in and whispered softly, words flowing like a lullaby, beguiling, alluring, creating a false veil of innocence.

"He's here, Jenny. The one that hurt you, the one you ran from. He's here and he's getting closer. You must move away from him. Protect yourself, Jenny."

She flinched, her body rigid, too afraid to look around, believing his every word. Her feet shuffled forward, inches from the platform's edge as tendrils of fear snaked around her.

"What the fuck are you doing?" I cried out incredulously, as my fear temporarily succumbed to shock, and my stubbornly fueled bravado disintegrated quickly. It moved even closer to her, its perverse satisfaction evident. I almost believed it had forgotten about me; a fleeting moment of guilty relief swept over me until the reality of the situation punched me hard in the gut. *This is for me!* A sick demonstration of its power and retribution for my defiance.

"Keep moving, Jenny. Don't let him get you again." The whisper of its words traveled like a soft mist permeating this poor innocent girl, fogging her brain, robbing her of her free will, rendering her completely powerless. Panic surged like bile in my throat as she continued to shuffle forward, her head down, eyes transfixed on the ground.

"No! No, no, no, don't, don't do it. Don't listen to him. Look up," I pleaded as the rumbling of the oncoming train echoed through the station.

One more shuffle, one slight knock, and she would no longer be on the platform. She couldn't hear me, couldn't see me, couldn't feel me, my efforts were in vain. I was watching it murder her right before me, and I could do nothing to help, nothing to stop it. It never occurred to me that anyone other than myself could be endangered by confronting it, by challenging it.

My body started to shake, my fingers clenched, clawing through my hair in desperation, knuckles white holding my pounding head.

The train was right there!

It looked at me, head cocked slightly to the side, savoring every moment of my horror, my torture, feeding it from it. Its eyes lit up, its timing was exemplary. "Jump, Jenny," it sang.

A horrified scream rose in my throat, bubbling like hot black bile, but didn't quite make it out.

As she teetered beyond the edge, time stopped, silence fell. One foot remained suspended inches from the roaring locomotive.

From nowhere, there was a whoosh of warm air, a gust so powerful I stumbled, and my hair blew sharply across the front of my face briefly obscuring my view. An arm shot forward and ripped her from her feet, from her suspended stance. Time caught up, and sound was suddenly unmuted as she crashed to the ground, the huge arm breaking her fall, the large hand attached releasing her slowly, carefully.

She let out a small yelp as fellow commuters rushed to her aid.

My wide eyes moved steadily from the hand, up the thick muscular arm, to the broad shoulder. I blinked, fixing my vision to take in the whole scene before me. There he knelt, one hand on the ground, one still outstretched from what was about to become a sobbing, somewhat hysterical, Jenny.

I thought I might be dead, again, but like *dead*, dead this time. I was sure my heart wasn't beating. Maybe it had left for real now. I wasn't sure I was actually still capable of breathing, and my brain was like a chewed-up VCR tape trying to replay and make sense of what I had witnessed.

The arm man locked eyes with a stunned Mr. Evil before turning toward me and back again. One word hissed from his mouth. "Run!"

And I did. If Captain Testosterone and Mr. Evil want to battle it out superhero-style, good for them. I was getting the fuck out of there.

I ran and I ran and I ran. If I hadn't been scared beyond my wits, I'd have taken a moment to marvel at the speed and deftness at which I traveled. I made no conscious decision to run in any particular direction, and yet there I was, home, yet again.

I stood on the curb, my eyes transfixed on the house. They were in there. I could feel them. Their energy, their life force, caught my breath in my throat. For a moment, I contemplated normalcy, imagined walking up the front porch steps, imagined reaching for the door handle, envisioned the door opening, opening to them, to my home, to my life when I still had it. But my eyes betrayed me, ripped the fantasy from me and replaced it with visual abilities far beyond human capabilities.

I struggled to remain in an upright position. I leaned forward placing my hands on my knees, counting slowly as I breathed in and out, blinking back tears.

I'm okay, I'm okay, I'm okay. The voice inside my head was stuck on repeat, trying desperately to convince itself that I was…what? Safe?

Distraction. I needed something to ground me, to keep me from being snatched from all aspects of self-control by an all-consuming panic attack.

My heart had returned from its brief hiatus. It pummeled the inside of my rib cage. Its beats reverberated through my body, its echoes filling my eardrums, deafening me to the world around me. I was lost, so lost I didn't hear or feel Captain Testosterone as he approached. So lost that it wasn't until he reached out to place a gigantic hand gently upon my shoulder that I was even aware of his presence. His touch was met with a high-pitched scream, and my legs finally saw through what they had threatened to do for days. I ended up on the ground, about as ungraceful and neurotic a mess as you could get.

From a heap on the ground, I looked up. I already felt minuscule in comparison to this herculean creature. Having him tower above me made me feel even smaller and more defenseless, a feeling I loathed.

He looked human, or an idealistic version of how a human should look. Unassumingly dressed in jeans and a gray shirt that hugged his broad shoulders, he had piercing hazel eyes with what looked like a thin silvery sheen over them. They glistened and smiled, even when his mouth didn't. He had lightly tanned skin and short-cropped dark blond hair. His beauty was breathtaking, which only added to my feelings of inferiority.

The energy he emanated wasn't like *it*, the shadow creature, Dr. Evil. It was warm, light, and comforting. I should have felt apprehension. I should have been wary.

He was too perfect. The glint in his eyes, the ease with which he held my attention—it was borderline controlling, but I was irrationally drawn toward him. It didn't make sense. Out of nowhere, a memory from high school science class hit me, Ms. Riley enthusiastically teaching us about the deceptiveness of beauty in the natural world. Some of the most beautiful flowers are the deadliest. In nature, attractiveness is sometimes used to lure victims into an often slow and agonizing death. *Is that what this was?*

"I'm so sorry. Holy crap, are you okay?" He tried to act as compassionately concerned as possible but failed miserably at hiding his amusement. "I didn't mean to startle you. I called out…I thought you were having some sort of…erm…"

"Mental breakdown?" I tried and failed to pull myself up. Adrenaline had reduced my legs to jelly. He slowly extended a hand, which I reluctantly took, allowing him to pull me gently to my feet.

Well, this is awkward.

"You followed me?" It was supposed to be a question but sounded more like an accusation.

"I wasn't sure what happened back on the platform. The girl…you were trying to help her?" He stared so intensely as he questioned me that a sense of unsettled nervousness started to claw its way back into me. The rollercoaster of mood swings was making me nauseous, and I felt like a specimen being examined under a microscope.

"You can see me?" I whispered.

He nodded slowly.

"Are you here to take me somewhere?"

Confusion swept across his face.

"I mean you just saved me, right?" I persisted. "On the platform, with that thing…" My voice trailed off; I didn't have the words to describe what I had just witnessed.

"Okay, well…" he began slowly. "I guess, I mean, that's kind of what we do, help people."

"Like an angel?" I asked wide-eyed.

He bit his lip in an attempt to smother a laugh. "Erm, not quite."

My cheeks flushed, and I looked down at my feet, silently praying the ground beneath them would open up and swallow me whole.

"We should probably go," he said softly, extending his arm toward me.

I flinched and stepped back, fear creeping through me. "Go where?" I snapped.

He held both hands up as he shook his head. "Whoa, I'm not abducting you. I'm trying to help you. It might not be safe here, for you." His words were gentle, and too slow, a futile attempt to keep the crazy lady calm, but his eyes, his eyes were so intense, too intense.

I might not have felt the same degree of danger I experienced every time Mr. Evil closed in on me, but for reasons I could not comprehend, I certainly didn't feel safe.

"Not safe because of you?" I ventured, casually stepping farther backward.

He raised one eyebrow. My not-too-subtle attempt to move out of arm's length had not gone unnoticed.

"Not safe because, for whatever reason, Kerwin is hunting you, and that makes it a very unsafe situation for everyone." His eyes were locked on mine, his voice restrained.

So many questions!

"Kerwin? That thing has a name. Why is it coming for me? This Kerwin person, or thing, whatever he, I mean it, is." The calmness with which I asked was not an accurate representation of the ever-increasing swell of fear that threatened to tip me back into a pit of hysteria.

"That I don't know yet, but I do have some answers, and we can help you, I promise." His voice was starting to change. His calmness was slowly dissipating, and his words were coming with a growing sense of urgency.

Did that mean Kerwin was coming? Wait, did he just say we? I wanted to know who "we" were, wanted to know what he was, where he came from, why and how he had appeared when he did. I had a million questions and no desire to go anywhere with him until they had all been answered, and maybe not even then. Until, that is, I realized how unbelievably stupid and reckless I had been, until it dawned on me the potential repercussions of standing exactly where I was standing at that moment. Prior to today I had assumed the shadowy one could only interact with me, only posing a threat to me. Until today I had never seen it interact with the living.

I was suddenly acutely aware of the proximity of this creature to my home, to *them*. I had literally just led this stranger, possibly unliving stranger, straight to them! And now potentially Mr. Ev…Kerwin again too?

Putting myself in a precarious situation was one thing, potentially putting them in one was another entirely. I took a breath, desperate to do anything I could to get him as far away from there as possible.

If that meant sacrificing myself, so be it. Like the mother bird drawing the hunter away from the nest, I had to lead them away from here.

Seeing him as the lesser of two evils, I took a step toward him. I avoided direct eye contact, opting to glance beyond him nervously for signs of Kerwin. "Do you have a name?" I asked.

"I'm Noah," he responded.

"And you'd be taking me where exactly?"

"Somewhere safe, not too far from here," he assured me.

I took a deep shaky breath, said a quick prayer to whoever or whatever may be listening, and before I had time to change my mind, I said to him, "I'm Alyssa, now let's go."

Chapter 3

We traveled with a sense of urgency, but not the blind panic that had sent me barreling for home earlier. Noah moved with the speed of an Olympian and the ease of a dancer as we sped beyond the suburban streets and small businesses of town. Within no time, we had reached the old mill district, an area that consisted primarily of disused factories, abandoned mills, and warehouses. Most of this part of the city was unoccupied. We passed what remained of a few small houses, wooden shack homes left behind and long forgotten, now almost completely obscured with overgrown plants, twisted ivy, and moss.

He'd offered me his hand, back on my street. I'd recoiled in horror, never good at masking my true feelings. He hadn't seemed overly offended by my reaction. An expression of slight confusion with that hint of amusement that never seemed to be far from his features had passed quickly across his face.

We entered from the far side of the sprawling estate into the grounds of one of the deserted mills. Although there were a few small-scale mom-and-pop businesses still operating close by, the majority of the once-thriving industrial estate was now derelict. We sidestepped an old, rusted iron gate that sat ajar, entering an overgrown courtyard surrounded on three sides by towering walls with tattered barbed wire coils perched on top. The outer walls of the building consisted of a patchwork of dark red and brown bricks. Large wall-mounted pulley systems, dilapidated double wooden doors that opened onto nothing, and the rusted remains of exterior steps adorned the external walls. The windows, which were large and lead-framed, glared down upon the tiny courtyard and the two scurrying creatures darting amongst the shadows. Many of the lower-level windows were either bricked up or broken, their rusted bars offering no protection against teenage vandals and the elements. Noah continued forward, sidestepping broken glass panes and small mounds of rubble. His step never faltered and, afraid to be left behind, neither did mine.

We entered the building through a heavy metal door, scuffed and dented with faded spray paint residue. Inside the dimly lit building, I paused, giving my eyes a moment to adjust to the darkness.

Off to the right, there was a wide wooden staircase with missing spindles and a metal handrail. We took the stairs five at a time, and once on the second floor turned right and headed to the end of a narrow corridor, illuminated by a single overhead light. At the end of the musty corridor sat an old freight elevator with a wooden horizontal slide-up hatch gate.

Noah flipped the top half of the heavy door like he was flipping a beer mat. Both doors parted with a groan, and we stepped inside. The elevator grumbled and creaked up through the shaft, finally resting on the seventh floor. The ride seemed agonizingly slow in comparison to the speed of our travel across town. We stepped out into a square foyer. Straight ahead, a wide rolling door sat ajar. Noah pushed it farther open but remained on the threshold. He bowed slightly and extended his arm in a sweeping motion, an outdated gesture giving me precedence because of my gender.

The loft was breathtaking, a sharp contrast to its dingy exterior. Adjacent to the doorway, across a wide, open room, east-facing windows stretched almost from the floor to the ceiling, giving an impressive panoramic view that expanded far beyond the run-down industrial site. Sprawled beyond the crumbling remains lay New Jersey's Paterson city, with the infamous New York skyline just visible on the dusty horizon. The elevated ceiling extended up three stories high. To the right of the windows was an open staircase, dark wood floating stairs and black wrought iron handrails leading to a first-level mezzanine, above which sat black iron girders supporting a third-floor space.

A built-in bookcase covered the whole wall behind the stairs stretching up onto the mezzanine level. A long rectangular fireplace was cut into the stone wall on the opposite side of the room. Small flames danced around the burning blocks of wood, throwing out a soft and cozy glow. The middle of the room contained an oversized L-shaped sofa facing two large armchairs. The seating and a couple of side tables framed a large low dark wood and metal coffee table. The lamps that sat upon tables and shelves were industrial style consisting of uncovered, oversized bulbs and black iron stands.

A brick archway directly to the right of the entrance created a hole in the book wall. Through it, I glimpsed the dark wood and metal accents of a kitchen. The soft brown and beige monochromatic color scheme that flowed throughout the loft created a sense of calm and serenity, much like the ambiance that radiated from Noah. In the distance through the window, the twinkling of orange streetlights snaked like a river throughout the city as dusk settled over it.

"This is where you live? It's beautiful," I said, turning to Noah who was leaning casually against one of the black iron girders supporting the mezzanine.

"Thank you," he responded with a humble bow of his head. "It is something, isn't it? But I can't take credit, the design was all Steven." As he said the name, he turned his head toward the glowing hearth. It was only then that I noticed a doorway to the left of the long fireplace and became aware of another presence in the room.

Steven stood motionless in the doorway, hands in his pockets, leaning casually against the frame.

Dressed in slacks and a dark knit sweater, he could have just stepped from the pages of a men's fashion catalogue. He was slightly shorter than Noah and had a slender, leaner build. His dark eyes matched his dark hair, which was cropped short on the sides with a little more length on top, textured and styled to look a little tousled. I noticed he also had what looked like a thin sheer film of silver covering his eyes much like Noah.

"You must have lots of questions," he said with a warm smile.

A low sigh escaped me, and tears swelled in my eyes. I nodded, afraid that any attempt to form words would turn into a sob. I had been so convinced I was going to spend eternity in a living hell of fear and fleeing from shadow people. These two people—beings? Whatever they might be—were the first sliver of hope I'd had since *that* day. I could wait no longer and blurted out, "Am I definitely dead?"

Steven was much better at hiding his amusement

than Noah was, who, with a smirk, responded, "Well, you aren't alive anymore."

"And you?" I ventured.

Steven extended his left arm, motioning toward the sofa. "Come, sit."

I perched stiffly on the edge of one of the armchairs. Steven sat on the sofa. Noah joined him with impeccable timing. It was like watching a choreographed routine, two people utterly in sync. They sat close. One of Noah's arms draped along the back of the sofa behind Steven who rested his hand on Noah's thigh. Their connection was palpable. I was hit with fleeting pangs of jealousy as I watched them, not from the desire to have a partner but from the loss of a love so pure, so complete, a connection I once thought unbreakable that had splintered into a million pieces just a few days ago.

"So, you're both...dead?" The answer seemed obvious, but I needed to hear them say it, to confirm once and for all that I hadn't lost my mind, not completely at least.

"It really doesn't matter what you call it. We were alive, as all humans are, believing that that was it, the one shot at living before the inevitability that is death chose to take it away. The first thing you need to do is to try and forget everything you thought you knew, everything you were told. It is all false, fallacies created from ignorance."

I took a moment to process exactly what that meant.

"So, there really is no afterlife?" I asked, surprising myself with the sadness in my voice.

"If there was no afterlife, how would you explain this?" said Steven gesturing between me and them.

This can't be it!

"No God? No Heaven?" As stunned by this revelation as I was, I realized that I was also experiencing an overwhelming sense of relief. I'd been so sure that I'd screwed something up, sinned so badly that Heaven had rejected me.

"It's not that they don't exist. It's that your interpretation of them doesn't exist."

Clear as mud!

Images of the dark shadowy creature slithering out from the shadows flashed before me. "I've seen places, gateways or holes, places of darkness. How do you know those places aren't actually Hell?" I asked.

Steven smiled sympathetically. "There are places, places of light and peace. Conversely, there are dark places, places of fear and conflict. But all three planes are here, within this existence. The living can't see beyond their own plane and typically can't cross between them, but we can. Most people when they die go straight to one place or the other. But some of us don't. We stay here."

"But why?" I asked, feeling all the self-doubt clawing its way back into my brain. Maybe I had done something wrong after all.

"We have skills. We have heightened senses, abilities far beyond the living. We believe we have those for a reason. We choose to use those skills to help others." Steven was trying to sound nonchalant and clearly attempting to gloss over the finer details.

The last thing I wanted to do was to anger the first beings I'd come into contact with since that day who weren't trying to kill me or others because of me, but my face gave me away. I couldn't help it; it sounded ridiculous. Delusions of grandeur to the extreme. I half expected one of them to pull out a mask and a cape.

Noah rolled his eyes at me. "We don't think we're superheroes!"

Wow, get out of my head!

"Can you read my thoughts?" I asked, alarmed.

"I don't need to read your thoughts; they're written all over your face." Noah continued, "Every person who dies acquires the same skills. Some stick around, and some don't. Like it or not, as a dead person you can see and be seen by all entities that are no longer living."

What did that even mean?

"Let's take a walk," Steven suggested, rising gracefully from the sofa. "I think a demonstration might help add some clarity. Are you game, Alyssa?"

They're testing me.

I shrugged, consenting halfheartedly, desperate to make some sense of what they were telling me.

We left the loft and headed in a northeasterly direction, the Passaic Falls thundering to our left. We formed a loose line walking side by side with me in the middle. Steven kept his pace even with mine. Noah, a few steps ahead paused impatiently every few minutes.

"Don't mind Noah," Steven offered with an apologetic smile. "He forgets what the first few months are like. It's a lot to take in."

I wanted to ask him how he had died, where and when. I had a million questions bubbling just below the surface, but my focus had to remain on Noah who had inconveniently decided to pick up the pace. I couldn't decide if it was impatience that was driving him or an effort to deter my questions.

The evening air was brisk as we headed toward the downtown area of Paterson. The darkness around the old site was thick and relentless, offering a heavy concealment for creatures drawn to it, making me feel vulnerable even when flanked by Noah and Steven. I was relieved by the comforting glow of the streetlights as we entered the outskirts of the city.

"So, it's just the two of you?" I asked as the pace slowed and so did my fear of being left behind.

"There are actually four of us that live in the loft, but you're more than welcome to stay," Steven said with a smile.

Complete strangers offering to put a roof over my head should have triggered red flags waving furiously, but all I could feel was more relief. I tried to conceal my feelings and feign shock, responding, "Oh, no, I couldn't possibly. I mean, I don't even know you. That would be weird, right?"

Steven shrugged and said with a wink, "Only if you made it weird. Griffin and Amelia will be back later this evening. It was Griffin who brought us together. He's been here the longest. Amelia is still learning; her passing was hard for her. She still struggles with parts of it now. You'll like them, Alyssa, I promise."

We turned onto a brightly lit street with ground-level storefronts sitting beneath three- and four-story apartments. Fluorescent lights beamed from the handful of small restaurants, a barbershop, specialty groceries, and convenience stores dotted between units that had closed for the day, silent and dark behind gray metal shutters emblazoned with spray-painted graffiti. A few people wandered up and down the sidewalk, greeting store owners, collecting takeout, or heading into one of the many apartment buildings that sat above the business units. We stopped at a corner, directly in front of a secondhand car lot.

"Okay, take a look around. Tell me what you see," Noah said, gesturing up and down the street.

I frowned at him but glanced briefly around. "Stores, apartments, cars, people. Am I supposed to be looking for something specific? I already know I can see exceptionally well now. What exactly is the purpose of this?" I was being overly defensive. My arrogance was unintentional, a byproduct of trying too hard to disguise my insecurities.

"Be patient," Steven murmured with a friendly smile.

With a huff, I turned my attention back to Noah, who instructed me to close my eyes. "Take a breath. Focus on what's around you and tell me what you feel?"

"Mildly irritated."

"Try again," Noah insisted.

I was acting like a petulant child. Fear of being patronized was not wearing well. I took a breath and focused on feeling my surroundings, focused on the surrounding energies of which there were many. I tried to filter through the clamorous vibrating clouds and differentiate between them. It wasn't easy. As people moved their energy moved with them.

I signed heavily. "I feel people, life." If the idea was to teach me how to feel people, their energies or whatever, I already knew. I pointed toward the convenience store farther down the road and said, "They're in trouble" as two boys in their early teens barreled out of the door and sprinted down the block to a tirade of expletives from the store owner as he chased them onto the street waving his fists. I pointed to the apartment building above the store where a woman in her late fifties stood by an open window smoking. "She's grieving." I pointed to a girl in her late teens leaning on a pickup truck outside of the barber shop, hands stuffed into the pockets of her jacket, head bowed. "Someone's hurting her; she's scared."

Noah threw a bemused, slightly confused glance toward Steven, who was staring so intently at me it was making me feel a little uncomfortable. I shifted from one foot to the other with a slight shrug. "So what? We all have the same abilities when we pass, right?" I shifted my gaze between them questioningly.

"I mean, yes, yes, we do," Steven admitted. "But it usually takes a while to learn them, understand them, learn to harness them. I mean, you only just passed over."

"It was days ago," I corrected him.

"It's a little unprecedented how quickly your skills have developed is all," Noah agreed, ignoring my comment.

I was making no conscious effort at that point to assess what or who was around me. I was focused on the conversation with Noah and Steven, or more accurately the unspoken dialogue that passed between them, when out of nowhere it hit me, an invisible black dart aimed perfectly at my right temple. Like a metaphoric lightning bolt, it zapped through the air skewering my brain before disintegrating into a thousand specks of dust. A quick and painful warning. My heart pounded; a thousand tiny volts streaked beneath my skin as the scent of smoldering embers blew by. It took all my restraint not to run.

My head whipped to the side, and I froze. I expected to see Kerwin, but this wasn't him. It was one of whatever he was, but distinctly different, standing in the shadows of the deserted basketball court, halfway down the dimly lit street adjacent to the corner on which we stood.

A second can pass by so slowly sometimes. Adrenaline is supposed to speed events and actions up, but on this side, it has the opposite effect. One second becomes ten seconds, every minuscule movement distinguishable. As my eyes settled on the figure, the energy surrounding us shifted, grew, amalgamated. Steven followed my gaze, alerting Noah by hissing, "Sygan." They both spun in its direction, half a step ahead of me, and assumed their flanking positions. For a few seconds, nobody moved, nobody spoke. It briefly surveyed us before backing up a few steps, turning on its heels, and fleeing.

It ran because it was scared. I could feel its fear. It wasn't just the power from Noah and Steven either. I was a part of it, a part of the force that invoked a fear strong enough to send it running. The feeling was euphoric, was exactly what I needed, was what I had desperately been searching for.

The past couple of days had taken their toll on me, reducing me to something unfamiliar, something weak, vulnerable, powerless. They had bestowed upon me traits associated with preconceived characteristics I had fought my whole life to avoid. But this, this feeling of power, this shift from the hunted to the hunter—it was like it was saving my lifeless life.

"Did you see that?" A hushed whisper on the wind passed from Steven to Noah.

With a nod, Noah replied, "I think our demonstration is over."

We headed back to the loft. My exuberance refused

to acknowledge the questioning glances Noah and Steven shared. It wasn't an awkward silence, they asked me questions about my encounters with Kerwin, talked about the merits of me taking one of the top-floor rooms, and laughed when I admitted the number of times I had jumped into bushes to hide from people I was invisible to. But it was there, unanswered questions, confusion, a line of conversation I was censored from.

The loft remained empty. Noah insisted I stay for at least one evening, meet Griffin and Amelia, maybe get some of my questions answered by Griffin. The prospect of gaining answers to my questions dangled like a carrot before me.

He led me up to the top floor, a level above the mezzanine. A staircase identical to the one in the living room sat at the end of a walkway alongside the huge windows, in an area obscured from the view on the first floor. At the top of the stairs sat a small landing with two heavy dark wood doors. Noah opened the door to the right and stepped back, allowing me to enter first.

The room was illuminated by a large freestanding lamp. To the left and against the wall sat a large bed with a dark wooden frame, with matching units positioned on either side. The warming glow of the floor lamp spread from its location in the corner opposite the bed, across an oversized love seat and dark wood dresser. The ceiling had exposed wooden beams and metal girders. A large cast-iron radiator stood beneath a wide window, its view blocked out by closed wooden blinds.

A door next to the dresser, opposite the bed, led to an almost empty walk-in closet and bathroom. The large shower was covered in white tiles contrasting beautifully with a gigantic black metal showerhead. A range of toiletries sat on a small shelf to the side of a basin and neatly folded towels were arranged on a stand close to the shower door.

The sight of the shower reminded me of how long it had been since I had actually paid any attention to my personal hygiene. I was immediately embarrassed.

Steven entered the open closet area with armfuls of clothes. "These should do you for now. Take your time. When you're ready, I'll have a glass of wine awaiting you."

The thought of participating in something so normal, so comforting, almost brought me to tears.

"I haven't eaten or drunk anything since…" I trailed off.

"It isn't the necessity it once was. It's more of a pleasure now," he offered with a smile as they both left the room pulling the heavy bedroom door shut.

The shower was amazing. So much so, I struggled to step out from the steaming stream of water. When I eventually did, wrapped in one of the luxurious bath sheets, I rubbed my damp hair dry with a towel and rummaged through the small cupboard beneath the sink to find a hair dryer and comb to finish the job. I stood in front of the basin, examining my image in the large wall-mounted mirror.

I still looked like me, for the most part at least. My eyes were still blue but now a brighter shade with what looked like a fine silver film over them, not dissimilar to Noah's and Griffin's. My skin felt the same, but the tone was different, no visible signs of freckles, scratches, scars, or veins. It didn't turn pink beneath the surface when I pressed it. I chewed on my lower lip and took a step back before dropping the towel. I turned slowly one way, then the other, gazing at my naked form, a small, satisfied smile played on my lips. I looked good. A small ego boost I appreciated given my present company. With a roll of my eyes, I grabbed the towel and headed into the closet. I pulled on sweatpants and selected a man's black T-shirt; I pushed my arms into it and was about to pull it over my head when I sensed the presence. I spun around, partially dressed, toward the bedroom as a huge form filled the doorway.

"Wow!" He stumbled backward, but not before getting an eyeful of a seminaked me. He turned his back to me but remained in the bedroom. "I am so, so sorry. I should have knocked. I didn't think. I—are you decent?" He attempted to glance over his shoulder as I pulled the shirt sharply over my head. "Oh God, I'm so sorry!"

"If you're sorry, why do you keep doing it?" I snapped.

Steven's familiar voice cut through the rising tension. "Hey, is everyone okay in here?"

"Everything was great before Peeping Tom decided to come perv at me," I hissed.

The pervert held his hands up. "I swear I wasn't watching you; I'd come to check you were okay. You were up here for a *really* long time."

"Oh, so this is *my* fault," I squealed indignantly.

He stood with one arm crossed as his other covered his mouth, clearly trying to conceal a laugh. Steven bit his lip; he was equally as bad at hiding his amusement.

"Just a thought—poker? Not your game," I seethed, gesturing between the two of them.

"I'm sorry," Steven said, still amused but at least appearing somewhat apologetic. "Alyssa, this is Griffin. Griffin, this is Alyssa."

Griffin was as tall as Noah, not quite as broad but still muscular. His skin was a darker tan, hair golden brown and thick. His eyes were chestnut brown with golden flecks and the telltale film, but his looked more gold than silver. He was dressed in jeans that hung perfectly from his hips and a shirt that emphasized his defined chest and arms. Like Noah and Steven, he was unnaturally beautiful.

"Shall we?" He motioned toward the doorway.

"After you," I responded curtly, still stinging from embarrassment. "You've just been staring at my top half; I don't need you watching my bottom half descending two staircases, thank you."

That shut him up. He lowered his head in defeat and walked a step ahead.

As we reached the lower floor, Noah and a girl I could only assume was Amelia rose from their seats. My eyes scanned past Noah and rested upon Amelia.

She was standing next to the coffee table, watching me carefully. Although only slightly smaller than me, she looked tiny in comparison to the three men in the room. Ombre box braids fell away into soft brown curls that framed her petite face. Her eyes were a shimmering shade of bronze, and she was dressed in skintight jeans, a figure-hugging vest top and a fitted oxblood leather jacket. A smile broke out on her face that spread into her warm eyes. "Finally! Another girl." Her smile was contagious, and I couldn't help but return it.

She introduced herself to me with a warm and genuine hug. I loved her immediately.

I positioned myself at one end of the sofa as Steven filled wine glasses and passed them out.

Griffin also settled on the sofa, but at a respectful

distance from me. "Do you mind me asking you some questions? I know we only just met," he asked, his intense eyes staring at me.

"Well, you've seen my breasts already. I'd say traditional decorum is out the window," I responded with a small smile and large sip, letting him know I was over my initial hissy fit.

His face flushed with embarrassment. "Do you remember passing over?" he asked me gently.

I shook my head slowly. "I don't even remember the days before it. I just woke up one day, and everything was different, and I couldn't understand what had happened and then that thing came after me and just wouldn't stop hunting me."

My voice trailed off as Griffin's demeanor changed. "Wait, why do you think he was hunting you?" He looked pointedly at Noah who seemed embarrassed, like a child caught doing something he shouldn't.

"It wasn't the first time it had chased me."

"Ah yeah, about that, we didn't actually discuss that. I just assumed that was their first, umm, encounter." Noah was choosing his words with great care, shifting awkwardly to the edge of his seat.

"Would you excuse me?" Griffin said with a warm smile to me, before he turned his attention back to Noah. "Can we have a word privately, Noah?"

"I don't think that's such a great idea right now, Griff," he responded slowly, his eyes wide as he glared at him.

"We got a demonstration of Alyssa's abilities earlier," Steven chipped in, trying and failing to keep the tone of the conversation casual. "They really are...developed."

God, this was awkward!

My gaze met Griffin's. "Did I do something wrong?" I whispered. There it was, the debilitating self-doubt that had haunted me in life, raising its persistent little head again.

"Not at all," Griffin responded reassuringly. "I guess I just have a lot to be filled in on."

The conversation stayed relatively light after that as Griffin took the not-too-subtle hint. Noah and Steven shared our experiences from earlier that evening, triggering matching eyebrow raises from Amelia and Griffin when they described how I was the first to notice the shadow man, or Sygan, as they referred to him. They fell into a conversation that went way over my head. I stopped trying to follow it and sipped my wine, drowsily content and feeling safe for the first time in what seemed like forever.

I drifted in and out of sleep, lulled by their relaxed chatting and soft laughs, awaking with a start as Griffin attempted to cover me with a blanket. I looked around the now quiet room, empty except for the two of us.

"I didn't mean to disturb you. I didn't think you'd appreciate me carrying you up to bed after you accused me of having voyeuristic tendencies," he said with a smirk.

I rolled my eyes as a laugh escaped me. He offered an outstretched hand, which I accepted, allowing him to pull me to my feet.

"Thank you," I said as I headed toward the stairs.

"For looking at your breasts?"

"For welcoming me into your home, Griffin. Good night."

"Good night, Alyssa, and Alyssa…"

I paused and turned to look at him, still standing in the middle of the living room.

"It's your home too, if you let it be."

I turned and continued up the stairs, thankful that the smile that spread across my face was hidden from his view.

Chapter 4

The following day I awoke before dawn. I dressed quickly and crept silently from the loft and headed home. I sat in my usual spot on the curbside and tried to organize my thoughts. I could feel their energy in the house behind me. It comforted me, but when my thoughts started to drift, I pulled them sharply back.

I felt him before I saw him, his presence caused me to inhale sharply and freeze, like I'd been caught doing something I shouldn't.

Griffin slipped out from the side of the house and sat next to me on the curb, respectfully at arm's distance away, watching me closely. At least I was dressed this time.

"You followed me." I sighed gently.

"Yes."

First, I'm tested, now I'm followed!

"Why? Don't you trust me?"

"Nah, I'm just nosey." His quip broke the tension, and relief flooded over me.

Griffin turned toward the house. "This is where you lived?" he said, nodding at it.

I wanted to answer him, but my voice got lost somewhere between my throat and my mouth. The anxious energy that had taken over my stomach on that very first day suddenly started to expand, pushing its way up into my diaphragm.

"I don't want to do this," I stammered.

Griffin's eyes held my gaze, reassuring but insistent as he responded, "You have to."

I shook my head, trying to free myself from his snare, pushing my hands down on either side ready to stand.

"Wait." Griffin reached for me, laying his hand on my arm lightly with a feather touch. "Don't you ever wonder why you always come back to this spot?"

My head turned instinctively to the house.

"No, not the house, Alyssa. I mean right here." His hand drifted softly from my arm to the curb.

I pushed my palms down harder on the ground, desperate to get away, but the skin-to-concrete contact held me, blowing unwanted memories before my eyes. The jarring flash of a paparazzi camera that was too close, close enough for me to see the thin metal filament of the bulb casting dazzling beams of white light. The vision made my head spin, and my fingers pushed even harder against the curb in an effort to remain upright. I turned my head to the side as the roar of a jet engine filled my ears. I pulled my hands sharply from the ground like I'd touched something hot and staggered to my feet.

Griffin leaped quickly next to me, and grabbed me as I swayed, saving me from gravity. "Alyssa, it's okay," he promised.

"No!" I growled, fighting against the nausea as it burned my throat. "I can't do this." I lurched away from him, moving toward the house. My steps faltered as I reached the carpet of velvet grass that sat before the porch. I froze. The thick grass, a forgiving surface for small knees and elbows. I didn't see the leaves that littered it at that moment. I saw the freshly raked version from that day. I shook my head, trying in vain to free myself from being sucked into the vortex of memories. I could feel the first smoky wisps of evening surrounding me despite the day's early hour, could see the football as it sailed through the air.

My breath caught in my throat. I was being pulled back, back to a different moment in time, back to a memory I did not want to revisit, although I still didn't know why.

The surroundings shifted, changing too quickly as everything around me took on a golden hue, and the perpetually changing sky cast hints of an approaching sunset, ushering the evening in with an array of orange, pink, and red shades, all deepening as they spread quickly above me replacing the early morning sky. The air became dry and crisp, aromatic with scents of cedar and golden aspen, blended with the fragrant aroma of sage and clove.

A sense of familiarity washed over me, reminiscent of feelings that had once embraced me like a warm blanket, but now suffocated me, restricting my breathing and dragging me to hell.

No!

With a cry I tried to run from it, darting away from the house, and the lawn and the memories, making it only as far as the curbside before falling to my knees. It had me. I could not escape. My hands flew to my ears as the roar of the jet engine filled the air. Just when I was certain I would die again, my feet left the ground. Warm arms encased me, and the steady thrum of his heart regulated my breathing.

Griffin carried me silently and effortlessly back to the loft. He refused to put me down until we reached the room in which I had spent the previous night. He sat quietly next to me, waiting patiently until the room stopped spinning, and I was able to pull myself into a seated position.

"I'm sorry. I had no idea how intense it would get. I shouldn't have pushed you," he murmured, his eyes wide and honest locked onto mine.

Tears pooled in my eyes and threatened to fall. I quickly changed the subject, and Griffin was gracious enough to let me.

"Griffin, did I fuck up? Did I do something wrong? Is that why I'm still here? Noah said Heaven doesn't exist, but if that's the case where are all the other dead people?"

I really could not let that go!

Griffin leaned forward with a small smile. "There are three planes in our existence," he explained slowly. "Heaven and Hell imply the presence of God and the Devil. Such entities don't exist. They were fabricated by humans, maybe as a control method or a comfort blanket for mankind. There are distinct differences between the planes—one is dark, chaotic, and full of war and pain. One is the opposite—light, calm, and full of peaceful contentment. How you refer to them is entirely up to you. Many here refer to them as Daeon and Laeon, the dark and the light."

He continued, "Every human soul possesses both good and evil elements in equal balance. During life, humans may feel an inclination toward one element or the other but are only truly aware of the existence and composition of their soul as they pass over. When a person is on the cusp of death, beyond the point of no return, they pass into a temporary domain. Here their soul is unveiled, and they truly see themselves for the first time. It is at this point they must decide, to either embrace their good and light essence or to embrace their dark and evil essence, and that choice dictates their eternity. There is no higher power to judge them, to redeem or condemn them. They are only answerable to themselves. They can only be redeemed by themselves."

"But that didn't happen to us," I probed.

"Correct. Although rare, there are those who refuse to choose. A glitch in the option of free will, maybe. Those who don't choose a path stay here. They have the same abilities as everyone else who transcends, but they exist on this plane. They retain free will. They can choose to use their powers and abilities for good, for bad, or for neither."

"So, every person is evil, to some degree?" I asked.

"Yes, but you must understand, this lies dormant during life. That serial killer you assumed to be pure evil…nope, he or she possesses the same balance of good and evil as Mother Theresa did. Sure, they may have surrendered themselves to their darker impulses, but the elements of their soul remain ordinarily impure and balanced."

He continued, "Humans are almost impervious to harm from non-living entities, at least while they are alive, but between the planes, at that moment of unveiling, at that moment of choice, the soul is vulnerable. This is the point at which some Sygans may try to take them, either working for inhabitants of the darkness or working independently and using the souls to trade, as they are considered collateral on the other side, in Daeon."

"So Sygans are like demons then?"

"Sygans are not demons. They transcended like us. They must retain a degree of humanity to enable them to walk freely on this plane. Full demons, if that's what we are calling them, are unable to walk the Earthly plane. Earth was intended for humans. Once the last ounce of humanity is lost, that door closes indefinitely."

I leaned forward, listening intently, afraid of missing anything.

"Sygans are like the unofficial gatekeepers of the Daeon plane. They can be ruthless killers, and overall, they function primarily for personal gain, often acting as intermediaries between the planes. Once a soul is lost entirely, that entity can no longer walk this plane. They will sometimes commission Sygans to carry out work on their behalf, usually to capture souls at passing. Some Sygans work independently, seeking out high-value souls and trading them to the highest bidder. Of course, being in such proximity to evil is not without its consequences. Sygans are unable to pass into the light plane. If they did, it would be debilitating, ending eventually in a certain death. Daeon is a dangerous place. The more time you spend there, the less humanity you retain. It is a place of constant war and a fight for dominance." Griffin's face darkened as he spoke.

"And you can't kill them?" My thoughts drifted back to the street corner, the Sygan that Noah, Steven, and I encountered was evidently scared. "Can they be killed; can we be killed?"

Every explanation seemed to bring with it another barrage of unanswered questions.

"If you die on this plane, there is no alternative existence." Griffin paused, allowing the enormity of what he had shared to sink in. "Dying here, for us, isn't as…easy…as it is for a human, but it is still a danger you need to be aware of."

My head was spinning with all the information, but still I pushed for more. "So, you can kill Sygans?" I persisted.

Griffin shook his head at me. "The situation would have to be extreme for that to happen. We conduct ourselves impartially. We don't get to decide which souls are worth saving. If a soul remains, we will make every feasible attempt to save it. Even if it could never enter Laeon, it could still exist with purpose here. We don't kill unless we absolutely must. Killing is self-damaging. What would be the point of saving the souls of others if in doing so we were condemning our own?"

"Killing on Earth is okay, but killing here is soul damaging. You do see the hypocrisy in that, don't you?" I pointed out.

"I wouldn't say humans committing murder doesn't matter. Every action has a consequence, but those consequences are contained on Earth. All actions are redeemable. Humans are ignorant. That minimizes their culpability. On this plane, what you do matters, to your soul at least."

"And what about Laeon. Do people travel between there and Earth?"

"Occasionally, if the pull is strong enough, they may visit for brief periods. They typically will visit loved ones soon after passing, but unfortunately, although their intentions may be good, their presence, more often than not, brings fear. If the living sense them, which could happen, especially if they shared a strong bond before death, or if they accidentally do something to alert the living to them, like knock over objects, or create inexplicable noise, it would be understandably terrifying. Once they create fear, they don't return, for obvious reasons."

"Hold on, you said humans can't be harmed, but Kerwin nearly killed someone. I watched him brainwash a woman; he almost made her jump in front of a train!" I exclaimed.

"Sygans have similar abilities to us," Griffin conceded. "Enticement is a powerful tool manipulated by some Sygans. Once you transcend from the living plane to this one, over time you can gain access to your full potential and eventually are afforded free rein over your abilities. Some Sygans can manipulate humans using a complex form of subliminal messaging targeted at a specific area of the brain. They use their empathic powers to identify past trauma and integrate it to invoke a reaction, like a subconscious, indirect form of mind control. They can't read human minds. However, trauma leaves an imprint on a person's aura which is easily identifiable to proficient empaths."

I paused, trying to allow my brain time to process the vast amount of information Griffin had shared.

Seeing I was content for the time being with the details he had shared, Griffin stood, pausing as he reached the doorway. "Noah, Steven, and I have some things we need to do, but Amelia should be back soon. Are you okay here alone for a little while?"

I nodded and sank back into the pillows. Emotional exhaustion had stolen away the last remnants of my energy, and I fell into a restless slumber.

I awoke a short time later, pulling myself stiffly from the bed. I headed into the bathroom and splashed my face with cold water before heading downstairs.

The loft remained empty.

I walked over to the fireplace, placing my still-trembling body close to the warming glow of the flames as they danced a slow sway between the ebony logs. My eyes traveled along the stone mantle above the rectangular hearth. Two display stands stood upon it. One held a gunmetal gray dagger, so plain and unassuming it looked out of place showcased in such a fashion. The other object looked more impressive. Balanced carefully on its wooden stand, it immediately caught my attention. I reached out and carefully scooped up the elliptical orb from its resting place. I turned the cool glass and metal container over and examined it. It was constructed from chrome and frosted glass, about the size of a large egg. It reminded me of a smaller version of the incense burner the Catholic priest used during one of the many masses I had been forced to attend. Realizing quickly the door that recollection would open, I forced the memory from my mind.

I was still examining the orb object when the other three returned, Noah bursting through the door first. That man had a disgusting amount of exuberance and enthusiasm.

"Wow, what you got there, Alyssa?" he bellowed, eyeing the orb.

My cheeks flushed as I gingerly replaced the object on its stand. "I'm sorry, I was just intrigued. It's really pretty," I offered weakly.

"That's okay." Griffin's voice, deep, warm, and reassuring drifted up behind me. "It's called a Vesk. Its function is to hold and transport souls."

Said so casually!

I'm confused. "Is that what Sygans use? Why do

47

you have one?"

"Just in case. It's a regular Boy Scouts brigade over here, Alyssa. Always be prepared," Noah mockingly boomed as he held up his three middle fingers in a scout salute while walking backward to the kitchen.

"How are you feeling?" Griffin asked, his concerned gaze searching for mine.

I chose to ignore his question, eager to steer the conversation in a different direction. "Griffin, you said earlier that you choose to help people, to protect souls. Do you know when a Sygan is hunting? Do you stop them? Is that what you were doing with Noah and Steven today?"

Griffin raised an eyebrow, but a smile spread across his face. "You certainly are determined," he mused. "Can you describe what alerted you to the Sygan last night?"

Answering a question with a question. What was he trying to avoid telling me?

I closed my eyes, casting myself back to the street corner, careful to recall every detail. "It hurt, just briefly, a sharp stabbing pain in my head. My skin crawled, and I could smell a charred, smoky scent." I opened my eyes. "Isn't that what you experience when you track them?"

Griffin's eyes narrowed. He appeared a little perplexed. "I mean, yes, it is," he admitted, "but it's just that, it usually takes a substantial amount of time to harness these abilities, to master them."

So I've been told.

We both fell silent, unanswered questions hanging in the air between us. I had no explanation, and neither did he.

"I want to learn," I said, my eyes fixed steadfast and

unwavering on him. "Whatever it is you do, I want to do it too."

He was not happy. "I don't want to put you in a situation you're not prepared for," he replied firmly.

"But how are you going to know if I'm prepared if you're not willing to give me a chance?" I argued.

"I'm not putting you in danger," Griffin insisted.

"I won't be in danger if you and Steven and Noah are there, will I?" I said with a soft coy smile.

Griffin raised one eyebrow. "Really? You really think flattery is going to win you this fight?"

Damn it!

"Maybe, maybe not. Maybe I don't need you with me at all to figure it out," I responded with a shrug.

His face darkened, and I gulped. Maybe I'd pushed a little too far.

"That's not funny," he said slowly, clearly reining in what he truly wanted to say.

I turned to walk away, my cheeks burned with embarrassment at my failed attempt to convince him, but I was also furious that he believed he had some moronic right to control any situation I chose to put myself into. I didn't ask to die, to be thrust into this existence. Maybe I didn't need him and his stupid loft and his perfect friends. I'd lived my entire life without a father figure. I sure as hell didn't need one now.

"I'm not trying to control you, Alyssa." His voice traveled hypnotically between us, calming my ridiculous temper tantrum like he was reading my mind.

"It feels like you're trying to do exactly that," I responded in a hushed tone.

Griffin's sigh was long and deep. "I'll teach you," he conceded, "but you need to learn how to walk before you can run."

"When can we start?" I persisted.

"We can start when I know you are ready," he muttered with a frown.

I bit my tongue, fighting back a response. The last thing I wanted to do was argue with him, but I was absolutely not ready to give up.

"Steven is cooking," Noah announced as he exited the kitchen. "Comfort food and love is all we need. Steven is an amazing cook!" The pride from Noah was evident. He was always happy, but whenever he spoke of Steven, his eyes sparkled just that little bit more.

I hadn't eaten in so long, and the thought seemed almost alien. I wasn't sure I'd be able to eat. If I wasn't full of nervous anxiety, I was a swirling mass of euphoria. The mood extremes left little room for anything else. I placed my hand on my stomach and grimaced.

"Part of accepting this new life is learning how to not only control your emotions, but also to learn how to create a buffer between you and everyone else's emotions," Griffin said. "Doing things that seem normal to you, human things, might help you to destress, help you transition a little easier."

"Normal things like eating?" I asked critically.

"Normal things like living," Griffin answered with a smile. "Eating, dancing, singing, having fun."

"But I'm dead."

"Doesn't mean you can't have fun!" he responded with a chuckle.

"Whoa! Hold on a minute, did you just say fun?" I mimicked his intensely serious expression and voice. "You're telling me you know how to have fun? Sorry,

Mr. Serious, I'm not buying it." I challenged him, crossing my arms as a smirk spread across my face.

"Oh-oh, did she just—wait, was that a challenge?" Noah called from across the room. "Dude, you got to show her. You can't let her get away with that, right?" Noah strode across the room to Griffin and slapped his huge palm on his shoulder.

Poor Griffin was clearly out of his depth and glanced between the two of us with bewilderment. "Ermm…I mean, I—we could…erm," Griffin stammered.

Noah shook his head and urged Griffin to do better. "Come on, man, I'm trying to help you out here."

"Yeah, thanks for that," Griffin answered sarcastically. "Wait, we could play a game."

Neither the silence nor the looks Noah and I exchanged deterred him. "Games are fun, right? We can have teams, and it will be, you know, fun!"

Noah slapped one hand across his eyes in his typically overdramatic fashion. "Tragic, brother, just tragic."

I shoved Noah hard. "Leave him alone!" I smothered a laugh, turned to Griffin, and reassured him that his idea sounded great.

He seemed genuinely confused. "I think it sounds like fun," he offered weakly.

"Course you do, Griff," Noah said, patting his back in mock sympathy. "Of course you do."

My trepidation about eating was cured when the smell of Steven's creation wafted enticingly from the kitchen, making everyone's mouths water. Amelia returned with impeccable timing, sharing nothing about her whereabouts.

It was an easy evening, everyone smiled easily,

laughed easily, shared easily. We played Griffin's games. Well, Amelia, Griffin, and Noah played, Noah in his true overly competitive fashion, the other two halfheartedly pulled along by his enthusiasm. Steven and I sat back and observed them with amusement.

"How, how can you be so competitive over a board game that no one really understands the point of?" I asked, watching Noah insist Amelia lose a point for some unheard-of board game etiquette indiscretion.

"That's my Noah. I'm so proud right now!" Steven replied mockingly, clasping his hand over his heart, before dissolving into fits of laughter as Noah strutted around the room claiming to remain the reigning champion of game night.

A mishmash of music played in the background. As an upbeat party tune started to play, Steven leaped from the couch, dragging me with him. I, in turn, caught hold of Amelia, and Steven pulled us both into the middle of the room. Noah turned up the volume and joined us as we laughed and danced around the room like a bunch of crazy people.

"Griffin! Get over here!" Amelia demanded, forcing him from the sofa to join us. I expected resistance, but he complied, his dancing was even worse than Noah's. The song drew to an end, and I wandered toward the kitchen. As I reached the doorway, a familiar tune drifted through the air, an upbeat rhythm entwined with the voice of Taylor Swift that stopped me dead in my tracks. The room around me disappeared, and the ground gave way as I plunged violently into a deep well of darkness. I couldn't scream, I couldn't move, and I couldn't breathe as images of *them* crashed through my skull, her face in the kitchen window, him bouncing across the grass, his voice replaced Taylor's as he recited the lyrics of his favorite song. I stretched my arms toward him; his name was about to burst from my mouth when the arm pulled me back. Back into the kitchen. Back into the now.

I looked down at my arm. Noah's hand was wrapped around it. "Alyssa!" From the tone of his voice, I got the sense he'd said my name more than once.

Griffin appeared beside him. "What happened?" he demanded.

"She just kind of zoned out," Noah hissed. "Is she okay?" He directed his question toward Griffin, like I was incapable of answering, which I suppose I was, but the humiliation stung regardless.

"I'm fine," I insisted.

Saying nothing further, Noah slipped quietly back into the living room. Griffin stepped closer.

The Taylor Swift song had ended, and a softer slower melody drifted through the air. I turned and walked briskly back into the kitchen. With trembling hands, I poured myself a glass of red and glanced back through the arched doorway to watch Noah and Steven, locked in a loving embrace as they moved in rhythm to George Michael's "Careless Whisper."

I could feel Griffin's eyes on me. I made the mistake of looking at him, and his gaze held me. I pulled my eyes from his, turned, and faced the sink, taking a large swig of cabernet. I felt him come up behind me. As I turned to face him, he gently plucked the wine glass from my hand and placed it down on the kitchen counter. Without saying a word, he pulled me into his arms, pressing me close to him as he swayed in time to the music. Embarrassed and confused I let him, enjoying the comforting feeling of his warm arms around me.

When the song ended, I pulled back and tried to step out of his hold. He loosened his arms, but his hands remained on the small of my back. His head bowed toward mine, and my heart rate increased. My body's reaction was a contradiction to what was going through my head. I could have kissed him, could have done nothing and let him kiss me, but as attractive as he was, something just didn't feel right. His need was too great. I wasn't ready to jump into anything with anyone, certainly not someone who felt so intensely invested so soon.

I coiled my hands behind my back, gently prying his fingers apart and guiding them to his sides, but his fingers continued to caress mine. I placed my palms flat on his chest and murmured, "It's time to go to bed," turning away from him.

Wait, that didn't sound very clear. Did that sound like I was inviting him into bed with me?

In a slight panic, I whirled back around, and blurted, "That wasn't an invitation!"

I was met with a bemused look as Griffin leaned back against the counter and crossed his arms, watching me digging a desperate hole. "I didn't think it was," he replied coolly, a smirk pulling at the corners of his mouth.

Wow, my foot really does like to live in my mouth!

I stepped forward feeling foolish. "I'm sorry. I just…I didn't want to give you the wrong impression. I mean, it's not like I'm not attracted to you—wait, no, that sounded wrong. What I meant to say is that it's not that you're not attractive, you are, very. I just…oh dear God, someone shut me up."

Griffin gave a low sultry laugh.

My cheeks flushed with embarrassment as I turned to leave.

"Alyssa."

I turned sharply, not realizing he had taken a step closer; my lips brushed against his. His kiss was gentle, warm, and brief, holding me for just a moment as his hand brushed my cheek. "Goodnight," he whispered.

I turned with cheeks still burning and slipped out of the room.

Chapter 5

Death is supposed to be the end. The religiously compelled will tell you it's a beginning more than an end, but it is undeniably the end of the only version of life any of us know. When you're alive, you imagine the worst, or one of the worst, eventualities anyone could ever experience would be death. Rarely do you think beyond that, that there could literally be a fate worse than death. That was the exact scenario I felt had been thrust upon me. The mind-numbing fear, the soul-crushing pain and desperation of being severed from loved ones, the finality death brought to every aspect of my being without delivering an absolute end.

Being trapped in an existence of bleak and dismal desolation seemed to be the epitome of rock bottom, but then discovering that rock bottom had an even darker abyss lying beneath it in the form of an evil undead monster that hunted me with malicious, possibly murderous intent, made my struggle for survival seem redundant and had annihilated every ounce of hope, extinguishing my fighting spirit along the way.

Griffin, Noah, Steven, and Amelia saved me.

The time spent with the four of them did not answer all my questions. Self-doubt still occupied a small space within me. The feeling that I had somehow messed up refused to adhere to its eviction notice. I still had no recall of my unveiling, had no idea why I had remained here. But being with them did give me something, something I had desperately craved in the days following my passing. It gave me hope.

Along with hope, it also gave me purpose, a rationale for the inexplicable, a reason for the rejection I'd felt so harshly cast upon me. Most importantly, it gave me back me. The fiercely independent, fearless girl I'd fought so hard in life to become.

Just one thing was holding me back. As much as the thought of revisiting the past petrified me, I was stuck in limbo. The smallest of things would trigger a memory flash. The fragmented surges brought with them a debilitating paralysis, both physically and mentally. The anticipation of experiencing one became almost as bad as actually experiencing one. I needed to know; I was unable to move forward with such a gaping hole in how I came to be where I was. It was haunting me. They were haunting me. I thought it was the job of the living to put the departed to rest, yet now the roles appeared to have been reversed.

I rose long before dawn and slipped silently from the loft, pausing outside to be sure I was not followed. Then quickly I made my way home, allowing the draw of the curbside to capture me once again. I may not have known the full story, but I certainly now knew why I was pulled each time to that very spot.

The residual energy. I recognized it now just as Griffin had. It hung thick in the air like static electricity before a storm, pushing me gently to that exact spot and holding me like a weighted blanket.

Driven with newfound determination, I sat perched on the cold cement and took a breath. I placed my open palms on the curb, fingers spread, hands pressed firmly down. I took deep steady breaths, each one slower than the last. I closed my eyes; the cement was warmed by my touch. I imagined it softening, imagined my hands sinking into it like warm wet sand on a summer's day by the shore. Everything stores energy. I had spent the last few days watching it, studying it, feeling it. Snippets of past events left behind to be absorbed and stored by plants and air and inanimate objects, by people and animals and nameless creatures.

The smell materialized first, barely a whiff, like a tiny wisp carried on a gentle zephyr. My slow steady breaths continued, deep and sedate. There was fear here, but it was numb, pacified. It flowed like an undercurrent, always there but deep down, causing no disruption to the surface.

The potency of the smells increased. They surrounded me, still dancing gently, carried by the breeze. The scents of metal, rust, and burning, friction from tires against the surface of the road. The scent of rust intensified, molecules from the metallic odor drifted into my nasal passages, down my throat, infiltrated my taste buds, and stirred memories.

Muscle memory snapped into action casting a thousand simultaneous sparks behind my eyelids, each one holding a tiny fleeting image of a small form with blond hair and a wide smile.

Kasey.

His voice sliced through my brain, shrill and breathless as he yelled, "Count how many it takes me, Mommy." I spun toward the sound, tears stinging my eyes, watching the replay as his tiny legs sprinted across the front lawn, running to retrieve the ball I had just flung across the yard. I'm right there, laughing and alive and oblivious to anything but him.

My breath caught in my chest, and a thousand daggers stabbed my head simultaneously.

Kasey.

I drifted from the curbside to the front lawn without any conscious effort.

The closer I got, the more I started to shake, and then I was no longer just watching. I was there. Back in my body, reliving a past I had run from, now powerless to stop what was already in motion. From the kitchen window, my mom watched while putting the finishing touches to dinner, sharing knowing smiles with me, coconspirator, as my counting slowed to allow extra time for little legs pumping fervently.

"Count quicker, Mommy. Do it properly!" he had shrieked, too astute for his five years.

"I am counting properly, Kase," I had insisted with a grin. "You're just too fast for me, buddy!"

He grabbed the ball and bolted back halfway across the grass before launching it with an effort-induced grunt in my direction. It glided swiftly through the air, approaching me with more force than I had expected from my tiny boy. I fumbled to catch it one handed as it struck my palm hard and bounced in the opposite direction, but not before it snapped my thumb painfully backward. "Shit!" I exclaimed.

"Mommy! You said a bad word," he indignantly yelled.

Oh, the shame!

"I did. I'm sorry, buddy. Mommy shouldn't have said that." I grimaced.

With a gasp, Kasey dashed the remaining few yards between us, the worried look on his face pained me.

"Mommy, are you hurt?" His big sapphire-blue eyes were wide from the prospect of having inflicted pain. Concern was etched across his beautiful features.

"I'm okay, baby," I reassured him, eager to expel the anxiety I had just caused. "Look, I just needed to shake it off." I shook my hand wildly as I bounced goofily across the grass singing loudly to his favorite pop song. Kasey bounced along in chorus with me, all giggles and silliness before we both collapsed in a jumbled mess of kisses and cuddles on the soft grass.

Our playtime was over. Dusk had crept upon us unnoticed. Our evening routine consisted of tub time before dinner, followed by stories and cuddles to wrap up the day. The air had chilled, making me eager to get inside. The football sat on the sidewalk, inches from the front lawn. Far enough from the quiet road for me not to think twice about asking Kasey to go grab it. As he danced across the front yard, he chattered about tubby time and bubble mountains while I quickly examined my injured hand.

I don't know what made me look toward the house, intuition maybe? I was confused by what I saw, my mom's features distorted by a horrified expression. Impulsively, my gaze followed her line of sight. I turned in the direction in which she stared, to the sidewalk where Kasey was just about to reach for his football as the roar of an engine filled the air.

What happened next, I have since replayed in slow motion a million times over. But right at that moment, it was like I was living it for the first time all over again. The truck, an old gray pickup sped too fast down the peaceful suburban street. It swerved manically, hitting the curb outside of the Cardona home, two houses down and across the street from us. The driver, in a futile attempt to regain control, overcorrected the erratically spinning steering wheel, turning it sharply in the opposite direction, which sent the truck tearing across the street, veering straight toward my precious baby boy.

I sprinted across the yard screaming his name. Kasey stood rooted to the spot, frozen in fear, a deer in headlights. *A baby deer in headlights, my baby deer in headlights*. His huge blue eyes glistened, wider than I'd ever seen them. I reached him with seconds to spare, my arms wrapped around him, and I turned us both sharply away from the speeding truck, our last embrace.

I remember the fleeting evanescent scent of his watermelon shampoo, the comforting smell of the fabric softener that clung to his sweater, the sweater that covered his fragile little form. All I wanted to do was to encase this tiny frame with my arms, with my body, to create a cloak of protection from the fast-approaching vehicle. But my subconscious knew better, knew this would not suffice. Instinctively, I used all the strength I had to shove him, hard, so hard his little feet lifted from the ground, so hard he flew across the concrete sidewalk toward the front lawn of cushioned grass where he landed with a soft thud and a wail. The sound of the runaway truck was like the thundering roar of a jet engine as it mounted the curb and engulfed me, muffling my screams. Its high beams blinded me, and then everything stopped.

I stopped.

Enshrouded by silence, cocooned by darkness, time tiptoed by, but I wasn't a part of it. No pain, no fear, no memories, I simply ceased to exist.

I wasn't. Then I was.

I gasped and raised my hands sharply. That wasn't the taste of rust, it was the taste of blood. My eyes blinked back into focus. I was shaken and horrified and heartbroken. But it still wasn't enough.

I didn't want to try again. I had so mercifully been spared the harrowing experience of remembering my death in its entirety. I had no desire to retrieve such long-lost memories. But something drove me forward. I could feel the driver's energy, isolated markers, familiar recognizable scents. The stench of stale beer, perspiration on clothing, gas fumes from the car. I just needed to hold on a little longer, move closer to really feel him, I needed to know who he was without really understanding why.

I took a deep breath and started over. My hands warmed quickly; empathic autopilot engaged. I swallowed hard, forced the warm metallic taste down my throat. Slow deep breathing kept me grounded, kept me calm as the smells continued to develop. I recognized the odor of exhaust fumes, old leather, possibly from the interior of the car, and then the flashes flared behind my closed eyes. Distorted and fragmented, small pieces of memories, like slivers of a torn-up photograph, the partial frozen frame of a moment passed.

A flash of headlights so close I could see the thin metal filament of the bulb casting dazzling beams of white light as they sliced blindingly through the darkness. The eyes of the driver, sluggish and unperturbed by what was transpiring before him, barely awake and clearly inebriated. Although dull, I could feel what resonated from him—arrogance and entitlement, jealousy and spite, every feeling ugly and dark.

I saw him.

Gently, I removed my hands from the curb. I avoided focusing on the roadside, knowing the tiniest specks of blood were still visible, to me at least. I walked back up to the house, stood on the porch, closed my eyes, and listened, homing in on the occupants, shutting off everything else that sounded around me. And I heard what I was seeking, the soft melodic sounds of my mom reading Kasey a story, the steady rhythmic beating of his heart, the smallest feeling of contentment and reciprocal gratitude for each other, comfort and love and longing and hope, grief still present, but swirling amongst a dozen lesser negative emotions.

My tears began. A warm and constant stream, sobs rattled my chest. My heart ached so badly; I was filled with a sorrow so powerful yet intertwined with the smallest ribbon of relief. They had each other, they would be okay. I was the one who would suffer the most, who had endured the greatest loss. If I'd had a choice, this was what I would have chosen infinitely. For them to live, for the sacrifice to be mine.

The pain in my heart worsened with the realization that this was all I would ever get to do, to listen and to watch, from the outside looking in.

And just like that a decision was made, cemented in my mind, absolute and steadfast.

Tomorrow, I would find him. Tomorrow, I would make him pay.

Chapter 6

The following day I was ready. Saying nothing to the others, I rose early and left the loft. When I was a decent distance from the industrial estate, I stopped and watched the sunrise, for some strange reason longing for coffee. A morning ritual I had been without and until this point had not missed. I was ready to hunt.

I headed downtown, straight to the closest bar. Fletcher's was familiar to me. I had bartended there for a little over eighteen months while attending nursing college. Something I had sensed yesterday had reminded me of it, something aside from the pungent smell of stale beer. It was a large red brick building that sat on the corner opposite the fire station and next to a strategically placed fried chicken fast-food restaurant that stayed open late to accommodate the bar's patrons.

Obviously, it was closed. Dawn was outside of the trading hours permitted by its liquor license. I placed one palm flat against the heavy wooden door. The bar was empty. All I could feel was a mishmash of residual energy, too weak to connect to my drunk driver.

I strolled through town, taking the opportunity to practice my developing skills. I was learning a lot. A single person was easy to identify, their energy, or essence, encapsulated by an invisible membrane that existed centimeters from their physical form. Like how someone may describe an aura but with less visibility.

Each energy was unique. Some may be similar, but none that I had encountered up to that point had been identical. Large group settings, public places like hospitals, office blocks, and schools on the other hand, were challenging, to say the least. The volume, the density, and the mass of collective energies were overwhelming, and isolating individuals within seemed impossible. The more I focused, the more I felt I would be sucked into a vortex that was deafeningly chaotic, a surge in which I was at risk of drowning.

Although I could only manage to maintain my focus on such places from a distance, I was starting to appreciate and develop an understanding of what was created by such an intricate web of energy. The hospital was an exquisite blend of hope, faith, and happiness interlaced with desperation, sadness, and loss. Elementary schools and churches beamed brightly with joy, comfort, and optimism, while in contrast the high school exuded dark swirls of angst, irritability, and frustration with intermittent plumes of love and pleasure.

Each place that held a high volume of people for an extended period emitted its own distinct form of blended energy, creating its own unique essence that became instantly recognizable. Each person frequenting these places added to its exclusive tapestry, but more than that, each person took with them a shred of that energy, a connection, a sliver woven within their essence, a way to link them back to it. Possibly a way to trace them from it.

The next few hours were spent wandering through town, resisting the urge to hide from the living as they dashed about their daily business.

As early afternoon came around, I headed back to

Fletcher's. I avoided the main streets where possible, still a little unnerved by my invisibility, and opted for the quieter back alleys and service roads instead.

About three blocks from my destination, while walking to the rear of a row of stores, I came across a strange alleyway. Small brick walkways leading to the main street appeared between every few commercial units to my left, the service road continued straight ahead, but to my right was a narrow stone brick alleyway, inexplicably dim and shaded despite the midday sun. Intrigued, I took a step toward it and froze.

At the end of the darkened alleyway, was a stone archway, leading to somewhere that was pitch black. Taking steps toward it triggered a strong and sudden fight-or-flight response. My heart rate increased sharply, and my skin began to prickle and sting as if an electrical current passed over it. Slowly and silently, I stepped backward, eyes fixed on the gaping entry, one step, two steps, three steps, until both feet were firmly planted back on the service road. Only then did I bolt, running the last remaining blocks to get to the bar.

Shaking away the eerie and ominous feelings, I entered Fletcher's and took a seat at the far side of the bar. The long walnut countertop stretched along two-thirds of the length of the single-room public house. A variety of shiny beer taps lined the inner side of the bar and glass shelves displaying a wide array of liquors sat along the wall behind it. Dark wood and faux leather seats in crimson lined the bar. Booths ran along the top wall and old dark wood tables with matching chairs dotted the open floor space. The walls were adorned with the memorabilia of local sports teams, framed sepia photographs, and light-up beer signs. Large flat-screen televisions were mounted behind the bar. About halfway along the wall opposite the bar sat an old jukebox, nestled amongst wall-secured high-top tables and stools.

The hours ticked by slowly. The people who passed through the bar at that time of the day shared similar traits. A couple of companionless older regulars, calling in as much to alleviate loneliness as to grab a beer. An off-duty firefighter who I hoped would not be heading to a shift after polishing off three beers and two bourbons. A couple of office workers getting very touchy-feely while taking a late lunch break, concealed in one of the back booths, their actions raising my suspicions.

Only one wearing a wedding band, nice!

Damn! Death had brought out my inner judgmental side.

One of the television sets was airing a house-flipping show, and in my boredom, I found myself watching it. A group of four college students took one of the high-top tables, ordered wine spritzers, and discussed their upcoming holiday celebrations. It was around four fifteen that he entered. The bartender nodded a cold and unfriendly greeting in his direction, addressing him as "Mike."

I had remained consistently aware of everyone around me, closing my eyes as I scanned the room mentally for something, anything that would alert me to his energy.

He was easily recognizable, his shameless swagger, the way he rudely clicked his fingers at the bartender, leering toward the college students, his shouts to two men sat at the opposite end of the bar. Every action a reflection of his condescension and disrespect for everyone and everything.

I estimated he was probably in his mid-forties. A trucker's cap sat on top of a mop of greasy dirty-brown hair, a beer belly protruded above his belted jeans covered by a plaid shirt. He took a seat at the bar, six seats down from me, leaned back draping one arm along the back of the barstool, took a long gulp from the bottle of beer placed in front of him and spun slowly around on the barstool, eyeing the rest of the patrons up and down. Arrogance and self-righteousness oozed from him. Not one ounce of guilt or shame could be felt.

The anger that had been on a slow simmer started to boil, increasing in volume and velocity in seconds. Like a river of lava, it flowed, seething and vengeful, burning up my insides, consuming everything in its path. It flooded my mind with murderous thoughts. It crawled and twisted like strangling vines around my heart, feeding hate, fueling images with bitterness and loathing.

I watched him finish off his beer and start on another one, loud and obnoxious, demanding the bar snacks be replenished or the next beer be served. He got to his third beer before he clambered down from the barstool and headed toward the restroom, and in doing so he passed directly by me. In one fluid movement, I spun my seat, simultaneously rising on the stool's footrest just enough to lean over the bar and scoop up the small paring knife sitting next to a bowl of limes. I didn't miss a beat as I slid from my seat, half a second behind him.

I got to the restroom door, placed one hand on it, and froze as a familiar scent wafted through the air, making the hairs on my neck stand up, an oppressive feeling of doom engulfing me.

It was here.

You have got to be kidding me!

This time I didn't run. I simply turned and walked through the rear fire exit. I would not fight it now; my fight would be saved for the driver. I would not risk being incapacitated by the Kerwin shadow entity today. Furiously I skulked away.

I arrived home quickly. Making a conscious effort to avoid the pull of the curbside, I took a seat on the front porch and looked at the small blade still in my hand. I hadn't formulated a plan. I'd been led by my instincts, but I knew with absolute certainty, had I entered that restroom, I would have killed him.

I was contemplating the potential ramifications of killing him when a car screeched to a halt at the front of the house, breaking through my thoughts. A familiar white car with a logo on the driver's side door. I slowly rose and quietly repositioned myself in the far corner of the front porch, obscured from view, an utterly redundant action given the circumstances, watching with amusement as the delivery guy bounded up to the front door to deliver the food, takeout from our favorite Asian restaurant.

"It must be Monday," I murmured to myself.

Monday nights my mom worked late, and therefore I had been charged with preparing dinner. After a few disastrous attempts, which at best rendered my culinary attempts inedible and at worst resulted in me nearly burning the house down, I had admitted defeat and utilized my dialing skills to order takeout instead. And so, our Monday Chinese takeout tradition came to be. A tradition that was being continued, it would seem. It warmed my heart and loosened the hateful vines that had entangled it.

As the delivery driver approached the front door, I

held my breath. I could hear my mother's footsteps as she hurried to the door, hear the pitter-patter of Kasey's tiny feet as he thundered down the hallway. That child was incapable of walking; everything he did was at high speed. I could feel them moving closer, each essence similar yet unique, as identifiable as if they were standing right before me.

And then they were.

I'd grown accustomed to walking through busy public spaces confident that I could not be seen, yet the thought of stepping out from my hiding place terrified me. I told myself the irrational hiding stemmed from a fear that my child might sense or even see me, potentially causing him more trauma. But in truth I was petrified at how I would handle either one of them not seeing me. Their passing next to me, oblivious to my existence, forced me to face the inevitable: in their world I simply no longer existed; the bond between us had been severed forever.

And so I remained, a mere few feet from them, hand clasped over my mouth and tears pooling in my eyes as I watched them.

It had only been a couple of weeks, but Kasey looked taller. My mom's smile didn't reach her eyes as she exchanged cash for the takeout and thanked the driver, making my heart ache even more. I waited for the car to pull out of the driveway and move a distance down the street before allowing my knees to buckle. With a heavy sigh, I slid down to the ground, pulled my knees to my chest and leaned slightly against the wooden railing, drinking in every last moment of the closest contact I would get with my baby.

My mom had carried the bag of food through to the

dining area, and for just a moment, Kasey was alone. The car had gone, but my little boy remained in the doorway, looking out across the gloomy front yard, squinting at something across the street. I turned to follow his gaze and nearly choked. Staring menacingly at him was the shadowy figure, his tall male stature motionless in the middle of the road.

Kerwin!

How had he gotten so close without me realizing!

He wasn't staring at me; he was staring at Kasey, who appeared hypnotized by him. Eyes wide and unblinking, he took one step beyond the door frame as Kerwin's arm reached out to him. I panicked, leaped to my feet and snatched up one of the smaller potted plants that decorated the porch. I held it above my head and dropped it. It hit the porch floor with a crack, its terracotta pot shattering on impact. The sound snapped Kasey from his trance-like state and alerted my mom, who dashed back to the doorway, pulling Kasey back inside, a puzzled look on her face as she surveyed the broken pot and soil strewn across the porch. Thankfully she closed the door, telling Kasey it didn't matter, and they would clean it up in the morning, ignoring his futile attempts at claiming innocence.

My child and mom safe, I turned my attention back to Kerwin. He cocked his head to one side and stared at me, hissing something inaudible. I couldn't understand the words, but the message was clear. I thought I was tougher, thought I could outwit him, thought I could outrun him. I was ignorant. I was wrong. I had underestimated him. His furious power hurtled toward me like a tsunami.

Still staring at me, he crouched, like an animal ready

to pounce, pushing me beyond the limits of my control. The flight instinct overpowered me, and I leaped from the side of the porch and ran.

Chapter 7

I ran without looking back, fear coursing through me as it always did, but this time it wasn't alone. I was angry. Angry at myself for succumbing to my fear and fleeing, angry at him for inflicting a terror that cast me into a freefall of pure panic. The anger-induced heat pushed me on long after he had ceased his sadistic cat-and-mouse game. I didn't stop until I reached the loft.

I entered breathlessly, which made me even more angry at my foolishness for not taking a moment to compose myself. I wasn't trying to deceive anyone, not intentionally. I just knew that no one else could possibly understand my need for vengeance. I didn't want to lose them; I didn't want them to judge me, but above all else I didn't want them to stop me.

I was relieved to discover the only person home was Amelia, curled up on one of the leather chaise lounges on the mezzanine floor, reading. She peered down with a quizzical expression at my dramatic entrance.

I gave a casual wave and ducked into the kitchen, gulping down a glassful of water and taking a moment to calm myself the hell down. I was really hoping she would return to her book, but instead I walked back into the lounge area to find her standing at the bottom of the staircase waiting patiently.

Shit!

In a feeble effort to steer any conversation away

from me and my whereabouts, I walked alongside the lower-level bookcase. I ran my fingers along the collection of books, some bound in paper, some in leather. It really was an impressive collection, arranged by genre, then alphabetized. First-edition poetry, history, folklore, mythology, and science.

I wondered if it was a shared collection.

"They're all Griffin's, for the most part at least," Amelia said softly, reading my mind. She stepped away from the base of the staircase and walked toward me with a small smile. I realized with dismay my diversionary tactic had failed but that she was graciously indulging my efforts by playing along.

"How old is he?" I asked, craning my neck to see the top shelves. Most of the books there appeared to be written in an array of different languages.

"Well, I know Steven was a seventies kid, died in the nineties. Noah is older. He was killed in like the 1950s or something."

He was killed!

"And Griffin?" I persisted; it was like trying to get blood out of a stone.

"I know he's older. I don't know exactly how old. Disclosure isn't really his thing," she admitted with a nonchalant shrug.

"What about you?" I asked. I watched her carefully, assessed her reaction, not sure if my directness had overstepped a mark.

"Is that what it's going to take?" she asked.

I frowned. "What do you mean?"

"For you to trust us? To trust me?"

I gulped.

She continued, "We do notice when you're not here,

you know. And just to be clear, Alyssa, you can come and go as you please. You don't have to sneak out in the middle of the night."

"That wasn't...I mean I wasn't doing it to avoid anyone. I just..." My voice trailed off. I'd never been great at lying.

Amelia's eyes narrowed. "Don't you think we know?"

My breath caught in my chest. "Know what?" I squeaked.

"That dying is one of the most emotionally painful experiences anyone can go through. No one is going to push you to talk about it."

I let my breath out slowly, feeling a guilty relief wash over me.

"When you're ready to talk about it, we're here." Her smile was back, warm and genuine.

"And you? Are you ready to talk about it?" I queried softly.

With a small sigh, Amelia turned and walked over to the lounge area. She sat on the sofa and tucked her legs beneath her. It made her look even smaller on the oversized seat. I hesitated and watched her movements curiously but stayed close to the bookshelf until she beckoned me over.

She looked nervous as I joined her, tucking my feet up underneath me in a similar manner to her. She offered me a small smile and turned to gaze out of the large window behind the sofa. We remained silent for a few moments. I waited patiently knowing exactly what she was feeling, feeling what she was feeling. Sometimes words are unnecessary. Fear and apprehension swirled around her. She wasn't avoiding my questions; she was mustering up the courage to respond and taking the time to try and calm herself. As I waited patiently, my heart ached for her. So fragile, so delicate, and so broken.

When she started to talk, it was barely an audible whisper.

"It happened two years ago. I lived in Queens, had done all my life. I met my fiancé in high school. It sounds so cliché, I know, but he was my soul mate. I knew we'd be together forever…" Her voice trailed off, hitting me with a huge feeling of guilt.

I cleared my throat to speak, but she shakily picked up again, her eyes fixed on mine with a glimmer of determination. I understood, she needed to do this, get through this. I closed my mouth and listened.

"We were so good together. We'd set a date for the wedding, May twelfth, but then we had to postpone it when I got pregnant. She was unexpected. I'd had…issues. We weren't even sure if I could get pregnant, but we did, and she was very, very wanted."

I understood that feeling.

Her eyes softened, and the memories made a small smile drift across her face. "She was two, when we died."

We?

"Cal, my fiancé, Malaika, my baby girl, and I were all in the car when it was hit. We all died."

"But only you stayed?" It wasn't really a question; the answer was evident.

I don't know what possessed me to assume such a thing, where it originated from or why it blurted so loudly from my mouth before my brain had even registered its existence. Maybe there was something too familiar in the haunting tone of Amelia's voice or the ashen color that seeped across her face as she recounted her story, but once it escaped, there was no going back.

Her eyes widened in shock as the words hung in the air between us, stated like a fact, like I knew the truth before being told, like I was literally a mind reader.

"It was a drunk driver!"

The frozen look of horror on her face made me wish I could snatch the words back, stuff them deep down my own damn throat!

"I can't read your mind, Amelia," I reassured her. "I have no idea where that came from. Well, actually, that's not true. I mean, I kind of do, but I honestly didn't mean to upset you. I didn't mean to shout that." My panicked words gushed uncontrolled in an effort to fix what I'd done. It seemed to work. Amelia closed her eyes and took a deep breath before opening them and looking straight at me.

"Alyssa, it's okay. I was just shocked because, well, you were right. It was a drunk driver," she said with a gulp.

Huge tears streamed down her face. My last ounce of strength crumbled and I succumbed to my own grief, tears falling fat and steady down my cheeks as I crawled across the sofa to embrace her. She clung desperately to me. Sobs rattled through her, matched with my own sobs. Shared anger, shared resentment, shared pain too deep and raw to explain, a shared despair brought about by the actions of a common enemy.

We cried until it depleted our energy, until red raw eyes were unable to shed anymore. No words were exchanged, no words were needed. Amelia fell into an unsettled slumber, and I got up from the sofa, covered her with a throw and walked numbly around the room, looking for something, anything to distract me from the dark thoughts invading my brain.

I was still adamant that I would take my revenge on the bastard that killed me. Maybe I'd make it my job to track down the bastard that killed Amelia and her whole family too, avenge her once I'd avenged myself.

"Is Amelia okay?" Griffin asked, concern shadowing his face as he gestured toward the tiny sleeping ball curled in the corner of the sofa.

He had arrived ahead of the other two, who were probably out saving the world, a sharp contrast to my afternoon that had been spent fantasizing about murder.

"She told me what happened, how she passed. I might have broken her," I admitted sheepishly.

"No, you didn't. You probably helped her. She needed to get it off her chest." Griffin remained in his spot, a master of intensity as he studied me carefully, making me feel like a specimen in a laboratory again. "I can feel hostility. Are you okay?"

Damn right there's hostility. There's only one way to alleviate my hostility, and it's called vengeance.

Despite my thoughts, my face remained impassive. I knew Griffin would disagree with my plan. Alerting him to it would probably push him into following me even more than he already was and would fuel his attempts to prevent me from inflicting harm on another. I needed him as my ally, not my obstacle.

I turned to him. "She has hostility and resentment for what was taken from her. We both have. I think that's to be expected given the circumstances."

"Resentment is a slippery slope. It will drag you down with it," Griffin warned.

"It's not like I can flip a switch and suddenly stop feeling," I snapped.

"That's not what I'm saying. You just need to channel the anger and resentment into something else, something more constructive," he offered.

"Well, maybe if you stopped bubble-wrapping me and let me learn, I would have less time and energy to focus on anger and resentment," I pointed out.

His mouth dropped slightly as he scrambled for a response.

"I'm ready," I insisted.

He sighed, knowing he was beaten but still refusing to agree.

Thankfully Steven and Noah arrived home, providing a much-needed distraction from what would undoubtedly have disintegrated into an argument and offered me a window of escape. I stole silently upstairs as the three of them talked, feeling Griffin's gaze on me with every step I took.

Chapter 8

The next day I rose early, just not quite as early as usual. I was still the first to be up.

I traveled home and stood on the far side of the driveway, only partially obscured from view, had I still been alive and with an actual visible form, that is. I watched my mom and Kasey conduct their usual morning routine. It stung a little but left me feeling I had accomplished at least something. A step in the right direction, acceptance that I would only ever be on the outside looking in.

Today was going to be a good day. I was so determined to learn, so desperate to do something, to practice my skills, to prove myself, and it was all a step toward my ultimate goal, the execution of my plan, my vengeance.

I'm coming for you, Mikey!

With excited anticipation, I quickly made my way back to the loft.

As I turned the last corner before the building, the low rumble of an engine filled the air, and there sitting patiently upon a huge black and chrome motorbike was Griffin.

My jaw dropped. "You have a bike?" I asked.

"Why is that so surprising?" he replied with a laugh.

"You just don't seem like the biker type," I said, quickly adding, "I mean, it looks good on you!"

Keep him sweet. He's doing you a favor, remember!

Griffin revved the engine and offered me his hand. "Are you ready?"

"Where are we going?" I asked, making no attempt to move toward him or his bike.

He raised an eyebrow quizzically. "Are you afraid to ride with me?"

I answered him with a roll of my eyes before clambering on behind him. My arms wrapped around his torso as the engine roared, and we set off leaving a cloud of dust and gravel in our wake.

We headed south toward the Atlantic coast of New Jersey.

The drive down to the shore should have taken a few hours at least, but astride an engine, it was apparent Griffin lost his staunch sensibility. We sped through the streets at dizzying speeds. As scary as the ride was, I liked this version of Griffin, a lot!

The roaring engine's speed and volume decreased as the cold December salt air whipped around us. Griffin pulled smoothly into a shaded area close to one of the many wooden walkways that accessed the beach. We walked through the empty dunes and sat amid the sandy hills secluded from the distraction of anyone who may have been taking a beach stroll.

It was peaceful and serene. Despite the season, the sky was blue, and the sun was shining, the waves lapped rhythmically against the shore, and the gulls dipped through the air. It was not what I had envisioned our training day to look like.

I eyed Griffin suspiciously. "This is beautiful, but what are we doing here?"

"There are things you need to learn. Fighting skills

are just one small part. Focus and self-control play a bigger role, for your safety and the safety of those around you. But before any of that I need to show you something."

"Okay."

Griffin's voice was low as he explained, "There are doorways. It's important that you recognize them. It's important you don't get too close." He continued, "I know you think I'm too serious and that I have too many rules. But I hope you understand it's only to protect you."

"I know," I answered softly. "It's just sometimes, the way you try to enforce them, the way it feels like you're trying to control me, you make me feel like a woman from the 1920s."

Griffin lowered his head, then glanced up at me and with a soft laugh said, "That was actually a time of great progress for women."

"Huh?"

"Women gained the right to vote in the 1920s," he said, his eyes downcast again.

"What are you, a historian now?" I teased him with a soft shove.

"No." He chuckled. "That was when I lived."

"You were alive in the 1920s?" I shouldn't have been surprised; his mannerisms aligned perfectly with that era. "Wow, you really are an old man." I laughed, overemphasizing the old.

He shook his head and rolled his eyes, standing and extending his hand to pull me to my feet. "Get up, child. We have work to do."

We walked down the beach until we reached a bend on the shoreline. A path of powder-white sand was visible between the rolling dunes and long grass behind us.

Griffin paused. "We're going into the dunes. I need you to tell me when you feel anything unusual."

We followed the hollow between the dunes as it spiraled around a large mound. It felt like we had walked in a full circle, but instead of ending up back at our original starting point, we had reached a long sandy path stretching beyond where the shoreline should have been. There was no doorway, no hole or tunnel, just a long narrow path with grassy dunes on either side. But something was wrong. The sounds of the ocean, the squawking of the gulls, and the sharp salty breeze had disappeared, replaced with motionless silence. My heart sped up. An anxious energy played with my nerve endings. My instinct was to step backward, back to the real world, to normality and the sounds of life from the water and the wind. It didn't feel bad, just wrong.

I turned to Griffin. "Is this where the planes cross? Is that Laeon?"

"Yes, there are a number of convergence points. Each looks somewhat different, but they all feel the same."

"And what would happen if I did continue walking?" I asked, unsuccessfully craning my head for a glimpse into it.

"We can pass between planes, but it's not our zone of existence. You may not recognize dangers, you may become weak or disoriented, and as we don't know why you chose to remain here, we don't know for sure either plane would accept you."

"Have you ever entered it?" I asked him.

"Not for a long time," he responded.

We walked back the way we had come, back to the

shore, retracing our steps up the beach, back to our hidden sanctuary. Once there he told me to stand in the center of the sandy space.

"The strongest weapon you have is your mind," Griffin said as he walked slowly around me. "Don't rely on what you see, rely on what you feel."

I closed my eyes. His footsteps stopped. I resisted opening my eyes and instead turned slowly toward the direction I felt him to my left. I could feel a distance between us, sensing him as he stood motionless. The shrill cry of a gull momentarily pulled my attention away, and within a split second, Griffin launched himself across the sand toward me. Keeping my eyes closed, I dropped to the ground and rolled in his direction. Instead of coming into contact with me, he flew straight over the top. I sprang to my feet and paused with my back to him, waiting till the very moment his hands brushed millimeters from my skin before throwing myself up and back, somersaulting out of his grasp. He ran at me again. I tried to duck, but he changed his tactic and dove at my legs, tackling me to the ground with a thud.

Damn it!

I turned to face him, breathless not from the exercise but from the exhilaration.

He seemed genuinely impressed. "That was really good. Just don't commit to any direction until the very last minute," he suggested, pulling me to my feet to go again.

We practiced for hours. Griffin taught me how to punch in the most effective manner, how to immobilize an attacker in three different ways with elbow blows, where to kick an attacker to sweep their feet from under them and how to avoid getting pinned and locked.

The sun was setting when we finally collapsed, sweaty and breathless from exertion.

Lying next to each other, our bodies warming the cold sand, Griffin turned to me. "Your fighting skills are impressive. Most people would need to train for weeks, months even, to get to the level you're at." He continued, "Developing fighting skills is important, but so is knowing when to run." He propped himself up on his elbows. "A Vesk is an instrument forged on a different plane from Earth. Its existence here is unnatural, therefore it emits a very strong, very distinct energy that is easily identifiable. The only weapons that can harm you are ones created on a different plane. Like the Vesks, any such object carries with it a strong energy, one you'll feel long before you can see it."

"So, in that situation, I'm just supposed to run?" It was hard to keep the disappointed tone from my voice.

"Yes!" Griffin said firmly, refusing to elaborate.

"Tell me about your life," I asked him.

"Maybe someday," he replied quietly, climbing to his feet and pulling me to mine.

With the golden hour setting the sky ablaze from the sun's last rays, we hurtled through the streets and towns back to the loft, the sun heating the air around me and a sense of contentment warming me from within. I pushed down the pangs of guilt that happiness brought. A life without Kasey should be anything but. I missed him with all my heart, but this new existence was becoming hard to hate.

When we got back to the loft, Noah was waiting for us with news. We had barely stepped through the door when he announced, "We have one passing. It's going to be soon, and the competition is strong."

"What do we know?" Griffin demanded.

"Location is an assisted-living facility near Columbus Park. Looks like there may be multiple factions after this one," Noah replied.

"Which means it's either a pure one or they're scrambling. Maybe the big one is closer than we thought," Griffin surmised.

"It's definitely Laeon bound. One of Kristoff's clan was there this morning. There's only one type they're interested in, and besides, I think he'd be too afraid to break Aamon's rules."

"I agree," Griffin replied.

"What does this mean?" I asked, stepping forward.

"It means we patrol," Noah answered, giving me a wink.

"I can come, right?" It really was more of a request for confirmation rather than a request for permission.

Griffin shook his head. "It's too soon. You literally just started training."

"No, I just started training with you. I held my own for weeks without you, and you said yourself that I'm a quick learner. I have a really good handle on my powers, *and* I fought like I'd been training for weeks, months maybe!" I argued, using his own words against him.

"Alyssa, this is the wrong time to throw you in the deep end!" Griffin's eyes flashed angrily.

"Or maybe it's the wrong time to be without me!" I insisted, my voice rising.

"She has a point," Noah mumbled, pointedly ignoring Griffin's furious glare.

"Stop treating me like I'm made of glass," I hissed.

"I'm not!" Griffin protested. "I just think you need a little more time; really test your limits before you—"

"Put myself in a potentially dangerous situation," I interrupted, finishing his sentence. "Thank you for your concerns, but I'm coming!" I turned and stomped up the stairs.

I rounded the corner on the mezzanine level just in time to hear Noah say, "You're holding on too tight. Loosen your grip or lose her, Griff."

Too annoyed to try and fathom out exactly what he meant I continued my stomp up to bed.

I awoke the next day long before dawn, eager to start the day, eager to do something productive.

Noah was his usual overly enthusiastic self. Griffin was his usual intense and brooding self. Steven had been absent all evening. The previous night I was told he was watching. When I asked what he was watching, Griffin had responded curtly, "I guess you'll see tomorrow."

Clearly, he was still nursing his bruised ego.

We headed east into Paterson and took the Bergen County line to Hoboken. From there, we headed north to an assisted living facility overlooking Columbus Park in NYC. Steven sat on one of the low-level sand brick walls that surrounded a frozen courtyard dotted with empty patio tables and chairs. He stood up to embrace Noah and threw a disapproving look toward Griffin over Noah's shoulder. As unimpressed as he clearly was with my presence, he still greeted me warmly.

"Any updates?" Noah asked. I was unsure if he was choosing to ignore the obvious tension or if he was actually oblivious to it.

"The old dear is still hanging in there, but it shouldn't be long. The vultures have been circling all night. They hightailed it as you approached, but they won't stay away for long," Steven replied.

I cleared my throat and instantaneously wished I hadn't as three sets of eyes turned toward me. "I was just wondering—people die literally every minute of every day. Why are you here for whoever she is?" I gestured toward the facility. "Why would anyone want her soul specifically?"

"Its purity," Noah responded. Steven and Griffin turned swiftly to him; twin glares told me he'd said more than he should have. He held his hands out and mouthed, "What?" before turning to Griffin. "You brought her here."

Griffin turned to me with a sigh. "Remember I told you some high-value souls were sought after; well, she happens to possess one of the high-value souls."

"And its value is dictated by its purity? I thought you said all humans had souls composed of an equal balance of good and evil?"

"They do, but like humans have evolved, so have souls. Like human DNA can be tracked back through generations, so can souls. Although everyone is born with an equal balance of good and evil, the composition of the good and the evil can vary. For most people, it's similar. But there are a few, very rare souls that have not evolved. Their good or evil elements are completely pure, making them the most potent, highly concentrated form of either good or evil. It may well be that they are direct descendants from the original source of dark or light."

I had a million more questions, but they would have to wait. Something different demanded my attention. I jerked slightly at the invisible point piercing my temple, breathed through my mouth to avoid the familiar chargrilled scent from filling my nasal passages, and turned my head in the direction of the frost-covered lawn that sprawled beyond the paved patio. My reaction garnered the other three's attention.

"Wow, dude, she sensed it before you," Noah taunted Griffin with a look of amused admiration on his face. The Sygan walked straight toward us. Noah and Griffin stepped in front of me. Steven remained beside me. Their assumption that I needed protection when I was the first one to sense the damn thing irritated me. It got within ten feet before hissing and darting left around the perimeter of the building.

"Noah," Griffin roared.

"On it," Noah responded, sprinting after the creature.

Griffin pointed at me as he headed in the opposite direction. "*Stay here.*"

It wasn't a request; it was a demand. It was not appreciated.

I stood statue still and closed my eyes. I focused first on Noah's energy until I could pinpoint his location precisely, then I swung my attention to Griffin's energy. He had circled around the large rectangular building in the opposite direction to cut the Sygan off. Next, I turned my attention to the nefarious smoky energy of the Sygan. It was faster than anyone had anticipated. It was inside the building already, moving upward, fast! Without hesitation, I darted in through one of the open french doors that surrounded the patio.

Some distance behind me, Steven cursed and frantically chased me as I vaulted up staircases and leaped over handrails between flights. I was focused on the Sygan, moving spontaneously, taking a back seat to my instincts, caught in the moment, no time for any other thoughts. I knew I was getting closer; I just hadn't realized how close I was until I abruptly turned down one of the many identical carpeted corridors and ran smack-bang into it.

Rebounding hard, we both crashed to the floor a few feet away from each other. I scrambled to my feet, but he beat me to it, leaping from a lying position on the floor back onto his feet in one fluid movement. I considered fleeing but fought against the impulse. Like being faced with a wild animal, I knew better than to display fear.

I didn't know Steven had caught up to me until he flew past me straight into the Sygan, throwing him over his head and back toward me where he landed literally at my feet. I stumbled backward as he jumped up ready to charge at Steven, turning his back to me in the process.

The opportunity was not missed. I high-kicked the center of his spine, sending him crashing back down to the floor. As he flew one way, something small flew in the opposite direction and landed on the thick carpet at my feet with a soft thud. It was a Vesk, but it contained something. A swirling mist was visible through the glass, and the energy was so strong, oscillating and pulsating. It was mesmerizing and beautiful.

She must have passed already. Damn! This Sygan was quick!

I was only snapped out of my hypnotic state by Griffin's deep booming voice yelling from the other end of the corridor. "Alyssa, smash it!"

I looked up to see the Sygan wrestling furiously with Steven, writhing free and pouncing at me. I stumbled backward as Griffin caught up to us, knocking the Sygan away from me. With a gasp, I flung the Vesk with force against the wall. A warm but invisible energy rushed from the shattered glass, dissipating quickly into the air.

The Sygan disappeared, defeated, in the other direction.

The fight was exhilarating, delivering an adrenaline high that was quickly extinguished when my eyes met Griffin's enraged stare.

"I told you to stay put!" he yelled angrily, storming down the hall.

I stepped forward to meet him, glaring defiantly. "And I told you that you don't own me, you don't get to tell me what to do!" I screamed back.

"What happened?" Noah interrupted, finally joining us. "Did you get it?" He looked between Griffin and Steven.

Steven stood with his arms crossed. He nodded in my direction and said, "She did."

Noah, with complete disregard for the obvious animosity, held his hand up for a high five as he enthusiastically hollered, "Way to go, Alyssa!"

Griffin was seething.

I purposely ignored him and high-fived Noah with a grin. Noah and Steven headed to the stairwell; I hung back, waiting for the opportunity to speak to Griffin alone.

Griffin was the oldest, the leader, the one with superiority, and I respected that, but this constant need to protect me had created contention. My fighting skills were second to none. I didn't need physical protection, and it irked me that he refused to acknowledge this.

Many women would probably have been flattered by such chivalrous inclinations, especially from the very tall, strong, and handsome Griffin. But as well as resenting it, I was afraid of it, fearful of the sense of comfort and security it afforded me. Afraid that I'd slip unnoticed into a dependency. As jaded as my outlook was, it was not without due cause. I had seen firsthand the dangers of relying upon others, how negatively an error in judgement can impact a person. My fear manifested as anger and indignation at the implication of my assumed weakness, especially when the basis for such beliefs were gender generated.

"I get no pleasure from pissing you off, Griffin."

He didn't look at me, but he did unclench his fists. Crossing his arms, he leaned against the wall.

I continued, "I shouldn't have to go to war with you for you to treat me like everyone else. I'm just as strong, just as fast, and just as capable as they are, even if you don't see it."

He opened his mouth to respond but closed it again and remained silent.

I didn't want to have to deal with the anger and hostility every time, but equally there was no way I was giving in to him. Tears threatened to fall and I turned away. Like hell I'd let him think he'd made me cry, even if he had.

"I see it."

I had already taken five steps away from him. I didn't expect him to say anything. His words made me jump.

"I'm sorry," he said, his voice hushed.

I took a shaky breath before turning to face him. "Are you going to stop?" I challenged.

"Yes," he promised.

"Why are you so afraid to let go of me? I'm not going anywhere," I assured him.

"Would you be open to a compromise?" Griffin

asked.

"How so?" I inquired.

"Work with me, just for a short period, let me train you, follow my…suggestions."

"How exactly are you compromising in that situation?" I retorted.

"Give me a week, then I'll step back, let you make your own decisions," he promised.

"You'll treat me as your equal?" I asked tentatively.

"I'll treat you as my equal," he said, placing one hand over his heart.

"Agreed." I extended my hand to close the deal.

"Agreed." He accepted my outstretched hand.

And just briefly I saw it. The look flashed quickly across his face before he concealed it.

Every now and again I would catch it, a look in his eyes, a longing for something more than I was willing to give. I knew at some point I would have to address it, but for now at least, it could be held at bay. For now, at least I could hide behind the façade of ignorance, the truth tucked safely away for another day.

As the others headed back to the loft, I took a detour. Nobody had mentioned that it was Christmas Eve, but it hadn't escaped my notice. Every time I thought about it, I experienced severe pain. It was another first to get through, for me, for my mom, and for Kasey.

My mom had gone all out with decorations, no doubt in an attempt to overcompensate for what would not be a part of this year's celebrations. Our front porch twinkled with a hundred multicolored fairy lights. I snuck around to the back of the house and peeked through the window, concealing myself from view, like I was actually still visible. Some old habits die hard.

The Christmas tree looked beautiful. Santa's plate was ready with a cookie for him and a carrot for Rudolph. Kasey's stocking hung on the fireplace with my mom's to one side and mine to the other.

Why would they put my stocking out?

My heart filled with sadness; their longing ached just as much as mine. Even in the most joyous of times it was there, like an old battle scar, closed but always visible.

I remained there until dawn. I did not sleep, nor cry, nor think. I just remained, numb and sedated by a relentless anguish that tormented me. For the first time ever, I felt dead.

I watched.

I listened.

I listened to the thud of little legs as they rushed down the stairs shortly after dawn. I listened to the squeals of joy and the shredding of the paper that concealed the gifts. I listened to Kasey whisper, "Merry Christmas, Mommy, I love you." I watched him kiss his fingertip before pressing it against the framed image of him and me that sat on the side table. I watched my mom hastily brush away tears before he noticed.

I remained.

The footsteps echoed through the dark and his force filled the air, but I didn't have the strength to turn around. I felt his strong hands gently squeeze my shoulders. Felt his arms as they wrapped around my icy body, but still, I could muster no reaction. He stayed with me. Rode the grief train beside me, patiently waiting for it to pull into its station. Time passed. How much I wasn't sure, but most of the day had dwindled away before I found my voice and regained the ability to move and function. And as gently as he had arrived, Griffin led me home.

Chapter 9

The next few weeks were spent venturing out into the city, honing my skills, learning how to identify the presence of a Sygan at a crossing. They walked among us every now and again, but unless they carried a Vesk, we gave them a wide berth.

Initially, I had watched from a safe distance as per our agreement, and I'm sure as penance for my first encounter. Although I remained staunchly defiant when it came to being told what to do, I was able to acknowledge Griffin's efforts at loosening the reins. I would allow him a brief grace period for two reasons. One was to adhere to the compromise we had both agreed to. The other was the freedom he extended to me when he believed he'd successfully attained some degree of control over me. It was a stupid and frustrating game we played, but I needed my space to ever stand a chance of exacting my revenge plan, so for now, I would play along with him, and knowing he concealed some unknown ulterior motive lessened the burden of guilt at deceiving him.

And so, while Noah, Steven, and Griffin chased Sygans, successfully freeing the souls they had stolen, I fulfilled a sideline role, becoming extremely proficient at pinpointing the location of Sygans who were carrying a Vesk.

I counted down the days, serving the time I had

promised to until eventually I was allowed to become an active participant in their quest, and as much as Griffin refused to admit it, my capabilities made me the protector of the group rather than the one in need of protection. Amelia even joined us a few times. Together we could outmaneuver, outrun, and overpower our opposition far quicker than Noah, Steven, and Griffin. There was a great sense of camaraderie, and it turned the hunt into a battle of the sexes game, all taken lightheartedly, of course. Often, I would catch Griffin watching me with admiration. However, he would look away quickly when my eyes met his. A reaction I was thankful for. That was a thread I had no intention of pulling on.

I paid my last nighttime visit to my mom on New Year's Eve. I was pulled by a force I didn't understand, at least not until I arrived and peered through the window to see my mom tearfully clutching an old photograph of me. It was about thirty minutes before the ball dropped. Kasey was sleeping peacefully on the opposite end of the couch, cocooned in blankets.

I understood entirely the painful significance of a new year. It's what it leaves behind. Time is relentless and without compassion. It relinquishes the fallen without a second glance, pulling all living things along with it. Kasey and my mom would be entering a different year, a year in which I never existed, I would be left behind, forever frozen in time. With each passing day, each month, each year, the space between us, between our last interaction, our last memories would continually expand, growing until the colors started to fade and I became a shadow of times past, a sepia image buried beneath an ever-growing pile of new memories and life experiences.

It was cruel and heart-wrenching, but it was necessary. No life would be lived if loved ones remained with the dead, trapped in the timeframe of their passing. No healing could occur. Healing involves not forgetting, but laying the dead away in a special place deep within the dusty unfrequented corners of one's psyche. Leaving those memories untouched, undisturbed, does not imply a lack of love or that the dead have been forgotten. Quite the opposite. It illustrates how revered and adored the lost ones were, how debilitatingly painful it would be to revisit their existence when the current day doesn't afford the luxury of interaction with them.

A new year brings hope and new beginnings, but for the loved ones we lose, it brings a painful distance and a reminder of what we now must live without.

The clock ticked on. The present slipped silently into a new year, greeted only by silent tears. From the outside, I looked in. The physical distance between us remained, but every other sense of distance grew, pulled by an invisible current like driftwood floating out to sea.

Quietly. Gently. Inescapable from the relentless undertow of time. Leaving me behind, powerless to do anything other than to watch the gulf grow.

January brought gray skies and grayer moods.

At first, I rose early every morning, returning home to check in on my mom and Kasey. Then it became every other day, and eventually only a few times a week. As my abilities matured, I found I didn't need to be in close proximity to check on them. Dropping in became more about fulfilling my own need, grounding me to who I was, grasping lightly to that earthly connection. I knew at some point I would need to let go, but it was yet another bridge I was not ready at that point to cross.

Every day we trained. I still wasn't entirely sure what exactly I was training for, but I did appreciate that I had something to focus on. Tracking required practice and patience. Combat required practice, as did understanding and handling weapons and Vesks.

Griffin was relentless. I understood, to a degree at least, how important training was. In truth, I had always been competitive and never lacked the motivation to be better at everything I did, but Griffin took his dedication to a whole new obsessive level. He would make me run drills over and over again. Anything less than perfection didn't count. He pushed Amelia, Noah, and Steven too, just not with the same intensity that was inflicted upon me.

At first, I assumed it was because my abilities were way below par compared to the rest of them. But over time my skill level increased, and I surpassed the abilities of Steven and Amelia. However, this had no bearing on Griffin's harsh regime, and his rigorous sessions continued, if anything also increasing in intensity. If Amelia, Noah, and Steven trained for two hours, I trained for three. Although harsh, it became apparent that I functioned at a much higher level than both Amelia and Steven, and maybe Noah too. I obeyed his grueling demands without a word of complaint, although the narrative in my head was an entirely different story.

I became faster, I became stronger, and my reactive abilities became better than even Noah's. I could read an opponent's moves seconds before they instigated a strike. Despite my improvements, Griffin's foot didn't budge from the gas. He continued to apply the same pressure with the same severity that he always had.

Most people would have reached their breaking point long before I did. Most people would have thrown in the towel, yelled, and refused to adhere to his ridiculous repetitive demands. I wanted to, many times. But the stubborn streak in me muffled my protests, silenced me, and willed me to continue, using the anger to further fuel my efforts, making me determined to reach the day my abilities exceeded Griffin's and I could finally tell him to go fuck himself.

It was in one of these extended sessions that the first shift occurred. We were in one of the dingy lower-level rooms of the building. It was roughly kitted out with a partially matted floor, taped-up punch bags that swung from the exposed beams, and a wooden paneled wall for knife throwing.

There was only myself and Griffin. Amelia had trained earlier but as always was released way before I was. We were participating in a timed chase, with Griffin chasing me. The objective of this lesson was not to get caught, and if I was caught before the timer ended, we would start all over again. If I remained free for the duration we would switch roles, and I would become the hunter, a role I much preferred.

I darted between brick pillars and training equipment, around the large industrial space with ease, reading Griffin's moves and avoiding his capture. This was my third consecutive attempt, and I was eager to avoid having to repeat the lesson for a fourth time.

Griffin's footsteps were heavy as he closed the distance between us. I faked a run in one direction and as he turned to follow me, I skidded between abandoned rusted oil drums in the opposite direction, twisting and leaping into the air, swinging from one of the exposed metal pipes that ran along the ceiling.

The timer was almost done. The excitement of a potential victory sped my adrenaline to double time throughout my body. I was seconds away when Griffin threw the axe, aiming it with meticulous precision to land inches away from me in the direction I traveled, causing me to screech to a halt and allowing him to catch me.

I was furious. Weapons were not a part of this lesson. Griffin had specifically forbidden the use of them, yet here he was reinventing the rules to ensure my failure.

I lost my shit.

Swinging wildly away from his grasp, I stormed into the center of the room, unable to calm the growing rage within me.

"What the fuck was that?" I demanded, gesturing to the axe embedded in the wall.

"I was stopping you. Let's go again."

"Like hell! I guess that means that I can use weapons too, then. It's your turn to run," I growled, shaking from the waves of red-hot anger that flowed through me.

"No, you failed, you need to go again," Griffin insisted.

"You fucking cheated!"

"You think a Sygan is going to obey rules? Let's go again." Griffin strode over to reset the timer.

The timer started, but I stood still, seething in the center of the room.

Griffin continued as if completely oblivious to my wrath. He charged at me and knocked me to the ground. It was the final straw. I exploded, leaping to my feet with a scream. Turning away from him, I kicked at the closest punchbag, a five-hundred-pound one that hung from the thickest beam. The triple chains securing it snapped, and with a deafening crash, it flew across the room and straight through the single brick wall separating the units. Griffin's eyes widened as I turned to him, still trembling with anger.

"Rein it in, Alyssa. Think of it as a ball of heat. If you squeeze it, you can smother it."

"I don't want to," I stammered, confused by what I was experiencing but not wanting to "smother" whatever it was that was giving me this power.

Griffin moved toward me cautiously.

"It's okay, I know it's hard, but you can do this. You must do this. Rein it in," he insisted, enunciating each word slowly.

I took deep shaky breaths in and out, willing the rage to calm without extinguishing it entirely. It worked. My heart rate slowed, the heat that had crawled to the surface of my skin drifted inward, and my fingers stopped trembling.

"You played dirty." I frowned at him.

He flashed me a wide smile and gloated, "It worked, though, didn't it?"

This was your endgame, to tip me over the edge!

I shot him a murderous look, and he held up both hands, murmuring, "Whoa, rein it in, remember?"

I stomped up to the loft, to the therapeutic stream of a hot shower and the solace of my empty bed.

Thankfully, outside of our training sessions, Griffin was a different person. He was kind and attentive to everyone's needs. He would have the occasional mood swings, but we all just learned to accept what was and avoid him, remaining quiet and unseen until his dark cloud lifted and normality resumed.

My training continued, and my commitment to each session persisted. However, I was careful to keep a thin line between myself and my level of engagement. What I held back was minute, so much so that it went undetected. What I held back was now barely the size and strength of a tealight candle, flickering weakly but still illuminated, hidden and protected from everyone but me.

Weeks slipped by, and my training sessions started to take place away from the loft and surrounding grounds. Griffin would take me to places that Sygans frequented, allowing me to practice tracking, and of course, practice the chase.

On one particular day, I was joined by Noah. Together, the three of us traveled across the Hudson into the city, to the southwest corner of Manhattan, to Tribeca. The hip and upscale neighborhood that was one of the most expensive places to live in the city was also a hub for Sygan activity. Read into that what you will.

We stopped on a street corner. The buildings were not dissimilar to the loft, with exposed brickwork and cast-iron architecture. A cobbled alleyway ran behind us, and a quiet street sat before us. Despite its peaceful façade, there was a bustle of activity concealed from human perception. Rival factions clashed often here. Fights over Vesks and God only knows what else were the norm. Dark energy pulsated from every direction. Noah and I were like wild dogs, leashed by Griffin, straining against his hold, eager to hunt. As always, there were rules. This was a training session, and as such, every move would be observed and assessed.

"There are three Vesks in the vicinity right now, all of them empty. The objective is to destroy two of the three, one each. You must do so with minimal engagement. Don't fight the Sygan carrying. Outmaneuver it, obtain the Vesk, and destroy it only when you are clear of its carrier. Understood?"

General Griffin had returned with force. He took serious to a whole new level.

"Understood," Noah and I responded in unison.

"Go."

Finally, freedom, of sorts. Noah bounded in one direction, I in the other. This wasn't a timed exercise, but whoever succeeded first, got gloating privileges over the other. I prayed that Griffin would trail Noah, but as usual after a brief head start, he was hot on my heels. I tried to ignore his presence and focused instead on meeting my objective.

There was a gateway to Daeon somewhere close by. I could feel its energy seeping out along the cobbled streets. I gave its epicenter a wide berth and circled around in pursuit of my Sygan. I could have utilized a better tactic, stalked my enemy stealthily, sneaking up upon him to steal away his possession before he had the chance to comprehend what was happening, but time was of the essence, and besides, where was the fun in that?

The Sygan felt my presence, felt me closing in on him fast, and as I'd hoped, he bolted. My adrenaline surged, and so did my pace. The primal rhythm of pursuit drummed in tempo to my thudding heart. It was exhilarating. I was almost disappointed to bear down so quickly on the Sygan.

In a blind panic, the Sygan made a catalogue of errors that accumulated in him cornering himself, meeting a dead end between the high-rise buildings. He turned toward me, his eyes flashing manically. He was not going down without a fight. This wasn't quite what Griffin had envisioned, but I was not leaving without my prize, and if that meant a fight to retrieve it, then so be it.

The Sygan snarled and leaped forward. I waited until the very last moment to sidestep him. Dropping to a crouch, I swept one leg to the side taking his feet from under him. He crashed ungracefully to the ground, and I leaped on his back. I forced my knee into the top of his spine, pinning him to the floor. I gripped his hair and pulled his head up roughly, as I hissed, "The Vesk—that's all I want. Remove it slowly, and I'll let you go."

"Fuck you, bitch."

"You wish," I taunted.

"Alyssa!" Griffin's voice boomed as he charged angrily toward us. "Let him go."

"What!" I exclaimed. "No!"

"Griffin, what are you doing?" Noah's voice yelled as he too turned the corner. "She's got this, let her finish."

Griffin strode over to where I was still astride the struggling Sygan. He grabbed at my arm and dragged me roughly off him. Furiously, I pulled my arm free of him, but I was too late. The Sygan leaped up and swung frantically for the both of us, catching my jaw and sending me reeling. I'm not sure who I was angrier with. The Sygan who had just landed a head-splintering blow or Griffin who had enabled the entire episode.

That little flame I'd kept hidden ignited the vapors of anger that coursed swiftly from the strike. The Sygan may have escaped my hold, but he was still cornered. Noah blocked his only exit. Griffin reached out to grab me again, further fueling my fury.

I twisted away and darted for the Sygan. Infuriated, I swung aggressively from behind. The strike threw him to the ground. With a groan, he rolled to the side and pulled himself unsteadily onto all fours.

With no time to waste, I delivered a swift kick to his gut. The action launched him airborne. His body twisted, and his arms flailed as he spun through the air before he struck the concrete with force.

Griffin pounced at me, but this time I was ready, dodging his grasp and again going for the Sygan. A ridiculous game of double dueling ensued as I bombarded the Sygan with relentless blows while evading Griffin's capture, his demands to stop ignored.

It was Noah who pulled me out of it. Noah who pulled the Vesk from the semiconscious Sygan and threw him to freedom. Noah who blocked Griffin and calmed me into a rational state of mind.

"Alyssa, breathe," Noah pleaded.

"I am breathing. Stop being so dramatic," I huffed.

"I told you to rein it in," Griffin hollered.

Incensed, I turned on him. "Why set me a mission to then prevent me from executing it?"

"It wasn't the mission you were executing."

"I had control. I only lost it because of you. That Sygan wouldn't have come close to smacking the shit out of me if you hadn't freed it!" I screamed back.

"This needs to stop now. This isn't how we do things." Griffin scowled.

"What are you talking about, Griffin? She did exactly what she was supposed to do," Noah argued.

"Wait, what?" My head was spinning, partially from the blow and partially from confusion. "You instigated this, and this is exactly what you do! The objective was to get the Vesk, an objective I was succeeding with until you fucked it up!"

"I had to stop you," Griffin stated calmly.

Noah shook his head, as baffled as I. "She had it, and you just let it go, and for what?"

"Stay out of this, Noah!" Griffin growled.

There it was, the confirmation that my suspicions were correct.

Noah turned, cursing, and kicked indignantly at the loose cobbles as he stomped away down the street.

"So this has nothing to do with the lesson, or the objective, or the Sygan or the fucking Vesk. This is about me and what I'm allowed to do, about your hold over me!"

"It's about saving you from spiraling. Is that what you want to hear, Alyssa?"

"I want to hear the truth, Griffin."

"Then there it is. I can see you slipping, and when I'm near you, I can feel myself slipping."

"What is it you're so desperately clinging to? Have you ever considered that just letting go might not be such a bad thing?" My thoughts darted back to my little flame. "You're constantly pushing me, almost beyond my limits, yet you do nothing but suppress yourself."

"I was testing to see how far you can go before you slip. You need to know your limits, just like I know mine. You don't know where it ends." Griffin's voice was quieter, calmer, and his eyes remained fixated on the floor.

"And you do?" I pressed.

"It's a downward spiral, one that you need to be pulled out from. Please just trust me."

I thought for a moment before echoing his

sentiments. "I'm the one dragging you down, is that what you think?"

"No, that's not what I mean."

"Well, maybe I don't need you to test my limits. Maybe I should be left to be accountable for my own self-discovery."

The flash of anger that crossed Griffin's face made me wish I could snatch back my last words. A thought that infuriated me, leaving a bitter taste in my mouth.

Without saying another word, I turned and walked away from him, jogging steadily to catch up with Noah. Silently, we trudged home, a bitterness hanging in the air that surrounded us, the seeds of resentment for Griffin planted by his own hand.

Chapter 10

The occurrences of that day remained undiscussed. I avoided Griffin for days after, ignoring his incessant tapping on my bedroom door while I faked sleep and stole from the loft at ridiculous hours to avoid a confrontation. On the third day, he lost the last of his patience and when knocking on my door yielded no response, he simply opened it and marched in.

I rolled over in bed and pulled the blanket over my head. He grabbed the corner and pulled it away, reaching for my arm and pulling me into a sitting position. I glared at him, but he ignored me and flopped down next to me on the bed. I went to stand to walk away, but he pulled me back down to the bed.

Now my patience was wearing thin.

"What do you want, Griffin?"

"To apologize."

"So write me a card," I hissed, attempting to lie back down. Again, he pulled me to a seated position, clambering in front of me and forcing our eyes to meet.

"I'm sorry," he pleaded. "Is your face okay?" He reached for my jaw, but I pulled carefully away.

"It was my ego that took a beating, Griffin, not my face." I sighed.

"It was both," he insisted.

I shrugged.

"Take a walk with me?" Griffin held his hands

together in mock prayer fashion as he pleaded.

As much as I didn't want to, I knew refusing would just prolong this exchange.

I unenthusiastically agreed.

We talked little as we headed away from the industrial estate. Despite the lack of conversation, there was no contention between us. Time had subdued my anger, leaving a sense of despondency in its place.

Griffin guided me toward the falls. We took the footbridge over the Passaic River and trekked along the edge of the rocky ravine as the water cascaded noisily down behind us, churning the river below. We rested against the tall flagpole that stood proudly atop the corner point of the rocky formation.

I had paused for all of two minutes when I felt it. Moving swiftly somewhere behind me, a dark energy and charred scent clung to the water particles that filled the air around us. I jumped to my feet and turned expectedly to Griffin, who offered me a small smile in return. This wasn't coincidental. He knew the Sygan would be here. This was his apology.

I waited, studying him.

"Go. I trust you."

Finally!

The primal entity that resided within me stepped forward to take the wheel, the control I handed over willingly. I didn't need to think, to second guess my actions. I just needed to submit, and I did.

Without a second thought, I bolted, darting through the thick undergrowth and dense trees, focused purely on the Sygan. Keeping up a sprint, I closed in on him quickly, my pace consistent as I overtook and rebounded off one of the thick tree trunks. The action launched me into a midair spin in front of the Sygan as he steamed toward me. He hit the ground hard as my elbow landed a blow deftly to his crown. I wasn't interested in the fight, not today. All I needed was the Vesk and to get the hell out of there. Still in motion, I snatched up the cold vacant orb and raced back to the flagpole. The entire incident took just minutes. The exhilaration continued for much longer.

I passed Griffin where I left him. Without breaking my pace, I threw him the Vesk and leaped across the steep ravine. My touchdown was flawless as I landed on the grassy embankment with a whoop.

I turned to Griffin, who laughed and followed suit, landing feet from me.

He was forgiven.

"Now will you back off?" I asked, softly punching his shoulder playfully.

"M'lady, I hereby grant you your freedom," he responded with a bow.

"And I can patrol without you?"

"I mean, I don't know why you'd want to, I'm such a joy to be with."

"Oh yeah, you're a hoot!"

Griffin extended his hand. "Friends?"

I placed my hand into his huge palm, agreeing. "Friends."

The adrenaline charge I had always experienced when a Sygan was close by was still there, but instead of originating from a place of fear, it was awoken by excitement. The desire to run had changed. I still wanted desperately to flee, but the flight instinct had metamorphosed into something different. I wanted to run at it, not away from it. I was driven to fight it.

When we could feel that there was a flurry of activity within our area, an increase in the number of Sygans, we knew this indicated the passing of a high-value soul; when this happened, we would patrol together.

We were never truly alone. Griffin's number one rule, safety in numbers. Since our agreement, he had tried to alternate between partners, and for this I was appreciative. Typically, though, Noah and Steven patrolled together, which left me usually with Griffin, but occasionally with Amelia.

It was on one of these rare girls-only patrols that Amelia and I happened upon a Sygan carrying an inhabited Vesk. I was pretty pissed that we'd somehow managed to miss picking up on the passing, and this only further fueled my determination to succeed in retrieving the Vesk.

Like a wild animal finally uncaged, I craved the hunt, and so when the Sygan ran, without hesitation I gave chase. As always, I slipped into a hyperfocused state, experiencing pure tunnel vision as every second the gap between us started to close. With speed and agility, I traveled over walls, around trees and cars parked along the street. Parkour extraordinaire, leaping from sidewalk to car to dumpster, launching from tree trunks and defying gravity by flying over humans, obstacles, and anything else in my path.

Closing the gap.

Around the corner and down the alley, like a runaway train, I pushed myself, beyond every speed record, beyond that fine line of control.

Closing the gap.

I saw nothing but it, the Sygan I would catch, the

Vesk I would smash, the soul I would save.

I noticed nothing about the alley we both took. Down it I flew, down the alley with no shadows. Down the alley with dulled, unnatural light. Down the alley and into the darkness. I was five strides in before I realized what I'd done, my body slow in catching up with my brain, attempting to execute an emergency stop as I slid across the floor like Scooby-Doo on ice.

Too little. Too late.

Daeon.

The air was humid and thick. My eyes took a moment to adjust to the stultified, muted surroundings. It was like dark gray storm clouds had settled a few feet above my head, sharply increasing the atmospheric pressure. There was a low buzzing sound like static electricity, and the familiar scent of burnt embers sat motionless upon the heavy air. The ground resembled hardened lava, jet black, uneven, and slick. A concoction of energy pulsated from everywhere, a reverberating mixture of malevolence and pain that caused an endless pounding in my head.

The longer I stood there, rooted to the spot, the more numb I became, like something had infected me, drugging me into a stupor. An uncomfortable blend of intoxication and a pain that throbbed, tugged me violently between pleasure and agony.

Then I wasn't alone.

I felt him before I could see him, and his essence took away my last dwindling breath. He approached me like a predator would approach their next meal, stealthy and unwavering. Slinking out from the shadows, bestowing me with paralysis. The enormity of his power was overwhelming. Somewhere deep within the recesses of my mind, the smallest part of me that was still compos mentis attempted to scream, willing my legs to run and my body to fight for survival, but her voice was muffled and barely noticeable.

Still I remained motionless. Still he approached steadily.

I was helpless knowing he could consume me in a second. He came so close his energy permeated mine. My flashpoint surpassed. I exploded from the inside out. Without hesitation, he wrapped his arms around me. I made no attempt to fight him. I couldn't; I was there, but I was gone. I slipped into his arms and closed my eyes, succumbing to my fate, feeling a rush of air as he moved with haste.

"*Breathe!*" Ripped brutally from a deadened ether, the voice roared in my ear, startling me into doing just that.

My eyes squinted against the brightness that seemed to appear from nowhere. I gasped and sucked in another deep breath. I was back in the alleyway, pinned up against the dingy brick wall by him. The predator.

I shuddered violently as the world around me lifted and tilted, making me feel nauseous.

I blinked rapidly, willing my vision to restore itself into focus. Coal-black eyes glinted inches from mine, holding me in a steady hostile glare. One of his arms was across my chest, immobilizing me in an upright position against the bricks; the palm of his other hand was flat against the wall, centimeters from my face.

My vision returned; I saw him clearly for the first time.

He had huge, thick broad shoulders covered by a dark shirt that clung to his muscular chest. The open top buttons revealed an intricate design of black ink and dark chest hairs. His skin was olive tanned and smooth. Thick dark hair crowned his head. His brow furrowed, and his defined jawline clenched, revealing his anger, an anger I had apparently caused.

Breathing the air in Daeon incapacitated me. Breathing in him stimulated me, electrifying my nerve endings. He didn't feel like a Sygan, at least I didn't think he did, but my mind was in turmoil. My head throbbed with fear and an urge to swing at him. My heart raced, my pupils dilated, and my body reacted in a way that left me shaken and confused. It throbbed for him, my back arching toward him involuntarily. I literally had no control, and I was scared that a part of me might have liked it.

My hands clenched into fists trying desperately to fight against it, against my own urges. "Get the fuck off me," I hissed. I tried to stare at him, but something happened when our eyes locked. I felt like I was falling into a black hole. He blinked and jerked backward, like he'd been slapped, releasing me to collapse into a crumpled heap on the ground.

He remained there for only a moment, surveying me almost hungrily. I silently prayed he would leave, knowing that if he touched me, I would not resist. He turned and skulked away, disappearing back into the darkened entry.

I tried to catch my breath. Shame and humiliation consumed me. This wasn't what Kerwin had done to me. It was far worse, bending and manipulating my free will, pulling my strings like he was a puppeteer. I climbed shakily to my feet and stumbled away. I got almost to the end of the alleyway before the thundering footsteps pounded the concrete, the fear and desperation emanating from Amelia and Griffin was almost tangible as they rounded the corner. Griffin caught me just before my legs gave way for the second time, scooping me up effortlessly as he muttered a wide range of profanities.

"What the hell happened?" He eyed the gaping doorway, thankfully choosing to answer his own question, transferring his assumptions into fact and saving me from having to lie.

"You got too close! You can't get this close to it."

Too close is an understatement.

I didn't dare tell him, how could I? He would snatch back the freedom it had taken me so long to acquire. He would never leave my side. Regardless, I couldn't explain what had happened to myself let alone someone else, and oh God, the shame! I said nothing and let them both assume my proximity to the opening had brought about my adverse reaction, locking away the real memories indefinitely and flinging away the key.

Chapter 11

A few days later, I was out doing the usual rounds with Griffin. I'd scared Amelia into taking a break from her already rare and sporadic patrolling duties, when I felt it. "I've got one," I called to Griffin bounding in the direction of the Vesk and the Sygan carrying it. The hunt was the best part, and I refused to allow my more recent encounter to deter me. It was like some primordial instinct took over, making me feel more alive than I ever had before.

Griffin had warned me many times to approach each situation with care, to exercise some restraint over my impulses, that not all Sygans were bottom feeders like the majority we'd encountered; some were powerful and could be very dangerous, but the threat of danger only added to the thrill, and evidently, I did not learn my lesson easily.

The Sygan we chased was fast. She was taller and broader than me, yet maneuvered between buildings and vehicles with a stealth I had never seen before. This only served to stir my competitive nature, which drove me harder into the chase. I couldn't feel Griffin's presence anymore, which should have slowed my steps, but it did not. I wanted revenge against the creature that had dominated me, imprisoned me within myself, and spellbound me. This was my opportunity to get a little payback.

I cornered her in an industrial depot close to the docks. To my surprise, she made no attempt to scale the walls surrounding her, instead ceasing her attempt to escape. She turned to face me, a smile on her face. My confidence wavered, but I stood tall and stubbornly resolute.

I guess we're fighting then.

Harnessing the anger I'd kept on a low boil inside of me, I ran at her, but she sidestepped me at the last moment. My arms swung wildly into thin air. The Sygan spun with speed. Her strong arms wrapped around me from behind before I had time to regain my balance. I leaned forward, bent my hands upward to grasp her arms, which were vise-like across my chest, and held her tightly in place before I launched myself from the ground, an action that propelled me into an up and backward motion. My head snapped up and smashed the Sygan squarely in the face. Her arms slacked, but I kept my grip as I jerked sharply forward and flipped her over my shoulder and to the ground in front of me.

My foot slammed down on her shoulder to pin her while my hand remained gripped to her extended forearm, which twisted sharply. With a yelp, she used her free arm to grab frantically at her pocket, retrieving something with an energy source so powerful it could not have been created on Earth. I didn't for one minute think it was a Vesk. The concentration of power was so different, but it was hard to decipher exactly what the source of the energy was when it took all my strength to restrain her. I was using both hands to immobilize her one arm and was preparing to bolt should I see a blade in her free hand, but to my surprise, she had pulled out a Vesk.

The swirling matter behind the glass looked similar to every other entrapped soul, but the energy radiating from it felt very unusual. I attempted to kick it free from her hand using my back leg, forcing my weight down on the foot that held her down. The glass orb flew through the air, but before it could hit the ground, Griffin appeared. I expected him to come to my aid as I struggled to maintain control of the Sygan who was fighting back like a rabid dog. Instead, he flew past me and dove across the concrete, catching the Vesk inches from the ground.

Then he lay there panting in relief.

Err, hello!

"A little help, please," I grunted, breathless. He jumped to his feet and pulled me off the Sygan, allowing her to leap to her feet and dart past us both. I was beyond confused and more than a little angry.

Really! Saving Sygans again, Griffin?

"What the fuck was that?" I gasped. "Why did you stop it from smashing?"

"Don't you feel that?" Griffin asked curiously, holding the Vesk inches from my face. "Is it not causing discomfort?"

Its energy was strong certainly, but not painful to be near.

"I mean, it's intense, I guess, different from what I've felt before."

"It's more than that, Alyssa. It's pure and it's evil."

Huh?

"The evil in this soul is all consuming, untainted and potent. It's devoured any good essence it might once have had. It cannot exist on this plane. It has to go straight to Daeon."

"So, what do we do with it if we can't free it?

119

Wouldn't she have taken it to Daeon? I mean I thought that was the whole point of them capturing souls, to take them to Daeon."

"It needs to go to a specific place within Daeon. If it had been left to pass correctly, it would have been delivered straight there. Remember how I told you Daeon is a place of constant war, a battle for power. There are Sygans who believe harnessing evil in its purest form will somehow empower them, raise them through the ranks. It wouldn't of course. It would just kill them, but the danger is that this"—Griffin held the Vesk between us—"this will end up on this plane."

"I thought you said once you lose your humanity, the door to this plane closes indefinitely."

"It does, meaning you can't leave Daeon to reenter this plane, but if you never entered Daeon in the first place…"

"Oh, well, shit," I whispered.

"Yeah, well, shit," Griffin responded with a sigh.

"What would have happened, if…"

"Hell on Earth probably," he said quietly, turning away. "You should go home, Alyssa; I need to take care of this."

"Wait, you're going to Daeon?" It was impossible to hide the horror in my voice, and the thought of that place conjured up an image of *him*, all smoky darkness and tattoos. Much to my disgust, the thought of him made my pulse quicken.

Griffin felt it and glanced toward me, mistaking my reaction for fear. "I'm not going there. I'm taking it to someone I know who will transport it to Daeon, safely."

Like my curiosity would ever allow me to just walk away from this encounter!

I said nothing but refused to return to the loft, following him a few steps back despite his protests. He gave up in the end and in true male fashion sulked with me instead.

We headed north toward the Falls, stopping at an upscale office block near the Point View reservoir. We entered the sleek and modern building through an empty main lobby and made our way to the third floor. Griffin continued to ignore me. He stopped before the double glass doors of an office space and pressed the call button. Within a minute, the echoed ringing was replaced by a sharp buzzing sound, and Griffin pushed open the door. He paused at the threshold and without turning asked, "Is there any point in me requesting that you please wait here?"

"Nope."

"Didn't think so," he growled as he stepped through the doorway before using his body to prop the door open and waved me in. Even in his worst mood, even being more pissed at me than ever before, he was still governed by his manners. It was sort of endearing.

We entered a small, unmanned reception area. Griffin walked through a second set of doors, and I scurried along behind. Beyond the doors sat a corridor. Without hesitation, Griffin strode to the double doors at the far end. They swung open as he approached, and we entered what appeared to be a conference room. At the head of an otherwise empty meeting table, a man was seated, dressed surprisingly well in a charcoal-gray suit. His tie had been loosened so it hung inches below the open collar of his white starched shirt. He slouched back in the large leather chair, one ankle resting over his other knee, relaxed, composed.

In the corner behind him stood a Sygan. Tall and broad as they all were, he had dark brown curls and a neatly trimmed beard. He was surprisingly handsome, and instead of an angry scowl he wore a bemused smirk as he watched the interaction between Griffin and the suit guy.

"Griffin." He nodded toward us, raising one eyebrow as his gaze fell onto me. Griffin didn't answer but gently tossed the Vesk toward him. The man barely looked in its direction, yet raised his left arm to catch it with ease.

He barely acknowledged the Vesk, instead focusing his attention on me. "And who do we have here?" He stared at me unabashed. I was uncomfortable but stared back belligerently.

Griffin stepped forward, placed both hands on the table and leaned toward him. "How about you focus on the matter in hand, Zagan, and while you're at it, maybe you can explain how the fuck this even happened," he growled.

The Sygan stepped out of the corner, his eyes narrowing as he looked toward Griffin. "Relax, Birsha," the seated man said with a deep laugh. The Sygan stopped but stayed just behind him.

"You know what this means, Griffin. You know what's coming," the man responded curtly.

The Sygan nodded toward me. "New toy?" he asked Griffin.

"Go fuck yourself, Birsha," Griffin retorted, his eyes still fixed on Zagan.

The Sygan laughed. "Now that's more like it."

"What do you propose we do about these occurrences?" Zagan asked.

"Sounds like an Aamon problem," Griffin spat, turning on his heels and storming from the room.

I started to follow, got to the doorway, and turned back, looking into the room, trying to make some sense of the interaction. The Sygan's leering smirk had reappeared. The suited man did not smile. He turned the Vesk over in his hands and held it up in front of his face, inspecting it closely. "Maybe it isn't on its way," he muttered to the Sygan. "Maybe it's already here."

I caught up to Griffin in the corridor. I was dying to ask him for an explanation, but he was still seething, so I kept my mouth shut and waited for him to calm down. I had never seen him so angry. It was a little unnerving.

I expected him to head home, but instead he made his way to the reservoir, only stopping when he reached the rocky shoreline. I hung back as he paced up and down, eventually stopping and staring out across the body of water, his fingers intertwined behind his head.

"I shouldn't have taken you there."

I picked my way across the rocks and clambered upon a large boulder close to him, closing the height deficit. I reached out my hand to his shoulder, turning him gently around.

"Griffin, when are you going to stop acting like it's your job to protect me. We had an agreement. You didn't take me. I'm not yours to take."

Griffin flinched; I'd hurt him. It wasn't my intention, but I spoke the truth. I didn't belong to him, and I wasn't his to protect. We'd done this dance before. Still, in that moment, it was a bad choice of words, so I attempted to fix it.

"What I mean is, we should be protecting each other, supporting each other. Griffin," I pleaded, "let me in!"

"Really!" He turned to face me fully, locking my eyes with his. "Do you let me in?"

I felt my face flush, and I swallowed. It was a fair point; I should have expected it.

He took a step closer, his face now only inches away from mine. I started to pull my arm back, but as my hand neared his wrist, he twisted his hand to catch it, lacing his fingers between mine. "Alyssa," he murmured, his warm palm pressed against mine, his eyes fixed steadily on me, "do you really think I would ever do anything to hurt you?"

My heart pounded in my chest. I tried desperately to maintain control. The scent of him was intoxicating. That desire I had locked away deep down inside of me began to stir.

"No," I admitted shakily.

But I'm afraid I might hurt you!

"Then why won't you trust me?" His eyes remained locked on mine; he edged closer to me.

I could almost taste him.

"Griffin!" Noah's voice thundered, snatching away the moment.

It was all I could do to remain upright as I turned toward the sound and stepped quickly down from the rock. Griffin kept a firm grip on my hand.

Noah, Steven, and Amelia appeared, wide-eyed and breathless. "Are you guys okay? We thought something had happened." Amelia's gaze darted between us before falling on our hands, still clasped together.

I tried in vain to subtly pull free, but Griffin refused to release me. Three sets of eyes stared bewildered, momentarily speechless before Steven cleared his throat and remarked that maybe they should give us a minute.

Not a chance Noah was letting this one slide.

"Whoa, whoa, whoa, what exactly do we have here? There we are, all panicked that you guys were under attack, and here you are taking a romantic stroll by the waterside. Nice." He bounded over, slapping Griffin on the back. The look Griffin shot him made me actually fear for his life.

If the ground could just swallow me now, that would be great, thanks!

"We sensed Zagan nearby," Amelia offered weakly, "but you're clearly not in any danger, so we can discuss this later." She pointedly ignored my glare as she backed carefully away, pulling a bemused Steven with her.

"Noah, give them some space," Steven yelled.

I turned to Griffin, now towering above me without my rock. "Griffin," I insisted under my breath, "let me go!"

He released my hand but pulled me close as I tried to step away. He leaned in, one hand at the base of my spine, his cheek brushing against mine as he whispered slowly, deliberately in my ear, "I would never, ever hurt you, Alyssa."

I was torn between the desire to kiss him and the urge to slap him. I honestly could not decide what was worse, having the other three think they had interrupted something or the fact that something almost had happened.

The three of them paused as I stumbled across the rocky ground. "We can deal with this later," Steven assured me, to which I responded with an icy "Shut up."

I stormed ahead but was pulled to the side by Amelia, who waved the guys on, insisting we would catch up.

"Well, that looked intimate," she said with a coy smile.

I groaned, leaning against the trunk of one of the many trees dotted about the reservoir grounds. "Oh God, I'm so embarrassed," I mumbled as I cupped my burning face in my hands and sank to the ground.

Because I wanted it, at that moment I wanted him.

"What! Why?" a puzzled Amelia exclaimed. "If it's meant to be it will be, and girl, he's hot! And he is clearly infatuated with you. You are without a ticket on this pity train." I peeked up at her and her voice softened. "Whatever it is you're holding on to, you got to let it go."

"Plus," she continued, a slow smirk spreading across her face as she pulled me to my feet, "you are wound way too tight; you definitely need to go get some!"

"Amelia!" I swatted at her, mortified at her directness. Despite my lingering embarrassment, it was quite nice to see her amused and playful.

We headed back to the loft. Griffin, Noah, and Steven were already there and deep in conversation. Griffin watched me closely; I could feel the heat of his stare but resisted the urge to turn toward him. I strategically placed myself at the opposite end of the sofa to him. As I sat, the conversation ended abruptly. Like that was going to deter me!

"Who is Zagan?" Might as well get straight to the point.

Steven lowered his head, suddenly preoccupied with something in his lap. Noah looked questioningly at Griffin.

I allowed my eyes to finally meet his. "No more secrets," I implored.

His face softened. "That's a two-way street," he

reminded me.

I nodded. "I know."

"Okay," he said reluctantly. "Zagan is a Sygan."

"Wait, why did I think he was a man?" It was only when I said it out loud that I realized how ridiculous it sounded, why would I think a man could see us...unless he was one of us.

"Zagan makes you see what he wants you to see. He isn't human. He is a Sygan, but not like the Sygans you're used to. He's a powerful empath, can manipulate people easily, and has no problem switching sides to advance his own agenda."

"And the other one?"

"Birsha, they...work together," he replied carefully.

"So you're, like, friends with them?" I queried, trying not to sound revolted.

"The fuck we are! Birsha is a nothing, and Zagan is an absolute piece of shit, but he isn't stupid, at least not entirely. He understands the order of things and what the consequences of messing with that would be."

I'd never seen Griffin so fired up; it made me wonder if there was more history between the three of them than he was happy to admit.

"Zagan isn't like a normal Sygan," Noah offered. "He isn't trying to climb the ranks. He's powerful enough working for Aamon, and he can be a useful...acquaintance in certain situations."

"He's a piece of shit!" Griffin insisted gruffly.

"And Aamon?" I asked tentatively, too intrigued to stop but also not wanting to tip a teetering Griffin over the edge.

Griffin's fists clenched and his eyes blazed.

I crawled across the sofa to him and rested my hand

on his arm. "Hey," I coaxed him gently, "it's going to be okay."

Maybe closing the space between us wasn't the best idea. Deep down my desire stirred. Being close to him wasn't getting any easier. I looked over to Steven.

He glanced at Griffin, who gave him a small nod. Permission to continue granted. "Aamon is sort of a god of Daeon," he explained.

"It's not as impressive as it sounds," growled Griffin, his knuckles white.

"So he's like a demon, trapped in Daeon, right?" I asked, running my thumb lightly over Griffin's clenched fist. His hand relaxed immediately.

The realization that I had such influence over him surprised me. Was this why he was so desperate to control me, to deny the power I held over him?

"Not exactly," Noah chimed in. "He still has a hint of a soul."

"But he only retains that so he can continue to walk between planes. Make no mistake. He's a cold calculating killer, extremely ruthless and without conscience," Steven emphasized.

"And with that said," Noah announced, standing with open arms dramatically, "we get to work for him."

"Wait, wh…" I spluttered.

"Not *for* him, *with* him!" Griffin's deep voice resonated angrily as he leaped to his feet.

"Okay, let's all take a breather." Steven stepped calmly between Griffin and Noah, defusing the angry situation.

Amelia ushered Noah into the kitchen, while Steven attempted to calm Griffin down. I headed into the kitchen, confident Noah would be much more forthcoming than Griffin.

The good thing about Noah was that he couldn't stay angry for long. It wasn't in his nature. He was sitting upon one of the barstools next to Amelia. They both looked up at me as I entered the kitchen.

"How is he?" Amelia asked, genuine concern etched across her face.

"I don't know," I responded brusquely. What was I, his minder?

They exchanged glances. I sounded like a bitch. My tone softened. "I'm not his girlfriend. I have the same relationship with him as you guys do. I figured the best person to bring him down was Steven," I explained with a shrug.

"Really, you really think Steven is the one to placate him when he's upset?" Noah's voice dripped with sarcastic contempt; the hand interaction clearly did not go unnoticed.

Amelia delivered a swift kick to his shins, and he winced in pain. I shot her an appreciative look.

"So, Aamon sounds delightful!" I said, steering the conversation firmly away from me while also attempting to lighten the mood.

"There's some big bad passing soon, some soul with an unprecedented level of purity, and not the good kind. As much as it pains me, Griffin is right. The safest and most effective solution is to work alongside that bastard and his band of merry monsters," Noah admitted without me even needing to ask.

"Prior to a big arrival we always see an increase in the passing of pure ones, like the opening act before the main event. Something powerful is coming—a dark soul of high purity, and when it passes, we need to ensure its safe passage to Daeon. We can't risk waiting until it loses its humanity. It will be the exception to the rule," Amelia clarified.

"Hold on, you're telling me it doesn't get a choice? Is that fair?" I asked. All the emphasis they had placed on free will and self-redemption was being completely contradicted.

"It doesn't sit well with me either, Alyssa, but our opinions are outweighed by the potential danger. I trust Griffin if he says it can't be saved, and so should you," Amelia replied softly before turning to Noah. "All of this I get, but why the dramatics?"

"The dramatics didn't stem from the suggestion of joining forces. It came when I insisted she join us." Noah nodded toward me. "We all need to be there, safety in numbers." He placed his hand over Amelia's. "It will be okay, I promise."

"Wow, back up! So you're telling me Griffin has no issue bringing Amelia along but wants *me* to stay behind?" I turned quickly to Amelia. "No offence, Amelia."

Wasn't that a direct violation of our agreement, our compromise?

Amelia held her hands up. "None taken. Griffin would be a fool not to want you there. Second to him, you're the best we got."

"Whoa, hold on a minute, sister!" Noah turned to Amelia and pointed at me. "Are you saying I couldn't kick her butt?"

"Well, you'd have to catch her first, and we all know she's twice as fast as you," Amelia taunted him.

"Yeah, I am," I teased him gleefully.

"Whatever! Continue with your delusions, at home

in your rightful place," he countered, gesturing around the kitchen with a wink as he dodged the oranges we simultaneously flung indignantly toward his head.

Steven entered the kitchen as Noah danced out, pausing to exchange a quick kiss and sidestepping the oranges.

"So, it's on," he announced. "We meet them tomorrow. Alyssa, I recommend you don't visit your mom and Kasey for a few days. There will be a lot of activity in the area, and you don't want to draw any attention to them."

I nodded in agreement. "I'm coming too?" I asked.

"Like wild horses could stop you," Amelia retorted with an eye roll.

Steven turned to me with a knowing smile. "You're coming too," he confirmed.

I thanked Steven and gave Amelia a quick hug, bidding everyone a good night as I headed up to my room. When I passed Griffin's open door, I caught sight of him on the corner of his bed, head in his hands. I leaned against the doorframe, restraining myself from entering. No point in putting myself in a position where it might be hard to maintain control.

"Hey," I said softly.

He looked up. "Come in."

I stayed in my spot. He raised one eyebrow, eyes staring intensely at me. "It's probably better I don't," I said, shifting my weight.

In one fluid movement, he stood and glided over to me, stopping tantalizingly close. The air hung dense and warm between us.

I crossed my arms and, with my eyes cast downward, whispered, "I just wanted to check you were okay."

He moved closer and leaned toward me, brushing his cheek against mine as he whispered, "I am now." His lips like a feather touch swept softly over mine.

"Griffin, this isn't the time," I begged him.

He didn't feel the same way, but ever the gentleman, he respected my wishes. He ran his thumb softly over my cheek, kissed the top of my head and murmured, "Goodnight, Alyssa."

I dragged myself away and into my room, my heart pounding. It wasn't that I didn't want to. Sex would have been an excellent and enjoyable way to relieve the tension, but I knew that it would mean so much more to Griffin, insinuating a commitment I wasn't ready to make. I was starting to understand the hold I had over him. I wanted to be careful not to abuse it, to cause him any pain.

I climbed into bed knowing full well sleep would not be visiting me that night. So instead, I lay staring at the ceiling, muttering a silent prayer to a nonexistent God that we all make it through tomorrow to live another day.

Chapter 12

As convinced as I had been that sleep would evade me, I did at some point manage to slip into a slumber of sorts. Rest may have found me, but it left tranquility and calm somewhere else, bringing instead turbulence and conflict that held me captive for hours, only releasing me as dawn rose. Despite the warming glow of the early morning's amber rays, my disturbing dreams stayed close, casting darkened shadows wherever I turned.

There was no definitive storyline, no meaningful sequence of events, just a swirling cocktail of energy and feelings, tugging me violently in different and opposing directions. Every molecule surrounding me was a harbinger composed of dread and trepidation. And then, brief intermittent moments of arousal, of a yearning so raw and deep finally fulfilled brought about by a faceless entity, a sharp contrast to the rest of the dream, appearing and disappearing like switching channels between television shows.

I dressed all in black. The standard Sygan color scheme, a sardonic one-finger salute to the enemy.

Steven raised one eyebrow as I descended the staircase into the lounge, to which I responded with a smirk and a shrug. Why not stir the pot? At least I'd be entertaining myself. Noah of course had to make a big deal.

"Damn, girl, nearly didn't see you then! What time

does ninja class start again?" His feigned shock was not in danger of winning any Oscars. I rolled my eyes but flashed him a wide grin.

Well, at least I'd lifted his spirits; Noah was never happier than when he had someone to tease.

Griffin remained his intensely serious self; I could feel his eyes on me but acted oblivious. I didn't need to see his fear or his longing. More important matters demanded his attention today. I would not be held accountable for deflecting his focus. Amelia was subdued, but her energy projected determination and strength, no fear. I was impressed at how well she had risen to the occasion.

We headed out of Jersey and into New York's Upper West Side, entering Central Park close to the Natural History Museum. Griffin kept a steady pace, only slowing as he reached Belvedere Castle, which sat majestically in the middle of the sprawling city park.

We entered swiftly, taking a narrow spiral staircase down two flights before heading down a stone-encased walkway, so narrow we had to travel in single file. A final dimly lit staircase led us into the bowels of the castle, a level I didn't even know existed despite visiting the structure on numerous occasions when I was alive.

I pushed hard against the memories, knowing they would only invoke weakness and vulnerability. Now was most definitely not the time.

The large open cellar was devoid of windows. Scant lighting illuminated only the center portion of the room; the unlit perimeter remained cloaked in darkness. I had no idea if there were any other exits aside from the narrow staircase we had just descended. We formed a loose line remaining on the side of the room closest to the only escape route we were sure of. Thick stone pillars formed an inner circle, further enclosing the insufficient light source. The gothic-style castle's dark gray stone slabs created a sense of claustrophobia despite the room's sprawling size.

I thought I sensed at least five Sygans, but such a concentration of conflicting energies made it hard for me to ascertain the exact number among us.

Off to our right stood a tall but slender male. His head was shaved with a single strip of auburn hair running down the middle. He had a long goatee and eyes that seemed to glow dark purple. His scalp was covered in black ink, and he stared unwaveringly at Griffin.

To our left was a much stockier male with short black hair. A twisted scar ran from just below his eye to his jawline. His exposed flesh sported the customary array of dark tattoos. Both were dressed head to toe in black. I mockingly raised a brow toward Noah, who sniggered, generating a frosty glare from Griffin.

A movement from the shadows directly across from us caught my attention. As a figure stepped forward, the smile fell from my face.

Kerwin!

His eyes bored into mine. I looked quickly away, but it was pointless. The heat from his stare continued to burn me.

"How goes it, Kermit?" Noah's voice echoed around the room, confidence and contempt bouncing between the damp walls as he glared challengingly at Kerwin.

It worked. Kerwin's smile faded, and his mouth twisted into an angry sneer, but it freed me from his sadistic glare as he turned his attention toward his humiliator instead. Noah, my savior, rescuing me from Dr. Evil again.

Dual footsteps from across the room notified us of another entrance. The silence reverberated and the tension in the room increased as two figures stepped forward. One I recognized immediately as Zagan. The other was a muscular female with hair that hung shoulder length and jet black on one side of her head but was buzz shaved on the other side.

Both sides stood motionless, each attempting to stare the other down.

In life, I had always had a terrible habit of laughing at the most inopportune moments, an unfortunate occurrence that had landed me in hot water on more than one occasion. Regrettably, it was a habit I appeared to have carried over into death. I looked around the room, eyeing the full coven I had been warned about. Now, don't get me wrong. They were a formidable and intimidating group, but the theatrics were excessive, to say the least. I felt like I was participating in some overly dramatic thespian production. I tried to suppress it but failed miserably. My laugh bounced from pillar to pillar, seemingly slapping each Sygan as it went. All eyes turned to me, menacing and furious, but that only served to amuse me more.

The lone female glared at Griffin. "Are you going to shut her up, or shall I?"

Without hesitation, Amelia sprang forward, hissing at the Sygan, "Try it!"

Wow! Amelia impressed me for the second time that day. Where the hell had this warrior version of my best friend been hiding? Turning to her with a wide smile, I exclaimed, "Check you out! You tell her, sister."

Griffin cast me a sideways glance, his eyes urging me to shut the hell up and stay focused.

His look did not go unnoticed.

"What's wrong, Griffin? Afraid you might not have quite the control over your little bitch as you'd hoped?" Kerwin sneered mockingly.

My eyes blazed, and Griffin, ever the chivalrous hero, leaped angrily to my defense. "Don't you fucking dare call her that!"

"What the hell, Griffin, seriously? You think being called a little bitch offends me?" I retorted with a laugh. "Oh please, I call myself much worse on a daily basis and have done for years." For the first time I stared unabashed at Kerwin, all fear consumed by anger at his insinuations. "I'm insulted that you assume I belong to him, to anyone for that matter. Unlike you, I'm owned by no one, *bitch*!"

"Finished?" a low voice uttered from the shadows.

The air in the room changed. I swear the floor shifted, tilting sideways.

I stopped dead, and my eyes widened. I could feel my pupils as they dilated, and I struggled to catch my breath. The force emanating from the darkness paralyzed me. I recognized him before he stepped into the light, emerging slowly, purposefully, again like a beast stalking its prey. I had crossed his path before. I had been his prey before. I had succumbed completely, surrendered without a fight when he dragged me out of the darkness, and ever since then he refused to leave me, violating my dreams, and infecting my thoughts. I tried desperately to look away, but his eyes met mine and stayed there, imprisoning me.

For a moment, I was in a vacuum, caught in the eye

of the storm. Nothing else outside of it existed, nothing beyond the twisted vortex he had dragged me into.

I wanted to reach out and touch him, an inexplicable and self-destructive notion. He held me in his poisonous stare for too long. Around us, chaos erupted. Griffin jumped in front of him with a roar, shoving him backward hard. Still his stare remained, unwavering, unbroken. Noah and Steven leaped to Griffin's aid, clearly expecting a reaction, but he simply stood still, rigid, as if Griffin had not just nearly pushed him through the damn wall. Griffin raged and leaped at him again, empowered by his lack of defense. Noah and Steven held Griffin back, struggling to restrain him. I'd never seen this Griffin before, all fire and anger, resentment, and jealousy. I wanted to turn away and watch what was happening around me, but he wouldn't release me from his gaze. Regardless of how hard I struggled, I was snared.

"Remember why we're here," Steven implored.

"Yes, please do, because it worked out so well last time." Kerwin's scornful voice dripped with sarcasm.

Griffin ignored Kerwin's comment, bellowing, "Don't you fucking dare," as he pointed at the man who had dragged me from Daeon. Standing between us, Griffin's broad shoulders momentarily obscured me from his view, breaking the hold, releasing me from my trap, and allowing me a moment to catch my breath. I glanced nervously around, meeting looks of confused bewilderment from both Amelia and the Sygans, all except for Zagan that was, who simply eyed me with fascination.

"Griffin, you came to me for help. Remember that," the powerful stranger growled deeply, thankfully turning his full attention away from me and back to Griffin.

"Like hell I did," Griffin hissed.

Zagan stepped forward placing himself between the two. "Actually, I was the one who instigated this meeting, but neither of you need an explanation, so get over your egos and let's resolve this once and for all so your paths never have to cross again."

"Griffin, you are not equipped to deal with what is coming solo, unless your soul has suddenly become expendable?" Zagan shot an inquisitive look toward Griffin, who responded with a small sigh. "Didn't think so.

"And Aamon, they"—Zagan gestured to us—"have tracking powers you will never regain due to the expendability of your soul." He turned toward him as he spoke.

Time froze momentarily; everything fell silent except for the ringing in my ears.

Aamon.

He was Aamon. That *was Aamon!*

A multitude of questions surged through my brain. I was drowning in the deluge. How and why would Aamon drag me from Daeon? Wasn't he more of a drag-them-*to*-Daeon kind of guy? What made him a god? Why was he wasting his time and energy playing mind-control games with me? Why was he not repelling me? Why the hell could I not stop my fingers from twitching?

"Tread carefully, Zagan," Aamon whispered gently in a voice that chilled the air.

Zagan held his hands up. "I mean no disrespect, sir, but time is of the essence." He bowed his head toward Aamon as he spoke.

Aamon crossed his arms. "We can trail any factions

passing between planes. I have groups scouring Daeon for infidels. The passage of Vesks between worlds is temporarily prohibited. Any being found transporting a Vesk will be killed. When you patrol, you patrol with one of us. You track the Vesk to the soul. We will do the rest." Aamon gestured toward all of us, careful to avoid eye contact with me.

My mouth dropped, and I glanced with disbelief at Noah. His jaw was clenched, but he said nothing.

So now we're taking orders from him, from Aamon!

I shot Amelia a confused look; she reciprocated it, clearly as shocked as I.

"Gill will take first watch." Kerwin nodded toward the goateed Sygan as he spoke. "I'll take the second."

Griffin turned to Noah. "I'll take the first shift. We'll reconvene here at dawn—"

"And I'll take over," Noah concluded.

Thank God for that!

The thought of working with any of them repulsed me, but spending any length of time with Kerwin would be unbearable.

I glanced between the stoic faces of the Sygans, stealing the briefest of glances at Aamon. His blazing eyes stared beyond me, refusing to make direct contact before he turned on his heels and departed via the hidden exit. His henchmen followed suit.

And like that it was over.

Leaving Griffin to patrol with Gill, we hastily retreated.

****

"The downside to remaining on this plane is that we get very little warning of potential cataclysmic events approaching," Steven explained.

We were back in our haven, gathered around the kitchen island trying to make sense of what exactly Zagan and Aamon were referring to during their cryptic exchange with Griffin.

"Do things like this happen often?" Amelia asked.

"Not that we've encountered," Steven responded, gesturing toward Noah, who was perched upon one of the tall barstools across from him.

Noah cleared his throat. "If Griffin has ever worked alongside Aamon so directly, I'm not aware of it," he offered grimly. "He has used Zagan to transport Daeon-bound souls when he's happened across them, but that only occurs every now and again. He is rarely in contact with him."

"Aamon governs Daeon's threshold relatively well. As much as he's impartial to the trading of light souls, he enforces the rules pertaining to dark souls, ensuring that preventing them from journeying to their intended place is forbidden, and for good reason. It's the one thing both sides accede to," Steven explained.

"So, our job is to locate and theirs is to kill," Amelia clarified.

"We know some ultimate evil is coming, but we don't know when? I mean, is there any timescale we're working with here?" I asked, continuing before anyone had the chance to answer, "I mean, do we know for sure it hasn't passed already?"

I was met with confused looks. "It's just that, the other day I happened upon a Vesk that had a dark soul in it. That was why you guys sensed Zagan nearby. Griffin took it to him."

I felt stupid and irresponsible for not mentioning it sooner but had been so caught up with the Griffin moment…"I thought Griffin would have said something," I added in a hushed tone.

"I guess there is no definitive way to know, but I think we'd be aware if the big bad was here already, plus would the factions seeking it still be focused on new souls passing if it was here already?" Noah pointed out.

Steven reached across the counter to grasp Noah's hand saying, "Babe, you need rest, you're taking the dawn shift."

Everyone ignored the elephant in the room. I'd expected Noah would be the one to question Aamon's reaction to me and the adverse effect it had caused on Griffin, but it remained thankfully unmentioned.

Unlike Noah and Steven, I was not able to rest. Nervous energy radiated from Amelia, who retired to her room, no doubt spending her evening pacing the floors, and memories of the previous evening's dark dreams poked at my conscience, leaving me jittery and unable to settle. At some point after midnight, I decided to take a walk to try and clear my head.

I made it about five feet beyond the exterior wall of the building when I felt it. Somewhere just beyond me, lurking in the shadows, was a Sygan. I stopped but did not retreat, instead I addressed the darkness. "What are you doing? You shouldn't be here; this was not the arrangement." One foot emerged slowly from the dark. It was the Sygan with the scar from the meeting. I eyed him suspiciously. "Does Griffin know you're here? He will find out, and when he does—"

"I answer only to Aamon," he interrupted with a growl. "Go back inside," he commanded, taking a small step back into the shadows and his on-guard stance. Agitated, I returned to the loft and spent the remainder of the night pacing. I was still in the kitchen when Noah crept carefully from the room he shared with Steven. I waited for him to tiptoe halfway across the kitchen before greeting him with a sharp "Hey!" scaring the crap out of him.

"What the hell are you doing up so early, you freak?" he bantered playfully after regaining his composure.

"Is it considered up if you didn't actually go to bed?" I asked.

He was immediately concerned. "Are you okay? Did something happen?"

"Did you know Aamon was posting a sentry outside?" I said, nodding toward the window.

"What? Are you sure?" Noah walked to the window, craning his neck to peer down to the ground.

"Oh, I'm sure. I nearly walked straight into the damn thing, the dude with the scar from the meeting."

"Alyssa, why the hell were you outside in the dead of the night?" Noah hissed, clearly pissed.

"I needed air," I protested.

"Then turn on a damn fan!" he snarled, adding more gently, "Girl, you cause me anxiety!"

"I'm sorry," I offered weakly. "I won't do it again."

"Yes, you will," Noah responded, gently kissing the top of my head before leaving to take over from Griffin.

I gave him a five-minute head start, then followed him, ignoring the Sygan still positioned in the tree line. I'd been cooped up inside for long enough.

I trailed at a safe distance, taking advantage of the fact that all of Noah's energy would be focused on his destination and the job that awaited him. He arrived at the castle before dawn, surveying the area before being met by his patrolling partner. Each eyed the other with mutual distaste. It was quite amusing to watch, especially as Noah was clearly the more powerful of the two. Seeing a less confident Kerwin was a novelty and incredibly enjoyable.

As dawn broke, Griffin and Gill approached. After a brief conversation, Noah and Kerwin took off in the same direction. Gill disappeared into the castle, and I started to move toward Griffin, eager to find out how his patrol had gone. However, to my surprise, instead of heading toward me, toward home, he took a moment to glance around the deserted grounds before heading in the opposite direction, traveling south.

I didn't hesitate, trailing behind him, just far enough to avoid his radar but close enough not to lose him. He didn't run but did keep up a brisk steady pace all the way down to the bottom part of Lower Manhattan, slowing as he approached South Sea Port. From there, he turned right heading for the Battery, stopping at the empty waterfront park overlooking the harbor. He circled around a large clump of bushes, taking a seat on one of the benches surrounding the thick shrubbery.

I sensed someone or something with him. Low voices murmured just ahead. I crept farther forward, eager to see who he had snuck off to secretly meet. Griffin would often disappear for hours at a time, avoiding divulging exactly where he had been. It drove me crazy. I knew what I was doing was wrong but reminded myself of the countless times he had tracked me, feeding myself a justification for the blatant invasion of his privacy.

I needed to get closer but remain hidden. I circled around in the opposite direction, creeping carefully to remain silent. I ducked down behind a trashcan, crawling around it to remain out of his eyeline, the hushed tones had stopped, and I worried I was too late. I kept my head down and crawled quickly, straight into a pair of stationary legs. Shocked, I fell backward with a yelp, looking up to see crossed arms across a broad chest and a very disapproving Griffin glaring down at me.

I scrambled to my feet. "Oh, hi," I blurted, cringing with embarrassment. Like I was convincing anyone that I just happened to be impersonating a bloody squirrel four feet from his secret meeting. He raised one eyebrow.

"Look, I know I followed you and that was really wrong, but I only wanted to know that you were safe, and besides, you really can't get pissy with me. I mean you've, you've followed me plenty of times and I…" I stammered.

"Shut up." Griffin cut me off.

Not going to lie, I was kind of thankful he'd shut me up.

"I'm sorry, I won't do it again," I whispered.

"Yes, you will," he responded matter-of-factly.

My indignation flared up. "Why do people keep saying that! Whatever, I didn't want to know anyway." I turned to stomp away, but Griffin pulled me back sharply, pulled me toward him, a little too close. I was scared he was going to try and kiss me again, but instead he flashed me a smile and said with an excited tone, "You should meet her."

He stepped off to the side, revealing the mysterious "her."

She was sitting serenely on the bench, looking at me with intrigue.

"Magda, this is Alyssa. Alyssa, this is Magda,"

Griffin said, gesturing between the two of us.

Magda was beautiful. She had silver-gray hair pulled back from her face, with soft waves that hung beneath her shoulders. Her eyes were silver, like mine, and her skin was pale and smooth like porcelain. She sat statue still with composure, and she nodded toward me, keeping her eyes on mine as she said, "Pleased to make your acquaintance, Alyssa."

Magda held her head high but cocked it slightly to one side as she studied me. She turned to Griffin and said, "A moment, please, Griffin."

Griffin bowed his head and moved quickly down the path that ran along the side of the harbor.

What the actual...?

"Come here, child." Magda held out her hands, summoning me to approach her. Feeling a little uncomfortable, I complied, placing just one hand apprehensively in hers. She held it for the briefest time before gently releasing it and murmuring, "You're different than I expected."

"Huh?"

"Your purity is strong, the strongest I have ever felt, but it's both," Magda mused, her head tilted to one side, as a shadow of confusion danced across her face.

"My what now?"

This woman is crazy!

"You don't believe me, do you?" she asked with a smile that extended beyond her lips. "The sooner you stop fighting it, the easier it will become, Alyssa. Let go of what is binding you to your old existence. Surrender, my dear."

I couldn't answer her. I wanted to, but the words got stuck in my throat. I had no idea what she was talking about, and yet as senseless as her speech was, it resonated with me. I didn't like it.

Magda turned toward Griffin, who had stopped a clear distance from us and was leaning on the railings, looking out across the harbor. "Go to him."

Anxious to escape the uncomfortable encounter, I hurried over to Griffin.

"Is she okay?" I asked, clearly questioning the state of her mental health.

Griffin choked on a laugh. "Magda is one of the elders. She's been here forever. She guides us, warns us when major things are going to happen. What did she tell you?"

"Nothing that made any sense. Why are you here, Griffin, and what's with all the secrecy?"

Griffin sighed, gazing out across the water that, despite its murkiness, still sparkled in the morning sun.

"Aamon is aware there is a dark soul preparing to pass, one whose purity is more potent than anything any of us have ever had to contend with previously. What he doesn't know is that it won't be alone. Another soul will also pass soon, one with equal potency but a sacred one, a light soul."

"And you don't trust Aamon with this information?" I asked.

"I don't trust Aamon with anything," Griffin huffed. "The real problem is, if either soul refuses to accept their destiny, does what we did and remains here, on Earth, Aamon will try to forcibly transport them. If that fails, he will kill them. Right now, we are working with Aamon and his Sygans to guide them to passings to prevent either of these souls being captured, for them to eradicate anyone stupid enough to try and steal them. But if he tries to kill the good soul..." Griffin turned to me. "I'll need to protect it."

"You mean killing a Sygan?" I concurred. "Do you know for a fact that doing so would actually cost you your soul, Griffin?"

"Yes," he responded. "And I don't want to go into how or why I know right now. Please just accept that I know," he insisted.

I was hit with a sudden revelation. I could do it! I was going to be damned for killing my drunk driver anyway, and Amelia's. Might as well go for broke, add another to my list. Maybe that was the way it was supposed to be. Maybe I was here to save Griffin, to avenge Amelia, to right some wrongs before...I didn't want to think of the consequences. My mind was made up. What would be would be. No point in thinking about the inevitable ahead of time.

I kept my thoughts to myself, knowing the only chance I had of succeeding was to keep my plan concealed from Griffin, from all of them.

Instead, I focused on learning about the impending arrivals. I asked Griffin what would make their existence on our plane so inconceivable.

"The higher the purity, the more power," Griffin explained. "Rather than having to learn new skills, they would have to control an unprecedented amount of power. One moment's loss of control could be devastating. Right now we don't fully understand how their power would develop. Once their powers were harnessed fully, they would become indestructible. In Aamon's eyes, that's too much of a risk to take."

"So, despite his nefariousness, he still wants to save mankind?"

"Don't be fooled, Alyssa. He wants to save himself. He's a depraved, vile sociopath. He kills without conscience, finds pleasure in inflicting pain and suffering, and is an untrustworthy piece of shit!"

"I get it, but as far as the impending arrivals go, you disagree with his opinion that the risks outweigh saving them?" I asked.

"How can I justify murder with ignorance?" he implored, turning to me.

I nodded toward the now empty bench. "And she couldn't help you, I assume?"

"Deciphering the prophecies is an art, not a science. The pure ones' arrivals are imminent, but an exact timescale cannot be applied as every human's death happens within a window. Where within that window it falls can depend upon the last decisions they make. Their free will can affect its exact timing but not affect the window in which it will happen."

Does that mean I was meant to die? Does that also mean Mikey is meant to die? As I swear, I will see that through.

"How do you know the dark soul you gave to Zagan wasn't the one?" I asked.

"Magda doesn't know when either one will arrive, but she will know when they enter either Daeon or Laeon. And that hasn't happened yet."

"She told you that?" I queried.

"No," Griffin responded, turning to me. "She told Aamon that," he said through gritted teeth.

"She talks to Aamon?" I felt my face flush as I said his name and turned quickly to look out across the gently lapping waves hoping Griffin didn't notice.

"Elders don't control. They don't impose rules or

judgment. They work with both sides to maintain the balance. Free will, remember. They are impartial and serve both sides for the greater good," he replied with a strained smile. "We should head back; I want you to rest before your patrol tonight."

My head jerked back toward him. "I'm patrolling, tonight? I assumed Steven would be taking over from Noah."

"You don't want to?" Griffin's voice was filled with hope.

"No, I do," I replied steadily. "I just expected to have to…" My voice trailed off; I didn't want to say anything that might change his mind.

"I'm not fighting you anymore, Alyssa. I know you can handle it. I just hope you refrain from rushing into problems," he said, staring straight ahead, the muscles in his arms clenched.

Why is it so hard for you to let go of me?

I responded with "I promise," fighting hard to contain my excitement.

Chapter 13

Although I was permitted to participate in the joint patrol operation, Griffin's one stipulation was that I be accompanied to the handover point. Initially, he tried to insist that he be the one to escort me, but Amelia was firm, knowing how badly I needed her calming energy rather than the distraction of Griffin's tumultuous mass of emotions. I could sense his regret and trepidation and was fearful that he would have a last-minute change of heart. As much as I loved him, I needed a break from the intensity that was Griffin.

Being with Amelia reminded me of being alive. She induced normalcy in an abnormal existence. Our time spent together was reminiscent of hanging out with my former girlfriends pre-Kasey. It was easy, safe, and fun. Our personalities complemented each other. We had the same kind of quirkiness, the same directness, the same level of craziness, and the same strong feminist views. And of course we shared the same traumatic heartbreak.

We caught the train over to NYC, like we were heading for a night on the town, sitting opposite each other in the almost vacant carriage, sharing funny stories of our first life experiences. Amelia was the one to bring up Aamon. Never one to skirt around the subject, that girl got straight to the point, an attribute I usually appreciated, though with this subject matter, not so much.

"I thought Griffin was intense, but damn! Aamon is on another level! In my opinion, there's more history between the two of them than Griffin's revealed, right?"

I couldn't tell if Amelia was merely gossiping or intentionally trying to invoke a reaction. I kept my face expressionless, absent-mindedly murmuring, "Uh-huh."

"I mean, he scared the shit out of me, and he wasn't even looking at me the way he was looking at you," she continued. I raised an eyebrow questioningly, "Like you were lunch," she verified.

Shit! I had really hoped only Griffin had noticed.

"Do you have any idea who I'll be working with tonight?" I asked, keen to steer her away from any subject involving Aamon. The mere mention of his name curdled my blood and invoked a feeling I was not ready to unpack yet.

"I mean, does it matter? Do you even have a preference?" she asked, with a look of distaste at the thought of patrolling with any of them.

"I guess not, as long as it's not Kerwin!" I shuddered.

"Oh hey, before I forget," Amelia exclaimed as she rummaged through her small crossover bag, "Griffin wanted me to give you this." She pulled out a cellphone and tossed it to me.

I rolled my eyes and scowled. "Of course he did!"

"He just wants you to be safe, girl. Now if you need his help, you can just call him." She bounced over to take the seat next to me, leaned over, and scrolled through the phone. "His number and Noah's have been programmed in already, see?" She indicated toward the screen.

"And you think it's just a coincidence that now he'll be able to track me?" I pointed out.

"You're paranoid." She laughed. "I mean, maybe not entirely inaccurate, but paranoid nonetheless."

"You're only amused because it's not happening to you," I noted.

"One hundred percent!" Amelia agreed, dissolving into uncontrollable giggles.

I swatted her with the back of my hand. "Next time, I'm coming alone!" I exclaimed.

"Next time, I'll let Griffin take my place. Maybe he'll take you for a moonlit stroll through Central Park before sending you off to be tracked and obsessed over!" she replied, rolling her eyes in a fit of giggles.

"You know I don't like him that way!" I insisted.

"Only because you won't allow yourself to. You've built walls that are impossible for anyone to break through," Amelia chastised.

"Okay, thank you for the deep dive into my psyche, Dr. A. Enough with the analysis now, please," I begged her.

"Okay, okay, I'm done," she promised.

A young couple with a baby stepped into our carriage, sitting two rows away from us. The child couldn't have been more than eight or nine months old. As always, habit caused me to hesitate, wait with bated breath as they passed by us to get to their seats. I smiled at the infant as they passed, an automatic reaction that was done without thought. To my astonishment, the infant smiled back, looking directly at me as he gurgled with excitement and waved his arms in my direction.

"Amelia, am I losing my mind, or is that baby smiling at me? I swear he sees me!" I whispered, unable to tear my eyes from him.

"He probably does. Some living beings can. I once

had an old lady try to have a conversation with me, wanted me to pass on a message."

"What did you do?"

"Freaked out and ran away!"

We both dissolved into giggles at the irony as the train rumbled slowly into Penn Station. We disembarked and took the subway to Eighty-First Street before making our way through Central Park, arriving at the rendezvous point just before dusk.

"Looks like you'll be patrolling with your bestie." Amelia snickered, nodding toward the female Sygan she had squared up against the previous day. She was perched atop one of the gray stone walls surrounding the large open terrace, her legs outstretched as she watched us approach with an angry stare.

"Alyssa." I introduced myself curtly. Another human force of habit, grace and courtesy ingrained within me, compelling social etiquette in unfamiliar situations. I hated myself for it. She merely responded with a grunt.

I really need to work on not being alive anymore.

I turned to Amelia with feigned enthusiasm, hissing, "Well, this is going to be fun!"

Amelia squeezed my arm and responded, "Good luck, sister."

We both felt Noah's energy nearing and turned expectantly to welcome his approach. In a typically dramatic display, Noah appeared, leaping over the wall from the side of the building only accessible by scaling the large rocky formation on which it sat. He did like to make an entrance.

With a wide smile, Noah bounded over and embraced us both warmly. "Amelia, Alyssa, and Miss

Seraphina." He gestured toward the Sygan. I swear the Sygan's lips twitched, almost forming the tiniest of smiles. Only Noah could do that. His exuberance was infectious. He leaned in closely and took my hand. "Don't worry about her. Remember, you don't need to be in close proximity to Miss Personality. She can sense if you give chase. If she's needed, she'll be there. Otherwise she'll leave you alone."

"I got this, don't stress," I assured him.

"See you in a few hours, I guess," Amelia said, giving me a quick hug. "Steven will meet you here at dawn, okay?"

"No problem," I said with a smile. "Now get out of here!"

I watched Noah and Amelia stroll down the castle's wide staircase, arm in arm heading home, before I turned to address the ever-scowling Seraphina.

Those damn human constraints dictating my actions again!

"How do you want to do this?" I asked.

Seraphina leaped down, catlike and graceful, from the wall, landing a foot away from me, and sneered as she looked me up and down. "How about you just stay the fuck out of my way?" she snapped disdainfully, then turned on her heels and sprinted into the park before I could even respond.

Works for me!

I spent the first few hours monitoring Central Park, the Upper West Side, and Harlem, before circling round to the Upper East Side and then making my way down to Lower Manhattan. For the city that never sleeps, it was incredibly quiet. I paused often to focus completely on locating something, anything, but I sensed nothing. Four souls passed in the time I patrolled, no Vesk was within the vicinity, and the only Sygans were Aamon's henchmen. In addition, each passing was completely uneventful. Only one word could accurately describe the experience, and that word was *boring*!

I'd always patrolled with at least one other person and never for an assigned duration. Time passed slowly. Each minute dragged painfully along. Just before midnight, I decided to cross the George Washington Bridge and head over to Hoboken in an effort to break up the night.

I can't believe I begged to do this!

The bridge was beautiful at night, illuminating the churning waters of the Hudson River between the cities, displaying stunning views of the New Jersey and New York evening skylines. It was at this point it occurred to me that, for the first time since the weeks following my death, I was alone. It's funny how peaceful solitude can be when you know you have a place and people to return to. For the first time in months, I felt free, liberated, and safe enough to allow the thoughts I'd kept buried deep within me to surface. Safe enough to reflect upon the past few days without fear of exposure.

Amelia's assumptions regarding Griffin were reasonable. I understood how she could have reached her conclusion, but that didn't mean she was correct. I did love Griffin, just not in the way she thought I did. I absolutely put up walls, but not for the reasons she suspected. Sure, I had a fear of vulnerability. Becoming completely dependent upon someone else was not in my nature. To me it implied weakness. But the main reason I held Griffin at bay was to protect him from my thoughts, to allow myself the clarity and space needed to execute my plan. The grudge I had nurtured and held close since the very first day of my passing had been my savior, giving me a reason to exist and the motivation to survive. What saved me would also ultimately end me, would be my damnation, my blessing, and my curse. I'd realized this long ago, but it was the path I chose regardless.

I loved Griffin like a brother and desperately didn't want that to change. I really hoped he'd understand that and not ask for more than I was willing to give.

My cynical, ever-critical conscience jabbed at me, echoing questions I didn't want to hear.

Are you trying to convince Amelia, or yourself?

I made my way into Hoboken, aiming to do a quick sweep of the city before traveling back over to Manhattan. I barely got two blocks in when I felt it, a familiar repugnant energy that awoke a vile memory. I stopped and stood motionless as I tracked it. Located it stumbling beneath the fluorescent lights of the sports bar a block over.

I hadn't planned on this today, but the brief period of contemplation on the bridge had brought my objectives sharply back into focus with impeccable timing. The universe was delivering me an opportunity, one that would not be wasted.

I felt it down low in my body, like some primordial entity had weaved its way beneath the Earth's surface and seeped up through the ground, infiltrating me, my body a welcoming host permitting the absorption via the soles of my feet. It traveled upward diligently, overpowering every cell it encountered. It consumed me, morphing me into something alien and frighteningly unrecognizable.

In a hatred-fueled trance, I trod heavily toward him, oblivious to anyone and anything around me, totally engrossed in only him, like a hunter stalking her prey. The dark loathing swelled and climbed, boiling and rancid in my throat, in my chest, radiating down my limbs, and it was not alone. Blended with it was an excited anticipation, a sickening desire to hurt him, torture him, exult in the pain I would inflict. The sane part of me didn't even put up a fight. She surrendered, stepping silently back into the shadows, finally releasing the twisted, damaged, and disturbed version of me, extending her the freedom to do her bidding.

The bastard that killed me, that left me dead in front of my child, feet from him, from my mother, from my home, swayed gently from side to side, ignorant to his impending attack as he enjoyed the last drags from his cigarette. He was undeniably inebriated; I mean, was he ever anything else?

I stood close to him, staring into his bloodshot eyes, willing him to see me or to feel me like the infant from the train. I followed him as he stumbled around the corner of the building into the dimly lit, empty parking lot. The longer I stood close to him, the angrier I became. But this anger was different than anything I'd ever experienced before. It was almost enjoyable. Fury became my friend; it nourished my darkness, allowing me to nurture it, to manipulate it. I purposefully stayed close to him, allowing my fury to expand and flourish. I breathed in his noxious fumes as he fumbled for his car keys. I laughed out loud, a demented and sadistic cackle, as he dropped them and shakily bent to retrieve them. He staggered against his truck, attempting to unlock it with fumbling hands.

"Enough," I hissed and reached for him. His essence prickled against my fingertips like static electricity. I felt the hairs on his neck stand up as my hands closed in around him. An internal alarm was triggered, but the sound was blanketed by my darkness, reduced to no more than a dull ringing somewhere far, far away.

That was how close I was. That close to quenching my thirst, to executing my plan when *he* intervened. I should have realized what the alarm was for, a survival instinct to signal his arrival, to warn me to run. In a heartbeat, the drunkard Mikey was ripped from my hands, swept up into the air, and thrown violently to the ground ten feet away from me. My anger flared, and with a piercing screech, I ran after him, lunging for him as huge hands grabbed him from my grasp again.

I stopped and turned to face Aamon, my eyes blazing as I demanded with a scream, "*Let him go!*" Aamon glowered at me, locking his eyes on mine as he held the whimpering semiconscious man above the ground with one hand fixed firmly around his throat. Aamon's eyes remained unwavering on mine, and with a flick of his wrist, he deftly snapped the drunk man's neck before dropping his lifeless, contorted body to the ground.

The power that had permeated every inch of my being exploded, incensed at what he had taken from me. He turned, seemingly unperturbed, and swept away through the maze of alleyways, disappearing into the darkness.

I surveyed the crumpled heap of twisted bones and flesh he had left behind, spat on it, and without hesitation gave chase, darting after Aamon, hunting him down through the back streets of Hoboken.

I tracked him to the outskirts of town and into an apartment complex, up the concrete fire escape stairwell, and into an empty hallway. My steps didn't falter as I continued my pursuit through a dark labyrinth of hallways. My footsteps only slowed when I realized he was no longer moving. I could feel him stationary and close.

I turned, carefully surveying the hallway behind me, and walked backward a few steps before I turned forward to take the next few steps, constantly assessing my surroundings, looking for any sign of him. Taking three steps forward, then three steps backward, I made my way cautiously down the shadowy passageway. I had taken two steps backward when his arm shot out of nowhere, yanked me off my feet, and pulled me roughly through a doorway, which slammed shut with a deafening bang behind me.

I should have been petrified, should have made strenuous attempts to free myself from his grasp as he held me against the closed door, but instead, with a pounding heart, I swung for him, hitting him squarely on the chin. He released me, dropping me abruptly to the ground, before he turned and walked away from me.

I wasn't close to being done. I leaped to my feet, raised my right foot, and kicked him hard in the center of his back. He stopped and turned slowly, throwing me a death stare. With a roar, I flew at him again punching and clawing. He backhanded me fiercely with a blow that sent me sprawling across the carpet. I lay there motionless as he stormed toward me, my eyes searing into his. At the very last moment, as he bent toward me, I lifted both legs and drove them simultaneously into his broad chest to send him crashing to the ground. Without hesitation, I leaped on top of him, swinging wildly with clenched fists at his face. He laughed a deep and guttural laugh before twisting sharply beneath me and throwing me to the floor, pinning me down with his body.

"Fuck you, Aamon," I hissed, trying to wriggle free, trying to ignore the energy shift between us and the heat that crept steadily beneath my skin. I clawed at his arms, his face, and his neck.

He grabbed my wrists and restrained them above my head. He leaned in close, his face almost touching mine as he growled, "Calm the fuck down."

As he spoke, he stared into my eyes, loosened his grip on my wrists, and lowered his head, close enough for his lips to brush mine with a snarl.

His words didn't stop me. Telling a furiously irate woman to calm down was about as effective as attempting to baptize a cat. It was something else that stopped me—the mood shift, the energy that burned hot between us intensified. It was dark and twisted, it was abhorrent and resentful, but it possessed another element, a deep dark lust so tempestuous, so powerful and dominating that in a heartbeat it stole away all of my self-control.

My chest heaved.

You have got to be fucking kidding me!

My reaction was not a conscious one. I closed my eyes; a swell of anger at being reduced into a submissive state consumed me, empowering me to make one last futile attempt to fight back before resigning myself to the inevitable. As his mouth met mine, I bit his lip hard, drawing blood. He pulled his head back and gave me a look that almost resembled admiration as he let out a low and husky laugh.

I hated myself and I hated him, but my body craved him, betraying my mind. The more I loathed myself, the more disgusted I was, the more turned on I felt. It was mentally torturous. I felt like I was standing on the edge of a cliff with the ground crumbling beneath my feet, unable to step back, unable to run to safety. And then the ground wasn't there anymore, and I was tumbling through the darkness with zero control. The point of no return breached.

I weaved my fingers around his wide neck and pulled his head toward mine. At first, he resisted. He was lying, his full weight on me. His scent was intoxicating. Sharply, I parted my legs and drew my knees up, an action that pulled him closer. My knees squeezed his hips and trapped him, hard and swollen against me. My body pitched and rolled reactively. Keeping my eyes locked with his, I released his neck, raised my arms above my head, and crossed my wrists, a willful surrender.

A small gasp escaped him, and his heavy breathing deepened. With hooded eyes, he peeled my shirt up over my torso, over my head, and stopped at my wrists, one-handedly wrapping it tightly to bind my hands together.

I lifted my legs, wrapping them around his back, and pushed one foot at a time against my boot heels to kick them off before dropping my legs back down to the ground. Aamon pushed himself onto his knees. With one hand, he flicked open the button at my waistband. Gripping the hem, he ripped my pants and my underwear savagely from my body.

He ran one hand from my wrist, down my arm, and to my throat, which disappeared beneath his huge palm. His broad chest pinned me to the ground. Bringing his head close, he brushed his lips against mine. This time I didn't bite. I kissed him. As his mouth closed around mine, I was pulled into a cyclone. I could feel the blood rushing through my body, could hear and feel the pounding of a heartbeat but couldn't tell if it was his or mine. His kiss was rough and hard, giving me everything I needed. In that moment, I craved him more than I had ever craved anything before, like an addict who'd found her fix. Again, my body coiled and rolled under his touch. He stood over me to remove his clothing, hungrily eyeing me. Falling to his knees naked, he kept his eyes locked on mine as he gripped my ankles and forced them sharply apart. My skin burned and my body squirmed, wild and desperate for him.

He watched me with uncertainty, still doubting what was happening, still doubting what my body was screaming for. Keeping my eyes firmly fixed on his, I lowered my still-bound hands between my legs and caressed myself, arching my back from the carpet with a gasp as my fingers explored my most intimate area, which throbbed and pulsated, wet to my touch. Like a wild animal, he sprang forward, pushing my thighs further apart and burying his head between them. He was ferocious and insatiable, bringing me to climax again and again.

His mouth continued to work as it traveled up my body, over my stomach, and up to my breasts. He ran his tongue over each, allowing his teeth to graze over my hardened nipples. When he reached my neck, his hands gripped my arms, forcing them back above my head and holding them there. As his mouth met mine, he pushed himself hot, huge, and hard inside of me over and over, deeper and deeper, rising up onto his knees and tugging my hips up to his, thrusting relentlessly. I cried out in euphoria. He flipped me over onto all fours, entering me roughly from behind. While still deep inside of me, he jerked me sideways so that I faced the wall, pushing me up against it as he continued to pound me. Breathless and still bound at the wrists, I pushed my forearms against the wall, using them to support myself as I shakily climbed to my feet.

He rose behind me. I could feel him towering above me. Having him so close without touching me electrified my burning skin, almost painfully.

I bent forward, pushing myself back toward him, still hot and throbbing. He slammed his arms against the wall on either side of me, caging me in before plunging into me, unrestrained and brutal, bringing us both to climax.

What we did was the furthest thing from lovemaking. It felt wrong to even describe it as sex. It was dark and primal and self-gratifying.

He stayed there, breathing heavily for a moment before tugging at my wrist constraints and lowering his arms, releasing me from my bindings and my cage. He wrapped his fingers around my hair and pulled my head slowly back, forcing my eyes to meet his, where I saw the fleeting shadow of confusion cross his features. I stared back unblinking with zero regret. He unclenched his fist, releasing my hair as he whispered gruffly, "You need to leave," before walking down the entranceway and disappearing around a corner.

With trembling hands, I snatched up my discarded clothing, pulling them on hastily over my mottled, damp skin. I hurried through the door and dashed from the building, sprinting down three blocks before pausing to gulp in the brisk night air. I could not bring myself to think about what had just happened, or who the hell that girl was. I carefully scraped together every molecule of recollection and shoved it deep into the recesses of my mind, slamming the door on my metaphoric box, concealing them for good.

I had no idea how long I had been gone. But I could tell from the ebbing darkness that dawn was approaching. I was running out of time to make it back to the castle's meeting point. The thought of having to fabricate some rationale for missing the changeover time gave me the drive I needed to speed through the streets of Hoboken, across the Hudson, and back into Central Park in record time. For the briefest of moments, I thought I had avoided having to face any uncomfortable questions, but as I circled the castle's grounds, my heart sank.

There, leaning against one of the pavilion's columns, stood Griffin. Just beyond him were Steven and a Sygan I did not recognize. I tried to greet them, tried to sound casual, and failed miserably. My voice sounded too shrill, and the words tumbled from my mouth too fast.

"Are you okay?" Griffin asked, a concerned expression distorting his perfect features. He took a step toward me, and I leaped back, petrified that he would pick up Aamon's lingering smell.

"I'm fine," I insisted. "I'm just wired, over-exhaustion or something, I just want to leave."

Steven opened his mouth to say something. I shot him a frosty glare, and he remained silent. He and Griffin exchanged confused glances. "I guess I'll see you guys later," Steven offered with a shrug.

"Stay safe," I whispered, before turning and briskly

striding from the park.

Griffin followed quickly. Coming up behind me, he swept me playfully into his arms. With a gasp, I jerked my rigid body from his embrace. Shocked at my reaction, he released me immediately, holding his hand up, a look of hurt confusion on his face. "Whoa, what the hell? Alyssa, what was that? Please tell me, did something happen to you?"

As if my shame and guilt weren't bad enough already, crap! I gulped and shook my head, my words stuck in my throat. "I just want to go home," I croaked.

Griffin stayed silent for the remainder of the journey, but he also stayed close, closer than I would have preferred. When we arrived back at the loft, I dashed straight upstairs to my room, pushed the heavy door closed tightly, and went straight into my bathroom, peeling my clothes off with each step. I balled them together and pushed them beneath the pile of laundry in my hamper trying to mask Aamon's stench. I stepped into the steaming shower and turned the water up to the highest temperature I could stand. Soaping my body over and over, then standing under the stream as the scalding water washed away Aamon from every pore.

Eventually, I stepped from the shower, rubbed my flushed skin dry, and turned to reach for my robe. I caught sight of my body in the large bathroom mirror and froze. My wrists had dark ligature marks; finger imprints formed bruises on my hips and inner thighs. Seeing the markings ignited a memory. It flashed through my mind, causing my breathing to deepen.

"No!" I growled to myself, pushing it far away from my mind. I wrapped the robe tightly around my body and climbed into bed, falling into a deep dreamless sleep.

I awoke with a start a few hours later. The moment I was awake, my mind started to wander back to the encounter with Aamon. I jumped out of bed and dressed quickly, choosing a long-sleeved shirt to cover my bruised wrists, before heading downstairs, eager for any distraction.

I was confused to see Steven back, standing in the living room deep in conversation with Noah. "How long was I asleep?" I asked half joking. "Aren't you supposed to be on watch duties?"

I was met with an awkward silence.

"What's going on?" I asked, trying hard to contain the panic rising in my chest.

"We know what happened," Noah said softly, his tone sympathetic.

The room felt like it was spinning. I battled desperately from losing my mind completely.

How could they know!

"Where's Griffin?" I croaked, as tears stung my eyes.

"It wasn't your fault. Alyssa. I know you probably wished for it, fantasized about killing him yourself, and now he's dead, you're experiencing guilt. But it wasn't you. He was killed by Aamon," Steven said in a hushed tone, walking toward me as he spoke. He gently scooped my hand from my side, cradling it in his.

"What?" I stammered.

"We know Aamon murdered the driver of the truck that killed you," Steven replied.

Well, isn't this just one big shitshow at the fuck factory!

I turned to Steven. "Wait, you know what killed him? You can tell that?" I was genuinely astounded.

"Griffin can. He followed your scent, retraced your steps trying to figure out what had happened to you. He found the crime scene and could tell you'd been there, as had Aamon. We know his death was absolutely at the hands of Aamon. His energy was all over the body. Whatever you witnessed, whatever Aamon did to you, it's going to be okay." Steven tried to reassure me.

Followed my scent!

"Where's Griffin?" I gasped, seriously alarmed. I already knew the answer, so the question was pointless. Obviously my knight in shining armor would *have* to dash off to protect my virtue, the bloody idiot.

"You let him go to Aamon?" I shrieked.

"Do you really think we could stop him?" Noah protested, uncustomary anger in his voice. "The only person who holds any degree of control over Griffin is you. You may not want to acknowledge that. We all tiptoe around the subject like you don't have your head buried in the sand, like you don't know how in love with you he is."

The room was spinning like an out-of-control fairground ride.

"WTF, Noah? Really, so because he feels some sort of way, it suddenly becomes her responsibility to deal with? She's suddenly obliged to do what? Reciprocate those feelings to appease him?" Amelia bellowed as she stormed in from the kitchen.

"Everyone needs to just shut up for a minute. The relationship I do or do not have with Griffin, or with anyone, for that matter, is nobody else's business, period. Griffin is an idiot for charging headfirst into a situation that could cost him his life!" I growled, adding, "I'm not the helpless victim he likes to pretend I am."

Noah turned to me, his face contorted with a baffled expression. "You really don't see him, do you? The only person in any degree of danger is Aamon. Just because Griffin controls his power, just because he doesn't flaunt it or utilize it for his own gain doesn't mean he doesn't have it. My money's on my boy Griff. If it's anyone's funeral, it's Aamon's." Noah sat down heavily on the couch, arms folded across his chest in defiance.

"Yeah, and what do you think killing Aamon will do to Griffin?" I hissed. "Aamon kills without conscience. You think Griffin can do the same?"

"Noah," Steven pleaded gently, "it's not her fault, and she's right."

"I'm going to find him," I announced, storming for the door.

Noah leaped to his feet exclaiming, "I'm coming with you!"

"The hell you are," I yelled. "I mean it, Noah, this is none of your damn business!" I glanced toward Amelia who gave me an approving nod as I swept out of the loft. My ride or die always had my back. She'd give Noah the dressing down he deserved.

Right now, my focus was on Griffin. Priority number one was keeping him safe. Priority number two was keeping my secret safe. I simply could not afford to lose the only family I had.

Chapter 14

I could hear and feel them as I approached the apartment complex. They were on one of the upper levels. Without hesitation, I sprinted wildly up until I reached the top floor, thankful they were not in the apartment where I had caught up with Aamon the night before.

I didn't knock on the heavy wooden door. Instead, I kicked it hard, sending it crashing open dramatically. Evidently, time spent with Noah was rubbing off on me.

Griffin and Aamon stood ten feet apart in the center of the wide-open room. Both sets of eyes flashed dark and angry. With shoulders elevated, they leaned forward slightly, poised to attack as they argued.

"She came to me," Aamon snarled.

"The fuck she did! You think I don't know what you're trying to do? That I didn't sense you tracking her? Over my dead body I'll let you do this!" Griffin bellowed.

"That's the most enticing thing you've said so far," Aamon hissed, hunching his shoulders farther forward ready to pounce.

Griffin raised one hand gesturing for Aamon to come to him, taunting him as he growled, "Try it, you prick!"

I rushed across the room and positioned myself between the two, facing Griffin.

"You've got it all wrong," I insisted to him. Behind me, the heat emanating from Aamon made it hard to stay focused and caused me to stumble over my words. "I wanted it!" I cried out. Aamon circled round behind Griffin, raising an amused brow at my choice of words. "I mean, I wanted to *do* it!"

Not much better!

I corrected myself again, feeling my face flush. "I wanted to be the one to kill him."

Finally!

"I chased him, I wanted to end him. He just got there first." I nodded toward Aamon.

"And so, some might say I actually saved her soul. Some might say you owe me an apology and your gratitude," he said smugly. He was thoroughly enjoying every moment of this.

"This is not his fault," I pleaded with Griffin. I didn't want to force his hand, to bend his will, especially not under the scrutiny of Aamon, but I needed to get out of that room, of that building. The longer I was there, the more I felt my self-control slipping away, like Aamon's essence was permeating steadily throughout my body and my mind, drawing me into a place I might not return from.

"Griffin." I stepped closer to him, placed my palm gently on his arm. He looked down with a start, and his eyes softened. I ran my hand down his arm, allowed his fingers to intertwine with mine, and tugged him in the direction of the door. Without a word, he complied. I could feel Aamon's stare, hot and incandescent behind us.

We left the building in silence. I was too afraid to say anything, terrified at what Aamon may have told him. We stopped while crossing a deserted park, Griffin finally speaking first.

"I'm sorry," he mumbled, eyes downcast.

"For what?" I asked, genuinely confused.

"For overstepping your boundaries again, for treating you like a helpless victim," he admitted, stealing a glance at me.

I released a slow deep breath of relief. We had each misread the other's nervous silence for anger.

"I'm sorry I didn't tell you," I replied, turning to face him. A half-truth at least.

"Steven left his patrol; you really stressed him out," I scolded him gently. "You should go speak to him; I can take over his shift." Griffin started to protest, but the warning look I threw his way soon shut him up. There was nothing he could say to justify denying me from patrolling. He didn't get to grant nor deny me permission for anything from this point onward.

Grateful for the break from everyone, I patrolled diligently for the rest of the day, keeping both my body and my mind occupied, changing out with Amelia at dusk.

"Are you okay?" she asked, concern etched across her face.

"It was pretty intense," I admitted with a shrug. "They really fucking hate each other!"

"Who doesn't hate Aamon? It must have been terrifying seeing him do what he did to that driver," she said with a shudder.

"I mean, he sure didn't deserve to live; I can't say I'll be shedding any tears for him," I retorted a little too harshly.

Amelia looked shocked, like she'd been slapped. I

changed my tone quickly. "It's over now. Griffin just needs to steer clear of him."

Amelia nodded in agreement.

"Stay safe," I said, hugging her before she sprinted off across the park.

The days passed by in a repetitive blur, morphing one week into the next. Winter melted into spring, and a new normal was spawned. We patrolled, we waited, always carrying a gnawing nervousness from the anticipation of the impending arrival. I fought hard to keep my distance from Aamon, both physically and mentally. During the daylight hours, the detox worked. Unfortunately, it remained ineffective at nighttime. Memories resurrected with the evening's darkness carried into my waking mind as much as my sleeping mind, relentless and unforgiving.

A change in temperature started to soften the frozen ground, allowing springtime flowers to push their way to the surface and alerting me to the changing season, alerting me to the arrival of another first. Kasey's sixth birthday. His sixth year of life, a year which he would enter motherless, another step away from me, from what was us.

The morning, six years to the day that Kasey entered the world, I rose long before dawn. I stole silently from the loft and watched the sunrise from my mom's front porch, realizing for the first time that my brain no longer regarded this as home. Somehow, over time it had transitioned in my subconscious from being my home and our home, to being just theirs.

An inevitable shift that left a sting.

I peeked, as I always did, into a life that once was mine. I watch Kasey with big bright smiles and excited giggles adorn a birthday crown and open an array of gifts while munching on a donut breakfast.

I tried to convince myself that the few drops that escaped and tumbled down my cheeks were tears of happiness. I watched for as long as my broken heart could take, leaving long before I was ready to return to the loft.

Rather than returning to my new home, I found myself wandering aimlessly around town, past the elementary school, the small local stores and cafes, the fire station and the church, ending up inexplicably at the cemetery.

This was where I stopped.

It had never occurred to me to question what had happened to my human body. If I had been cremated or buried, if I had a grave. The thought sent icy chills down my spine. Given my emotional state that day, I opted not to seek that answer out and instead picked my way through the mass of concrete headstones, all the way to the far west corner. Two rows from the wall separating the cemetery grounds from a busy highway, within the shade of a leaning oak tree, sat my grandmother's final resting place.

The light gray headstone, discolored from lichen exposure and hard water stains, detailed in the briefest of forms, the life and death of my grandparents and great-grandparents. I placed my hand on the cold stone but felt nothing. The only energy to be found in a cemetery originates from its visitors. The groundsmen, the gravediggers, and the mourners.

I could feel the few visitors as they stood silently by the graves of those they had lost. In life, the worst thing a loved one can do is to die and leave you drowning in an insurmountable ocean of pain. If only the living knew the truth. The pain of separation would remain, but the fear of the never again could at least be alleviated. But I suppose that would be dependent upon which eternity a person chose at passing. I wished there was a way to let my mom know I was okay. That death didn't signify nonexistence, that a beginning followed even the most severe of endings.

I had avoided going straight from my mom's house to the loft in the hopes of lifting my mood a little. Visiting a place of grief in its most concentrated form was not the wisest choice I had ever made. Feeling even more depressed than when I had left Kasey and my mom, I trudged back to the loft, with every intention of crawling into bed and remaining there until tomorrow came.

Arriving back, I tugged open the heavy door to reveal a gathering in the living room; four sets of eyes assessed me silently, surrounded by a haze of nervous energy.

It was not what I was expecting. I jumped a little and eyed them suspiciously.

"What are you doing? What's going on?" I anxiously glanced around the room trying to ascertain what exactly I had walked in on.

Griffin was the first to speak. He ignored my question and asked, "How are you feeling?"

"A little concerned by whatever this is…" I gestured between the four of them.

"We wanted to do something, to commemorate the day," Amelia started.

"We didn't want it to pass by unacknowledged," Steven cut in, continuing, "but also we didn't want to upset you."

My eyes narrowed; did they know it was Kasey's birthday? I was so confused.

"We know it's Kasey's birthday," Griffin confirmed with a sympathetic smile, stepping sideways to reveal the coffee table, its center dominated by a double-tier frosted cake. The wooden surface of the table had been sprinkled with shiny pieces of confetti, and a rectangular gift wrapped in pale blue tissue paper and secured with a yellow ribbon sat to the side of the cake.

Tears pooled in my eyes. I wanted to thank them, to tell them how amazing they were and how very loved I felt in that moment, but the words got stuck in my throat. Amelia was the first to hug me, holding me tightly. The embrace further warmed as each person joined us, heads pushed together, and arms intertwined.

Sniffing and wiping away tears, I was pulled gently over to the sofa. Steven sliced up the cake, and Noah handed me the gift. I tugged at the ribbon and carefully tore away the paper to find a small framed painting. The watercolor artwork depicted two figures, a mother holding her child in her arms against the backdrop of a beautiful sunset, their foreheads and noses touching, lost in each other. The two had matching blond locks. It was Kasey and me.

I looked at Noah. "You did this?"

He shook his head with a smile and nodded toward Griffin.

My eyes widened. "Griffin, it's beautiful, thank you."

"We just want you to know we're here for you, Alyssa. Today is an important day. When a baby enters this world, it's more than the birth of one being. Six years ago was a new beginning for you too, the birth of your new identity. That's something you should always celebrate."

Amelia linked her arm through mine. "And you're still a momma. When you're separated from someone significant, you don't just mourn losing them. You mourn losing that part of you, who you were because of them. But you never lose the title. You'll always be a daughter and a mom and a sister."

"I didn't have siblings," I murmured.

"Well, you do now," she said as she rested her head on my shoulder.

Although tinged with sadness, the tears that fell were finally tears of real happiness.

The days got a little brighter, the load a little lighter. The family unit we built fulfilled a need in all of us. Amelia and I became sisters, comrades, and best friends. Noah and Steven were like brothers to us, supportive, protective, occasionally irritating, especially Noah, who was clueless when it came to personal boundaries. I would often step out of the shower or roll over in bed to find him there waiting impatiently to ask my opinion or share some story with me. He rolled his eyes when I yelled, and he insisted that he didn't have to adhere to the same boundaries as other men on account of him being gay and in love with Steven.

He had saved me in more ways than one, and so it wasn't that I didn't trust Griffin. I absolutely did, and I felt safer with him there, not that I'd ever admit it. I just had to exercise great care not to become dependent on him. Never letting that final wall down, and I think he knew it, felt my reservations, and probably knew I was hiding something from him, which I was.

I always felt that there was something Griffin held back from me, aside from the secrets he refused to share, maybe because I knew I held something back from him. It had nothing to do with Griffin per se. Deep down, I was afraid of the repercussions should I become too close to anyone and lose them again, lose myself again. As strong and unbreakable as my persona was, it concealed a damaged, insecure individual who loathed the thought of another being possessing the power to control and manipulate me. Emotion was a dangerous thing. If not held tightly in check, it could slither away, leaving an unending trail of heartbreak and devastation in its wake.

It wasn't just the fear of vulnerability. Something else held me back. Griffin longed for me, but the yearning he carried for me was not reciprocated. I wished sometimes I could just feel the same way he did. I even contemplated faking it, trying to fool myself into believing I felt as strongly for him as he did for me. But even imagining it created a ball of hot anxiety that sat heavily in my gut.

And even worse, whenever I contemplated becoming romantically involved with Griffin, in slithered the memory of Aamon, filling my mind with a dark toxic fog.

Each time my thoughts would start to wander, I would remind myself that I had far more important things to focus on anyway with no time for pointless distractions. To be completely open with another person meant allowing vulnerability in. My desire to be wanted, to be loved, was buried deep within me and would remain that way.

Chapter 15

In the times that Griffin patrolled, I would slip quietly away, watching Kasey from a safe distance. I kept a healthy distance from Griffin too, telling myself the space between us was for his benefit as much as mine. Had the overarching tension of what was happening around us not been there to distract the others, they might have noticed the growing gulf between us.

One evening, months after Griffin's confrontation with Aamon, after multiple failed attempts to capture sleep, I slipped silently downstairs, creeping back up a few minutes later with a large glass of wine. I needed a companion for the long night, and that was the best the loft had to offer.

As I climbed the final step, Griffin's door opened. He shuffled out still half asleep, his hair tousled from an obvious slumber. It made the sleep-deprived me envious. One hand rubbed his half-closed eyes. The other stretched upward causing his shirt to ride up a little, revealing his toned midriff. I could have slipped right past without him noticing, but I didn't.

I paused for just a second. I desperately didn't want to spend another night alone, but the thought of doing anything that could possibly be conceived as selfish and inconsiderate of his feelings would only cast me into further turmoil.

But maybe he is the soap I need to wash away the

lingering memories of Aamon. Or the bleach to burn them away!

"Hey!" escaped from my mouth.

His eyes snapped open with a start. "Hey, are you okay?" he responded with concern as he eyed the very large glass of wine in my hand.

"Can't sleep," I replied with a small shrug.

Griffin raised one eyebrow and nodded toward the glass, asking, "And that's going to help you?"

"She's my company," I explained with a small smile.

"If you didn't want to be alone, why didn't you just come in to me?" he asked, gesturing to his room. "I'm right next door, a lot closer than the kitchen and the wine rack."

I glanced behind him, toward his rumpled bed and back to him. Words were not needed. He read my expression perfectly.

"Alyssa," he said with a sigh, "I love you. I think you are amazing and beautiful, but when are you going to believe me when I tell you that you are not above my ability to resist you. What do you think I am going to do to you?" he asked slowly, staring intently into my eyes with a half smile.

My concern is what I might do to you!

"Just for one night, let me look after you," he pleaded, pushing his door wide open and stepping to the side for me to enter. I paused, conflicted, but desperate not to be alone. "Like I said, you're not that irresistible," he teased playfully.

We crawled into his warm bed from opposite sides. Griffin wrapped his huge arms around my body in the darkness and assumed a spooning position behind me. At first, I stiffened slightly at his touch.

"Did you know that hugging actually releases oxytocin in a far more effective manner than a bucket of wine," he whispered.

I laughed and relaxed into his arms.

"You asked me once about my life," he said. "I was a different person back then, that's why I don't like to talk about it."

"Different how?" I asked, intrigued. I had no idea what had brought about his sudden desire to divulge details from his past, but I was appreciative of the opportunity to catch a glimpse into his first life.

"I didn't always follow the rules." Only Griffin could sound so pained saying something so innocent. "My mother was British. My father was American. They were good people. They'd fought so hard to be together. My mother left everything she had, crossing oceans to be with my father, literally. I grew up on a farm in Iowa, an only child. My mother had a lot of health issues. She died when I was nine years old. When my father became sick a couple of years later, he sent me to live with my mother's family in London."

My heart ached for the little boy who had lost everything.

"I suppose most people would say I fell in with a bad crowd, but then they were the only crowd that accepted me." His words were barely audible, floating between the small stretch of air separating us. I inched myself farther into his embrace, listening closely.

"They weren't bad people; unfortunate circumstances gave them very few choices in life. Back then, you had to fight to survive any way you could, or you gave up. They were really the only two options. And so, I broke the rules. Nothing extreme of course—petty theft, bootlegging—but still crimes nonetheless."

I laid my head back against his chest, lulled by the steady drumming of his heart and the low murmur of his words as he continued.

"We were efficient at what we did, and that didn't go unnoticed. We started to get involved in things we shouldn't have. Once you slipped into London's underworld, it was hard to get out. A friend and I were running a job for one of the big names at that time, a man with links to the mob. We were sent to collect something. I don't know what, we never asked. But we were set up. We walked right into a sting operation orchestrated by a dirty police officer, one of the worst in the city. Authorities were closing in on him and his criminal activities. We were his scapegoat. He screwed us over, then told the mob we had been the ones who screwed them over. We tried to escape London, but he'd falsely claimed a police officer had been stabbed trying to apprehend us. The entire city was looking for us, for me especially. I was blamed for inflicting the fatal wound. I would have hanged for it unless I got out."

He continued, "My uncle worked on London's docks. He'd made arrangements for us both to jump ship to Australia, but the mob found out, threatened to kill him, my aunt, and their daughters unless he put us on the wrong ship. I don't blame him for what he did. I'd brought nothing but trouble since the day I arrived on his doorstep. Suffice to say, we never reached our intended destination. Five days after boarding, our ship docked in New York where they were waiting for us."

"They killed you?" I asked in a hushed tone.

"Oh, they didn't just kill us, they made an example

out of us. We were tortured for days."

His words hung heavy in the air between us. I could feel the pain and suffering he had endured radiating from his disturbed memories, a box of anguish that had to be opened to be shared.

And just like that I understood him more, appreciated him more, and loved him more.

I didn't say a word, there was nothing more to say.

Whether it was brought about by a desperation to rid myself of Aamon's festering memories, a reaction to him lifting the lid on his chest of secrets, or simply a response to feeling closer to him than I'd felt before, I don't know. I didn't think about my actions, or their potential ramifications. I was tired of thinking, assessing, and analyzing every situation. I just did, surrendering to what felt right in that moment. As completely selfish as it may have been, I wanted him, and so I would have him.

I pulled his arms tighter around my body, wiggled myself back so that I pressed firmly against him.

"Alyssa," he warned, like I didn't know what I was doing, what effect pushing myself against his groin would have.

I placed my hands over his, guided one to my breast and the other between my legs. He inhaled sharply. "I want you, Griffin," I whispered through the dark. His lips found my neck, and his hands slid deftly beneath my clothes, softly, rhythmically exploring and caressing, making me pant. I rolled over pushing him onto his back and sat astride him. Grinding gently against him.

He pulled off his top first before reaching for mine and discarding it. He pulled himself up into a sitting position and wrapped my legs around his back as he shuffled up the mattress and out of his pants. The point of no return had long passed—may as well enjoy the ride.

Kissing my lips, my neck, and my breasts, he ran his fingertips down my spine, around my hips, over my groin, hooking one finger along the edge of my panties and pushing them swiftly to one side, freeing me to him.

Griffin lifted my hips gently upward and positioned himself perfectly before pulling me toward him. I let out a soft groan. God, he felt good.

He made my body feel ecstatic, physically connected, loved, wanted for something more than his own satisfaction. His eyes remained locked on mine through every moment. He never faltered, gripping my hands and riding through the rapture with me. It's crazy how lonely sex can be with an unconnected partner; I'd never felt like I'd actually been with someone for the whole experience except for with him. Long after it ended, I still didn't want him to move away from me. And he didn't. I should have slept soundly with my body wrapped around him like a vine, but as much as I tried, I just could not settle.

Long before daybreak, I carefully slithered out from Griffin's bed and slipped quietly into my room. I showered quickly, wrapped my body in one of the oversized bath sheets and walked into the bedroom.

Griffin sat on my bed waiting patiently, dressed just in his underwear, legs stretched out casually. I eyed him suspiciously, hoping I hadn't awakened some needy obsessive alter ego within him.

"I'm not stalking you. Calm down, woman. I just wanted to check you were okay." He watched me intently for any indication of regret.

I walked over to the bed, crawled across the mattress

to sit next to him. "I don't regret having sex with you."

The relief on his face was evident. But still he held my gaze. His eyes locked on mine as one hand untucked the top of the towel and let it fall away. His eyes remained on mine as he pushed me gently backward and ran his hand down my body, cupping my knee and pulling it upward.

This time it felt like making love. It was satisfying and safe, and the way he watched me with intensity, reading my reactions to every touch, every thrust, every taste made it erotic. When we were satiated, sleep still evaded me, but this time I stayed in his arms until dawn finally crept upon us.

We slipped into an informal relationship. I didn't have the same need for physical interaction as Griffin did, but I permitted his hugs, his touches. He was breathtakingly good-looking, kind and attentive, protective, and fantastic in bed. I trusted him, felt safe with him. It should have been picture perfect. From the outside looking in, we were a flawless match. But try as I might I could not stop a feeling invading me in the most random of moments. Out of nowhere, I would feel that snake of doubt, the feeling of incompleteness as it wheedled its way into my consciousness. And when it did, it would bring an Aamon memory with it.

At first, I convinced myself that the extreme events of the night with Aamon and the heightened emotional state I had been in had made the interaction with him seem more intense, more fervent, and made every feeling more exceptional than it actually was. Misplaced lust, a convenient outlet for the trauma endured.

I knew that I was longing for the same sexual gratification that being with Aamon had given me. But I tried to tell myself the experience had been circumstantial and not directly related to Aamon specifically. A futile attempt at convincing myself that the experience had little to do with him, that the same level of arousal was achievable regardless of the partner.

Sex barely seemed like the same act in comparison to what I'd experienced on Earth. First and foremost, I was completely selfish, and somehow within that, it became utterly gratifying for both parties. There was no conscious effort, you just had to let go. Sex as a living human being, in particular a female, had little to do with what you received. The emphasis was on what you gave, what you could help the other person achieve. Just another example of female inferiority.

Sex with Griffin was beautiful. I wanted to love him back with the absoluteness he extended to me. He was my protector, my ally, my anchor. But when he touched me, when he was with me in the most intimate way, it felt like surface pressure, amazing and fulfilling, but giving me just about what I needed and no more.

With Aamon, it had been dark and raw, fueled by anger and lust, but despite that, when he touched me, it felt like we ceased being two entities. When he touched me, I felt him everywhere, physically and mentally. And it wasn't all just about the sex.

When Aamon was close, I slipped into something, something so powerful I had no choice but to surrender myself to it. By this rationale, I should have felt powerless, but I didn't. It actually made me feel more powerful. A different me took over, a me whose inferior size meant nothing, even in comparison to someone as strong and menacing as Aamon.

I wasn't surrendering myself to him, I was

surrendering myself to me.

I thought I hid it pretty well. To almost everyone I did. But not Amelia. Maybe I let my guard down a little when it was just her and me, or maybe she was just a better empath than the rest of us.

I confided in her often, admitting an apprehension I did not understand. I wanted what I portrayed with Griffin to be authentic and true. I loved him and wanted him to be my happily ever after. I hated myself for whatever it was that was holding me back.

Amelia was always kinder to me than I was to myself. She suggested it was a degree of guilt at accepting contentment in an existence without Kasey, nervous anxiety for the impending arrival, or simply the adverse effect of being constantly surrounded by Sygans. All reasonable notions. But none felt accurate.

I couldn't come clean to her, couldn't bring myself to admit what I had done with Aamon. I struggled with the guilt and the shame. Being disgusted with myself was hard enough; at least I could avoid looking in the mirror. I didn't want to have to avoid looking into my best friend's eyes. When the truth edged close, denial took me by the hand and steered me in the opposite direction. Denial was something I did well.

We still patrolled. Weeks had passed and little had happened, but Griffin insisted that something was imminent and that continuing to work with Sygans was a necessity. I would usually patrol with Seraphina. I didn't like her, nor her I, but I had lots of opportunities to watch her. She and I were similar in a lot of ways, with the exception of her being an evil murdering bitch, of course. We still detested each other, but there was an unacknowledged degree of mutual respect that formed over the time I spent with her. Well, for the most part at least.

It was over a month since I had laid eyes on Aamon. Even having an awareness of the length of time since I'd last seen him irritated me. I didn't want him on my radar for anything at all.

I had patrolled with Seraphina. We were waiting out the last hours on the outskirts of the park, sitting upon one of the high gray stone walls that separated the city's densely populated roads and sidewalks from its urban gardens.

Another monotonous night had left us both frustrated and in a crappy mood.

"God, why can't this just happen already," I muttered, much more to myself than to her.

Her laugh was meant for me to hear, antagonistic and patronizing.

"What's so funny?" I bit back.

"Just looking forward to you eating your words when it does happen," she sneered.

"Oh, so you've had experience with the incoming level of purity before?" I asked mockingly.

That wiped the smile from her face.

"No, but Aamon's told m—" she began.

"Oh! Aamon's told you. My apologies, you really are the expert if Aamon's *told* you," I jeered, cutting her off mid-sentence.

"You really think you're equipped to deal with what's coming," Seraphina scoffed.

"Probably not. Maybe, I should go get some ink done to better prepare myself, find a shade darker than black to wear, abuse the shit out of my eyeliner. Apparently that's what counts here," I taunted.

"Fuck you, Alyssa. Do you even see yourself and your fucking Brady bunch? You and Griffin floating around like the Barbie and Ken of the afterlife. Whatever's coming will eat you up and spit you out, you prissy little bitch!"

"Oh my God!" I feigned shock. "I can't believe I didn't realize until now. *You* like Griffin! Do you touch yourself at night thinking about him? Do you get off imagining him inside of you?" I hissed dryly. "Is poor Seraphina not getting any? Are the men in your life impotent, or do you just not turn them on?"

"What is wrong with—? You sick fuck!" She jumped up, eyes blazing with angry indignation.

I laughed and swung my legs down from the wall, turning my body fully to face her. "Don't be fooled by the blonde hair and blue eyes, sweetie. I am the meanest motherfucker you will ever cross paths with. Don't fucking test me!"

I'm not sure where our little exchange would have taken us had we not been interrupted by an even bigger piece of crap in the form of Kerwin. To be fair to Seraphina, she looked just as disgusted by his arrival as I did.

He turned to her with a sneer. "You're needed elsewhere, leave now," he demanded.

Her eyes narrowed. "Says who?"

Kerwin's mouth twisted in contempt at her obvious resentment toward him. He really did know how to bring out the best in people. "Aamon," he responded with a glare.

My skin prickled at the mention of his name.

Seraphina paused briefly before leaping gracefully from the wall and sprinting down the sidewalk.

"Go heel, bitch," I yelled after her as she turned back fleetingly to give me the finger. I resumed my position on the wall, refusing to appear in the least bit bothered by Kerwin.

Kerwin's eyes tracked from my head slowly down my body. He ran his tongue over his teeth and made a clicking sound. "Death suits you, Alyssa," he drawled sleazily.

"Don't look at me," I snarled.

"Would you rather I touch you? I think you might like that," he badgered, his cold eyes glinting.

I had taken as much of Kerwin as I could stomach. Thankfully, the sunrise was just over the horizon. Without exchanging another word, I jumped down from the wall and into the park where I made my way over to the castle.

He followed, whistling an unrecognizable tune, low and eerie. I knew he was trying to get under my skin, constantly pushing me for a reaction. He thrived on inflicting fear upon others. As much as his tactics worked, I was hell-bent on masking my nervousness. I would not give him the satisfaction of thinking he had intimidated me. I hummed to myself, calming the air around me and at least partially drowning out his incessant repetitive whistling.

He was not happy. Typical bully. But the angrier he got the more I did it.

Not today, Kermit!

I got to the open pavilion to see Noah ready to take over from me. His face paled slightly when he noticed Kerwin trailing a short distance behind me. I embraced him happily, pointedly ignoring the loitering Kerwin.

It should have ended there. Each of us departing our

separate ways. For Noah to patrol, for me to return home, and for Kerwin to crawl back under his rock.

I turned and started to walk one way; Noah turned and headed in the opposite direction. Kerwin remained motionless in the middle. His voice, chilling and songlike, drifted through the air between us, low but piercing. "Oh look, this must belong to Amelia."

Confused, both Noah and I stopped and turned to him. He stood up from a crouching position on the floor, like he had just bent to retrieve the object, shiny and flat, that he held in his hand. That despicable gash-like smile played across his face as he flicked the small object toward me. I caught it one handed, looking between him and an equally perplexed Noah. Opening my fingers revealed a flat coin or token maybe. It took me a minute to realize what it was. A bronze sobriety medallion. I laughed at his pathetic attempt in which he had completely sidestepped the facts relating to Amelia.

My laugh only served to further infuriate him. I tossed the coin back at him. "You should try the drunk that killed her, maybe it belongs to him," I spat.

It was Kerwin's turn to laugh. "Oh, poor Alyssa, always the last to know everything."

My stomach lurched inexplicably. I glanced at Noah. The expression on his face chilled me. Out of nowhere, he stormed toward Kerwin screaming obscenities. I stepped slowly back. Kerwin dodged out of Noah's charge and bolted through the castle. His objective had been met.

Instead of giving chase, Noah turned to me.

"What did he mean?" I demanded with a wavering voice.

"Alyssa…" he pleaded, reaching for me.

"No!" I screamed, panic rising in my chest. "Don't fucking touch me. What did he mean, Noah!"

The silence hung between us like a toxic fog. A thick smoky curtain preparing to drop and reveal a hidden truth.

"Noah"—my voice cracked—"please."

My desperation broke his resolve.

"Amelia was the drunk driver that night," he muttered in a hushed tone.

"What? No, that's not possible. She was driving her family. Their car was hit by a drunk driver..." I said slowly.

"No," Noah insisted gently. "Their accident was caused by a drunk driver; their accident was caused by her."

Chapter 16

I don't remember traveling back to the loft. I do remember Noah following me, constantly there just behind me, begging me to slow down, to stop, to talk to him. But I couldn't, I had to see her, and Griffin. I needed her to tell me it wasn't true. I needed my best friend's reassurance. I needed my lover's warm embrace to remind me I was safe and supported, not lied to and betrayed.

I don't know how they knew I was coming or what was going through my head. Actually, that's not entirely accurate. They could probably feel my energy from a mile away as I barreled toward them. I burst through the door to be greeted by the sight of three frozen figures. Steven was sitting on the sofa, his head in his hands. He glanced up as I made my entrance, revealing red-rimmed eyes filled with shock. Griffin stood in the middle of the room, facing the doorway, awaiting my arrival. Amelia was half a step behind him.

Griffin tensed as I entered the room, gesturing for Amelia to remain back, shielded by him.

Guess you're her protector now!

I had so much to say, but my words failed me. I couldn't make a sound. I just stood mute and shaking, looking from one to the other. I thought I'd been the only one kept in the dark till Noah ran through the doorway. Steven looked up for a second time, hurt and anger etched across his face.

"I'm sorry," Noah stammered.

Steven said nothing; he rose from the sofa, turned, and walked into the downstairs bedroom, slamming the door loudly behind him.

"I'm sorry," Amelia whispered, her head bowed.

I blinked. So, it was true. What a way to find out. Thanks, *family!*

"I didn't lie. I just didn't correct you," Amelia began shakily.

"You think you're getting out of this on a technicality?" I asked incredulously, finally finding my voice.

"You have no idea how hard it's been…" she started.

"Enlighten me!" I yelled.

Griffin stepped between us, but not to comfort me. Not to calm me. He was protecting her.

Duly noted!

His betrayal stabbed sharply like a blade to my chest. I stumbled backward, feeling every ounce of every emotion drain from me.

"It was a horrible accident. A stupid argument at a family party. I drank way too much, had no idea what I was doing. All I know is that I was mad at Cal. I put the baby in the car and started to reverse off the driveway. He begged me to stop, and when I didn't, he jumped into the back of the car to try to get Malaika out of her car seat. I lost it and accelerated down the street, past a stop sign, and into oncoming traffic," she sobbed.

My heart ached at her pain. As betrayed and alone as I was in that moment, I still felt pain for her. For just a moment, the anger started to subside.

Then Griffin grasped her hand, embraced her, comforted her, leaving me where I always ended up, on the outside looking in. It was only then that it truly hit me. His betrayal was every bit as bad as hers. No, it was worse! I'd never slept with her. She didn't promise never to hurt me. She didn't tell me I had to open up and trust her. He did!

Fuck her, and fuck him, and double fuck Kerwin and…*Aamon!*

With tears stinging my eyes, I turned and walked out of the door. Noah was still outside Steven's door begging for forgiveness, and Griffin was comforting a sobbing Amelia. How ironic that the one time I did need to be treated like the victim I was, Griffin wasn't able to deliver.

No one followed me. No one cared enough to. Through no fault of my own, I had lost everything, again!

Why am I never anyone's first? Why have I ever only achieved third or fourth place on anyone's priority list at best?

Aamon must have sent Kerwin to do what he did. He ordered the switch with Seraphina and that was why. Probably revenge for my defending Griffin.

Bastard!

I was thankful for the little flame of hatred that glowed within me for Aamon. Right then, it was all I had left.

It was midday by the time I made it to Aamon's apartment. I entered without knocking. He stood across the wide-open room against the window, his back to me, barefoot and bare-chested, staring out across the city. The dark sweatpants he wore hung low on his hips, and his back was a mural of black tattoos that stretched down his arms. I stopped in the center of the room. Fury resonated from every part of me.

"Did you orchestrate that little performance?" I spat at him. Like I didn't already know that Kerwin and Seraphina were following his direct orders.

He moved quickly toward me but stopped a clear foot away. Having him so close was tantalizing and painful. He was just on the cusp of the safety zone, the zone of no return. The space between each other that allowed us to be able to still exercise a small degree of self-control. I edged forward, testing him. He stepped back, maintaining the safe space between us.

"I have better things to do. You should leave now," he growled. His eyes, as black as onyx, pierced me.

I edged forward again, constantly experimenting, trying to figure out how he always managed to pull me in.

Again, he stepped back. "You enjoy this, this sick little game?" he hissed.

I was a little perplexed. Why would the puppet master blame the puppet?

"Or is it Griffin," he continued, "the holier than thou sanctimonious piece of shit that he is. Is this his attempt at breaking me?"

Anger flared up inside of me. "Are you fucking insane? You think any of them know what we did! What you did to me. You think I'd share that with them? With Griffin? It would destroy him, and you know it. This is all *you*, you sick bastard!"

He was so close to that imaginary line. His toes twitched, his hands trembled, and his breath came fast and heavy. I was teetering on the edge of an angry euphoria, a furious high. My emotions conflicted beyond reason. I wanted to be angry. I was angry. I hated him so much, but when he got too close…*Oh God!*

I tried not to breathe. Inhaling his scent sent me spiraling somewhere I was afraid I wouldn't return from. My legs were shaking. A pulsing beat reverberated throughout my body. He spun away, darting across the room and back again within seconds, giving me barely enough time to gulp in a gasp of air that wasn't heavy with his essence. I couldn't tear my eyes from his, not until the clatter of metal on the ground between us snapped me out of my reverie. I stared at the dagger he had just flung at my feet, identical to the one on display in the loft; a wave of dread slowly crept over me. The energy that pulsated from it made it evident it was not forged on this plane.

Griffin's words drifted through my thoughts, chilling me like a Baltic breeze.

The only weapons that can harm you are ones created on a different plane.

"Just do it," he hissed. "Get it over with. I'm handing you your endgame, Alyssa. You want to redeem your fucking soul? Kill me mercifully and end the torture."

Oh my God, this can't be. If he isn't instigating this attraction, I sure as hell am not. What does that even mean…

I couldn't possibly possess any feelings aside from hatred and loathing for him. I couldn't even bring myself to think of the alternative word tapping away inside my head like an annoying woodpecker. His eyes were pleading with me, a look I didn't think he was capable of. I stumbled back a step, reeling from the thoughts that had hijacked my brain.

"You didn't set this up to reveal Amelia's past? This was Kerwin, not you?" My voice was barely a whisper as the sickening realization crept in.

His eyes broke away from mine. He stared down at the dagger, his voice husky and dripping with resentment. "Fuck you, I'll do it myself." In one fluid motion, he swept the dagger from the floor, spun the blade toward his chest, and plunged it straight toward his heart. I didn't make a conscious decision; my body went into autopilot. My left foot roundhouse kicked him, striking the handle of the danger just below his clenched fist, a blow that sent it flying across the room. With a roar he lunged at me, too late realizing his error. He grabbed me by the throat, and we both flew across the room, crashing into the wall.

It happened with such speed and ferocity, yet I hardly noticed. I was transfixed by a moment frozen in my mind, the nanosecond he broke the safety zone, the instant the surge of *him* hit me like the waves from a bomb blast. *Relief, the deepest strongest need about to be fulfilled.* I grabbed the hair on the back of his head, yanking him toward me. I didn't need to be so aggressive—he offered no resistance—but my last sliver of control was long gone. I knew what was coming, and God, I wanted it.

His lips met mine, and tears scorched my cheeks. Right at that moment, I couldn't have cared less about anything, not my life nor my soul. There was nothing that existed besides him and me. I needed him, every millimeter of him covering every part of me. I was insatiable and vulnerable and ached to remain locked in this chaotic erotic prison for eternity.

His kiss was raw and desperate. His left hand ripped

the clothes from my hot and writhing body. His right hand released my throat and grabbed my wrists, forcing them above my head against the wall. My legs snaked around his waist and pulled him hard toward me. My toes hooked into his waistband, pushing his sweats down his thick, tense legs, freeing him to push into me hard and hot, a frenzy of flesh and sweat, rolling and turning in rhythm, climaxing over and over, incessant and feral.

I don't know how much time passed, or how we managed to stop. We ended up a tangled mess on his bedroom floor, his legs wrapped around mine, his arm heavy across my chest entwined with my arm as I lay on my back. His eyes blazed, still jet black but ignited, imprisoning me, a willing victim, a victim with an insatiable thirst that could only be quenched by him. He leaned close. His lips brushed mine, and I felt it, the thing I dreaded, the thing I refused to acknowledge. Necessity, want, desire, some twisted form of *love*, not pure and light, but dark and deep and soul consuming. And I wanted it, I longed for it, exactly that way, the only way that made sense to me, the only thing that seemed right in such a fucked-up situation.

"I'm broken," I murmured. We had remained on the floor for the longest time, entangled, unmoving.

"We're all broken," he replied softly. "How do you get inside my head?" For once there was no bitterness in his voice.

"It's not a conscious decision, Aamon. You're inside my head all day, every day, pulling me." I looked into his eyes. "Pulling me somewhere I want to go."

He drew a sharp breath. He leaned forward, slowly, brushing his lips against mine. As soon as our mouths connected, the energy combusted, my back arched reactively, his kisses deepened, turning forceful and desperate. It drove me wild, and I didn't pull back. I pushed further into the darkness, further into him.

"Do you see what you do to me?" he said with his chest heaving.

For the first time, I saw his beauty, I saw his glow, and insanely, I felt safe. For the first time in forever, sleep found me.

To say I slept soundly would be an understatement. I awoke hours later, no longer on the floor but on a bed, still in the same room I realized. I hadn't even noticed there was a bed in the room. When Aamon was near, I could only see him. Probably not the healthiest of relationships. But then striving for a balanced and healthy relationship hadn't served me very well so far, so fuck it!

He wasn't my Romeo; he was my crack pipe, and the only time I felt okay was after a fix. I found the thought very amusing. Maybe it was just the serotonin remnants dwindling throughout my system, but nothing about my current situation felt wrong.

The door opened tentatively, and Aamon entered, carrying a steaming mug of coffee.

Coffee! The demon god is bringing me coffee, in bed. This really is too much.

I had never seen him look more human. Watching him made my heart skip a beat.

He handed me the coffee and sat on the bed. I put the coffee down and pulled him close. His fingers slid through my hair, holding my head close as he kissed me. God, I was insatiable around him.

"We're about to have visitors," he said breathlessly, still gently kissing my lips, my cheeks, my neck.

I pushed my palm against his chest, eyeing him hungrily as I warned him, "You start this, I'll finish it!"

"Promises, promises." He continued nibbling my neck.

I let the sheet drop, revealing my breasts. "So, you want your visitors to see me like this?" I bantered, lying back against the pillow.

"This is for no one else." His words flowed thick and seductive between us as he carefully tugged the sheet back up, covering me.

If anyone else had said that, implied I somehow belonged to them, I would have reacted furiously. But his response stoked the burning glow of desire deep within me.

He looked up at me, dark eyes flashing, reminding me who and what he was. But what I felt wasn't fear. His essence, his power, it made me hot.

I glanced around the room. "Where are my clothes?"

"Erm, I have bad news. Sadly, they didn't survive." Aamon motioned toward the scraps of shredded clothing that littered the floor.

Oh!

"I assume it's Sygans? Your visitors, I mean," I asked, still trying to figure out how I was supposed to acquire replacement clothing.

"Don't worry. Seraphina will be here soon. I sent her to find suitable alternatives."

I nearly choked. "Seraphina?"

Aamon regarded me with an amused smirk. "I mean, I could have asked Zagan, but I didn't think you would appreciate what he would have chosen."

"No, Seraphina's great. I can't wait to see what she's got me," I remarked with a sour expression. "So, this meeting..." I started to ask.

"I assumed you'd be joining us, hence the need for clothing?" He was looking at me like he may have done something wrong.

"Yes," I answered quickly. I had spent months being treated like a child, being told what I could do and when. Not having to fight for my rights was refreshingly new. "What if you didn't want me there? What would you have done?" I wondered out loud.

"Why would I not want you there?" Aamon looked genuinely baffled. "I don't give a shit about anyone else's opinion; people don't tell me what to do. There are no gray areas with me, Alyssa. If I didn't want you around, you wouldn't be in my bed. As that isn't the case and I do want you around, I want you around indefinitely. Of course, you're your own person. You're free to make your own decisions. I'm not keeping you bound under lock and key, unless of course, you'd like me to?" he queried, his voice low and husky.

I could feel the flush rise from my neck to my cheeks.

The doorbell rang shrilly, pulling Aamon from the room, giving me a moment to flop back on the bed and catch my breath.

Pulling the massive bedsheet around me, I tiptoed through the huge closet doors that sat to the side of the bed. I walked along the immaculately organized shelves and hanging spaces, running my fingers over his extensive range of clothing. The air was heavy with his scent. I breathed in deeply.

Getting my fix.

I pulled out a sweatshirt and trunks, pulling them on before creeping back over to the bed. My clothing was literally shredded, even the jeans. Aamon returned to the room with a selection of bags from various high-end stores. He eyed my current outfit. "Suits you," he said, strolling over to me; his kiss was fleeting, pulling back carefully before the riptide could carry us both away.

I started to thumb through the bags, pleasantly surprised, until I got to the underwear. Scanty was an understatement. I pulled out an array of panties that contained less material than my shredded clothing. "What am I supposed to do with these? Floss?" I asked, holding up a pair.

His eyes flashed. "Are you trying to tip me over the edge?" he growled.

I rolled my eyes trying to disguise the ridiculous grin as it crept across my face.

I had literally just lost everything, and here I was feeling stupidly content and grinning like the Cheshire Cat! Maybe I had finally lost my damn mind!

Aamon left the room, making a wise choice given the heat between us. I pulled out dark denim jeans and a lacey bralette from the heap of clothes, opting to keep on his underwear, and selected a crimson crew neck tank top. So, Seraphina *was* aware clothing came in shades other than black.

As I walked into the living area, a hushed silence fell. Aamon sat across the room on the arm of a sofa, one foot resting on the seat cushion, dressed in light gray sweatpants and a crisp white T-shirt that contrasted sharply against his olive skin and dark tattoos. The heat of his stare shrouded me, making me feel warm and safe. I remained strategically on the other side of the room, a necessary choice to maintain control.

Although the energy in the room was dark and

dense, there was far less hostility than I'd expected. Many of the faces were familiar. Seraphina glared angrily at me but swiftly looked away when my eyes met hers. Predictably, Zagan seeped his usually sleazy energy, his eyes traveling slowly up and down my body. Birsha looked constantly bemused, and Gill demonstrated zero emotion. The last Sygan I had never seen before. He eyed me curiously but remained silent. There were five of them in total, plus Aamon.

"Sir?" Zagan's voice snapped Aamon's attention from me back to him. I hung back from their circle, leaning against the kitchen counter as their conversation continued.

"I always knew he was a conniving treacherous little leech, but he really has outdone himself this time," Aamon snarled. "Do we know how many he has?"

"A substantial number. He's been planning this for a while," Birsha replied.

"Enough to succeed?" Aamon replied.

"That's impossible to predict," Birsha remarked.

"We need to make it possible to predict. I want everyone we have on recon. Others must have known about this. I want their fucking heads!" Aamon demanded.

"Anyone who had any knowledge of Kerwin's activities are either dead or standing with him," Zagan assured him.

"And his father?" Aamon asked.

"Still missing," Zagan responded.

Seraphina held her hands up. "Hold on, do we know for sure the lying little rat actually does have what he claims? How the fuck would he have managed to get his hands on the dark soul, even with his father's help? It doesn't make sense that he managed it, period, but not right under our noses."

"He would have to have something to amass his army," Aamon countered.

I shifted from one foot to the other, desperate to understand what exactly Kerwin had done, who his father was, what he was planning on doing. Had it arrived, the thing we'd all been waiting for? Had we missed it? Did he have it?

Aamon glanced over at me. I tried to look away, tried to avoid distracting him.

"Stop being so self-sacrificing. Ask what you need to ask, Alyssa," Zagan said with an eye roll.

Aamon looked like he was going to kill him! I spoke quickly to distract him from his obvious homicidal intentions.

"Who is his father?" I asked.

"Just one of Daeon's soulless entities, desperate for a power he will never possess," Zagan responded dismissively.

I continued, "Kerwin has the dark soul we've been searching for and an army of sorts, but why? Do you know what he's planning to do?"

Don't you just love an awkward silence!

"Enter Laeon with it," Gill stated, his voice as devoid of emotion as his expression and stance.

"What would happen if he succeeded?" I stammered.

"The planes can't withstand such a crossing of energies. It would be catastrophic," Birsha answered.

Aamon's eyes remained transfixed on me, trying to hold me together. It wasn't working. I was unspooling.

"It would likely be the beginning of the end," Zagan

agreed.

"Oh fuck!" Aamon stood up. "What the hell are they doing here?"

Huh? I didn't feel their energy until the knock on the door echoed around the room.

"I'll deal with this," Aamon growled, striding angrily to the door.

Zagan glanced at me; unspoken words hung between us. I knew exactly what he wanted to say, and he was right. Aamon "dealing" with Griffin, Noah, and Steven was a very bad idea.

I intercepted Aamon midstride. "I'll handle it," I promised.

He paused but didn't return to his seat. Birsha slipped in front of us both and opened the heavy wooden door. Griffin stood center, flanked by Noah and Steven.

I slipped past them all into the hallway taking a few steps away from the doorway.

"How did you know where I was?" I demanded, turning to Griffin. Both he and Noah glanced between me and the two large bodies leaning either side of the wide doorway.

"You tracked me?" I seethed; the damn phone must be in the apartment somewhere!

Steven ignored my obvious irritation and swept me into a warm hug, whispering, "Are you okay?"

I returned his hug, replying, "I'm okay."

Birsha and Aamon remained in the doorway, watching with emotionless stares.

Steven released me and turned to Griffin and Noah. "I don't think she needs rescuing."

I cringed and glanced toward Noah and Griffin, hissing, "You have got to be kidding me! Why don't you go take care of Amelia? That's clearly where your priorities lie."

"Alyssa, it wasn't about protecting her. It was about protecting you from doing something you'd regret," Griffin pleaded.

"Tell me, Griffin, does it never worry you that this intricate web of lies you have weaved yourself might one day entangle you beyond any means of escape?" Aamon growled from the doorway.

Griffin's anger flared, and he turned to Aamon. "What have you done to her?"

Aamon kept his arms folded as he swaggered over to Griffin. He laughed as Griffin's face contorted in anger and leaned in close, whispering, "I didn't do anything to her, but you might not want to ask what she did to me, multiple times."

Yup, that'll do it!

Griffin lifted his right hand to swing at Aamon. Steven and Noah jumped on him, dragging him back.

"Way to keep it classy, Aamon," Noah hissed.

"They should probably know," Birsha suggested to Aamon. Five sets of bewildered eyes turned to him. "Not about...*that*!" He gestured between Aamon and me. "About Kerwin!"

Oh. My. God. Ground swallow me now, please!

Aamon didn't grant them permission to enter, but he didn't reject Birsha's suggestion either.

And that's how we ended up gathered in Aamon's apartment. Five Sygans, Aamon, Noah, Steven, Griffin, and me.

Zagan quickly reiterated what had already been discussed.

"So, the apocalypse. Kerwin is bringing about the

apocalypse," Noah confirmed.

"How the fuck did he get his hands on the dark soul?" Griffin asked through clenched teeth.

"If we knew that, he wouldn't have it!" Seraphina berated him.

"Does he even realize how suicidal his plan is?" Noah asked incredulously.

"He's a bloodthirsty sociopath and a narcissist. I doubt he cares," Steven answered.

"So do we know where this crossing will occur?" Griffin turned to Aamon.

"We're looking into it," Aamon responded sharply without looking in Griffin's direction. He stood rigid, his hands stuffed in the pockets of his sweatpants, glaring straight ahead.

"And given that Kerwin fucked you over right under your nose, how do you know these are trustworthy?" Griffin grimaced as his arm swept around the room.

"Whoa, Griffin!" With wide eyes, Noah turned to him. "What the hell are you doing?" he whispered through gritted teeth.

"Careful," Zagan chided. "You're in the lion's den now."

"I think you should leave," I suggested.

"I'm not leaving without you," Griffin replied firmly.

"And why would I agree to that?" I rebuked.

"Kerwin was the one who did this," Griffin insisted.

"No! Kerwin may have played us"—I motioned between myself and Seraphina—"but he didn't betray me. He didn't lie and deceive me. That was you and you and Amelia!" I spat, jabbing my finger angrily through the air toward Griffin and Noah. I crossed my arms and took a step back, repeating, "You should leave."

"I am *not* leaving you here!" Griffin yelled as he bounded toward me.

Aamon padded softly forward. I felt him close behind me. Instinctively, I turned my head to him. His hands were still in his pockets, his head slightly bowed, but his eyes seared Griffin's.

Aamon kept his voice low. "She's capable of making her own decisions. Now get the fuck out of my house."

"Take care." Steven nodded at me, his eyes pained, before walking to the door.

As Noah pulled Griffin toward the door, he locked eyes with me. "I'm sorry." The sorrow was real and agonizingly painful.

I shook my head slowly. "So am I."

Chapter 17

Of all the derogatory things Aamon could ever be accused of, lacking determination was not one of them. He was merciless in his pursuit of Kerwin, spending hours scouring Daeon for information on those who Kerwin had enlisted. Pulling in Sygans from all corners and wreaking revenge upon those who had betrayed him and broken the rules of Daeon.

Kerwin knew Aamon and Griffin would find out and ultimately oppose his rebellion. He also knew very few Sygans would stand against Aamon. He had to possess something significant to have amassed the army he had. Regardless, by all estimations he was still outnumbered. Over the following days, many unfamiliar faces visited the apartment, illustrating how understated was the authority that Aamon held in Daeon. The concentration of such an ominous blend of dark energy remained encapsulated within the building long after its visitors had departed. Aamon started to hold meetings in a different unit on a different floor, and for that I was grateful.

For a period, I was effectively homeless. I had no intention of staying at Aamon's abode permanently, although the thought of leaving made my heart ache. But I had no desire to return to the loft, knowing doing so would mean facing Amelia, and even worse, Griffin. Besides, it didn't feel like home anymore, just one of the many things their betrayal had destroyed.

I missed Steven, and once my anger for Noah had subsided, I missed him too.

Amelia and Griffin, at this point, not so much.

Aamon's hours spent in Daeon were not without consequence. He masked it well, but each time he returned he brought with him an air of malevolence. A darkness that I'd find myself getting lost in. It wasn't entirely unpleasant, especially when we were intimate, but I did wonder how far I could fall before breaching the point of no return.

It was Birsha who finally succeeded in capturing one of Kerwin's felonious mercenaries.

He would not break easily. But if anyone could rise to the challenge of crushing the will of another, it was a Sygan. His torture went on for hours that turned into days before he broke, and then death was his reward.

The question of Kerwin's hold over his clan remained a mystery. But the how and when was now known, and a plan of attack was put into place immediately.

Kerwin would target one of the quieter gateways to Laeon, nestled among the Adirondack Mountains north of New York. The area was mapped out swiftly, as was our itinerary. We would all travel to High Peaks Wilderness. An unused and empty ski lodge would be our base and center of operations. According to Zagan, we would arrive a few days before Kerwin, giving us time to train, scope out the area, and produce a detailed tactical plan to hopefully terminate both him and his scheme.

That meant working alongside Griffin and Amelia.

I was less concerned about fighting shoulder to

shoulder with Sygans than I was with the prospect of joining forces with Griffin and Amelia. How had we gotten to such a point?

I had to find some resolve to make working with them tolerable. I would reconcile with Steven and Noah at the lodge. I would make efforts to render the relationship with Griffin and Amelia tenable, but I had to remain alone at the lodge. Being with Aamon diverted both of our attention from where it needed to be and would have a detrimental impact on Griffin. I had no interest in preserving his feelings. This was all being done to preserve my own life, to preserve everyone's lives, including my mom's and Kasey's.

I visited them the day before we left, watched quietly as they carried out their day-to-day routines, blissfully ignorant of what was transpiring around them. I whispered words of love and left before the tears started.

When I arrived back at the apartment, Aamon was already home. I could hear the shower running and resisted the urge to join him. Instead, I stood by the window watching rolling gray clouds fill the sky, ominously signaling a storm on the horizon. I felt him enter the room. The surface area of my skin tingled as he moved closer. Every molecule of my being craved him.

The smell of him seeped through the air toward me. His cedarwood bodywash mixed with the scents of incense and musk. The sound of his heartbeat, and the sensation of his breath on my neck sent me spiraling long before he touched me, turning me gently to him, into an infinite gravitational pull from which escape was impossible and unwanted. My own personal black hole. At least that's what it looked like to the rest of the world, a pitch-black abyss of nothingness. But I knew better. I'd stepped into his darkness before and found not emptiness and hatred, but comfort and exhilaration, and more than that, I'd found his light.

"I need to talk to you about the lodge," I said, squirming out of his embrace. Forming a meaningful sentence was impossible in his arms. There was only one outcome from physical interaction with Aamon, and it didn't involve conversation or straight thinking.

He pulled one of the heavy wooden chairs across the floor, stopping in front of me and straddling it. He crossed his arms loosely as he leaned over the back of it and looked up at me.

"I'll need my own room, and you'll need to keep your distance from me." The words made my chest feel constricted.

His eyes narrowed, and with a thickness in his throat, he replied, "I see."

"You need to be focused, and so does he."

I saw his misinterpretation immediately. Stepping closer to him but taking care not to touch him, I murmured, "You're not my dirty little secret to hide anymore, and when this is over, if you'll let me, if you want me, I'll be leaving with you."

For the first time ever I freed it, the vulnerability I fought fiercely to imprison. I swung open the door and allowed it to creep free from its confinement. And for the briefest of moments, I was petrified.

Dark eyes flashed, his breathing deepened, and I had my answer. He hooked his fingers through the belt loops on my pants and jerked me toward him. Still seated, his head was at the same height as my stomach. I relaxed my hands, running them over his broad shoulders, through his thick hair, gently tugging and teasing. Looking up at me, he snapped the button of my pants open and slowly pulled down the zipper.

What we did this time was different. It was still dark, was still wildly raw and ferocious, but it was intertwined with tenderness. I loved him, and I'd come to realize, for the first time in any of my existences, I finally loved myself. I was the person I wanted to be when I was with him. And he didn't just let me be me, he cast a helix of protection around me, keeping at bay all of the judgments that prevented me from being okay with being me.

I think that's the difference between love and infatuation. Love doesn't just take. It gives, beyond what you thought you needed.

The next morning, we rose long before dawn and began our journey to the mountains. Aamon spoke very little. A short conversation with Zagan confirmed his apprehension and suspicions about Kerwin's intentions.

"You think he's capable of double-crossing you? Here? Now?" Zagan asked.

"I think he's capable of far more than we give him credit for, which is why I don't like this. It's too easy, we're missing something," was Aamon's only response.

The mountainside lodge was a sprawling three-story building constructed from stone and thick log beams. It sat nestled between fir and spruce trees in a remote area of the range. The lower levels consisted of communal areas—a large dining area, kitchens, a library, a gymnasium, and a games room. The top level had multiple bedrooms and suites that branched off from a long snaking corridor. It was rustic and beautiful, with soaring ceilings, arched stone-clad walkways, and timber accents.

I opted for a room on the top floor at the very end of the extensive hallway, as far away from everyone else as possible. I dumped my bag and set off to explore the lodge and grounds. On the second floor was a huge wraparound balcony complete with firepits, seating, and tables. The view was stunning, with blue-gray mountains rising in formation, one behind the other, continuing as far as the eye could see. Above the misty low-lying clouds sat rounded snowcapped peaks towering over forests and lakes. It seemed like the perfect place for entry into Laeon. If I didn't know better, I might have even believed in Heaven and God himself.

Faltering steps revealed uncertainty and trepidation, highly uncharacteristic of Noah. Of course I had heard him, sensed him long before he approached me, clearing his throat, waiting nervously for me to acknowledge his presence. I turned with a sigh. This had to be done and the sooner the better, but I wouldn't enjoy it.

"I lied to you," he announced. No hello, no how are you? Or can we talk? When it came to ripping off the bandage, you had to give Noah points for directness and speed.

"I'm aware," I replied curtly. I took a deep breath, running my fingers through my hair. "I don't want to argue with you anymore, Noah. What's done is done. Can we please just move past this?"

His relief was evident. Refusing to adhere to personal boundaries in typical Noah fashion, he swept me into his arms with a whoop. I laughed and squealed for him to put me down. My smile remained as Steven stepped out onto the deck through the gaping open doorway, but when Griffin stepped out a second later, I froze.

I had every intention of extending him professional courtesy, of being polite and avoiding all drama, but seeing him, feeling his eyes on me, full of self-pity and regret, made me want to punch him in the face. "I'm not ready," I mumbled. I turned my head away from him and rushed for the door on the far side of the balcony, ducking inside and down to the ground level. Without pause, I headed away from the lodge, taking one of the trails rambling up the mountainside behind it. I was half a mile in before I realized I was being followed. I whirled around angrily, ready for a bloody confrontation only to be greeted by the sight of Steven.

"I told him not to. I told him you'd need time, but you know Griffin," he said with an apologetic shrug.

"No," I whispered, "I thought I did, but I was wrong. I definitely do not know Griffin."

"Heading on a hike?' Steven nodded to the trail ahead, adding, "Mind if I join you?"

"Sure. I didn't peg you for the outdoorsy type." I smiled playfully as we continued up along the trail at a steady pace.

"I was more of a hit-the-gym type than an outdoor hiking type. There are definitely better things to look at in a gym," he said with a wink.

I rolled my eyes at him. "Now you sound like Noah!"

Steven glanced toward me. "Did Noah ever tell you how he died?"

Oh, Steven, where are you going with this?

"He didn't, but then I never asked. I guess I could never figure out the correct etiquette for that. I mean how personal to a person is their death? Would it be like asking them about their sex life?"

Steven snorted. "Ha! You're joking, right! I know Noah isn't shy when it comes to discussing his sex life!" We both laughed.

"He lived in a different era from us. He was a fighter pilot, flew one of the first Skyraiders during the Korean war."

Wow! Impressive!

"Is that how he died?" I asked.

Steven stopped and turned to face me. "I honestly think if he had died in battle he would have passed without hesitation to his eternity. He had a much darker death, I'm afraid. First, he was dishonorably discharged when the President of America declared all homosexuals a threat to national security. Stigma like that doesn't leave you. The night he died, he was in a bar close to the Mexican border. He was murdered—jumped by a hate mob and beaten to death—and all because he was gay."

My stomach lurched. "That's horrible. But Steven, why are you telling me this now?"

He continued slowly along the trail. "I guess I'm trying to help you understand. It's kind of a theory I have, that if you're like Noah, if you died in the way he died, it's hard to let that go. Noah's a protector, but he couldn't protect himself, which is why protecting others became so personal to him. What may seem inconsequential to you or me becomes of paramount importance to him and his quest to protect. Kind of similar to Griffin."

There it is!

"It doesn't excuse their deception," I argued.

Steven agreed. "They both made a bad situation worse by lying. Their actions were self-destructive. They weren't trying to hurt anyone, quite the opposite, but they became compelled beyond control. It's the damage they carried over from a traumatic death they were powerless to stop. But you know in your heart that they are good people, right?"

"I don't want to talk about Griffin. Rehashing what happened is going to be detrimental to everyone. This is neither the time nor the place," I said firmly.

"And what about Amelia?"

"What about her?"

"Would you at least let her clean her conscience, tell you her story? You have the power to help another being heal, Alyssa."

We were close to the overlook, but Steven stopped and leaned against one of the tall white pines. I was about to repeat my time-and-place spiel when he softly said, "There were truths you kept from her too."

My head snapped up and I stared at him, trying to ascertain what exactly he knew.

"No one else was aware, Alyssa. I only suspected, and when I was sure, I said nothing. This isn't a threat. Just pointing out the parallels."

I narrowed my eyes, but a smile tugged at the corners of my mouth. "You play dirty!"

"Only when I have to. It's for your own good," Steven assured me, nodding toward the opening on the path ahead.

"She's waiting for me! That was bold! What would you have done if I'd said no?" I asked, genuinely shocked at the audacity of Steven's ploy.

"Honestly, I was still formulating a plan B," he replied with a laugh.

I knew I needed to face it at some point, so figured

I may as well get it over with, alleviate one of my many dreaded future tasks.

I took a deep breath and walked into the clearing.

The flat rocky overlook at the top of the vista was deserted. Its steep elevations would have deterred even seasoned hikers. Amelia sat off to one side of the rock edge. Silently, I sat away from her, pulled my knees to my chest close to the edge of the steep cliff with the sweeping panoramic views. I could just make her out using my peripheral vision, and for now that was enough.

Her voice was low but determined, like she had prepared for this moment. "I just want the opportunity to explain, to walk you through what happened. To be honest the way I should have been from the get-go." Amelia's voice drifted gently across the void between us.

I said nothing but nodded.

"I loved my life. As cliché as it sounds, I didn't realize how much I loved it until I didn't have it anymore. I was happy. I was loved. I had an amazing fiancé, a beautiful daughter, a job I liked, and just one small gray cloud that cast a dim shadow over an otherwise sunny sky. There wasn't some earth-shattering cataclysmic event that started my slow dark descent into alcoholism. There was no trauma beyond what any other female experienced in the early nineties. It just happened."

She took a shaky breath before continuing, "I was always wound so tight. Nowadays, I'd probably be diagnosed with some kind of anxiety disorder." Amelia sighed before quickly adding, "Not an excuse, just maybe a contributing factor."

I turned slightly toward her. She too was hunched up on a precipice, gazing out over the wilderness. "My drinking started at house parties, nights out, and celebrations, then extended to weekends, to every weekend. It gave me something to look forward to at the end of a hard week at work. The local club did promotional nights every Thursday. Suddenly the weekends became four days long. Mondays were always so depressing, and the most effective cure for the Sunday Funday tailgating hangover was of course, the hair of the dog. Taco Tuesday without a beer was just wrong, and then was there really any point in excluding Wednesday? Before I was even aware, I was drinking every day that ended in Y. Of course, there was always some form of what I deemed reasonable justification. I drank to destress, to help me sleep...ignoring the glaringly obvious fact that the groggy wine-induced brain fog of the next day was far worse than an hour of tossing and turning prior to sleep. I say I wasn't aware, but that's yet another lie. I knew. I'd get that uncomfortable niggling feeling in the pit of my stomach, hear that chirping of my own little cartoon cricket, but I chose to ignore both. And when that became harder to do, guess what became the most effective silencing tool. Another drink of course!" She gave a bitter laugh.

Unwavering she continued, "I think Cal knew, and for the longest time, I was angry at him for ignoring it, further enabling it. But now I realize he was as lost as me. I'd plunged us both into a situation we were ill-equipped to handle. And besides, it wasn't his job to fix me."

Amelia turned her head to face me. "You know how I died. You know who paid the ultimate price. There wasn't a cat in hell's chance I could forgive myself. And why would they even want me in the same place as them after what I'd taken from them. That's why I remained. That day in the loft I was going to tell you. It scared me that you already knew. You knew it was a drunk driver. So, when you assumed that meant somebody else, I didn't correct you. I should have, and I didn't and I'm so sorry for that."

"You still don't get it, do you?" I marveled.

I kept my eyes steadily on the horizon. "I don't care how badly you fucked up, what you did or didn't do," I affirmed. I tried to keep my voice steady, emotionless. I had to clench my hands together to stop them from shaking. "We were supposed to be friends, yet you didn't even give me a chance. You assumed I'd judge you, that you thought so little of me you believed I would criticize you, walk away from you, stab you in the back! That was your betrayal. That's what I didn't deserve, to be condemned before ever being given a chance. That wasn't fair."

"The way you spoke about the driver that killed you—"

I turned to her, all control slipping away as I screeched, "That's not even comparable! You didn't see the person he was! There was no regret there, no guilt, no remorse. You don't get to hold me accountable for something I didn't do, something based on your fucking assumptions!"

I stood up, wiping away angry tears. "I guess you really didn't know me at all," I concluded with resentment. I turned back to the trail that led to the lodge, brushing silently past an ashen-faced Steven.

I was relieved to slip undetected into the building, stealing silently up to my room. I locked the heavy wooden door, discarded my clothing, and climbed into the shower. The steaming cascade of water obscured both my tears and my sobs. I couldn't comprehend what I had done to be held in such low regard. Was I really such a shitty person? Such a shitty friend?

I stepped out from the shower and bundled myself into the oversized robe that hung on the bathroom door. I spent as long as I could getting ready. Drying my hair, rubbing lotion into my skin, pulling on clothing, and applying mascara. Keeping busy kept me from capitulating to my impulses. I yearned for Aamon. Repressing my urges and maintaining restraint was torturous.

Maybe a cold shower would have been a better idea!

In search of a distraction, I finally left my room. I got to the end of the hall before Noah appeared and insisted we take a walk.

"Noah, I've had about as much drama as I can take for one day," I pleaded with him.

He held his hands up in the air. "No drama, I promise."

I tried to walk around him, but he blocked my path. "Okay, so no walk then. How about a training session? I'll give you an opportunity to finally prove you're faster than me?" He took slow steps in the direction I had just come from, cajoling me into following him.

Oh, challenge accepted!

"Oh, Noah, I'm just not sure I have the energy…" I began as I fell into step beside him.

He laughed and started to run down the corridor. I took two strides after him before doubling back and sprinting in my original direction.

I sensed Aamon as I descended the open staircase into the lobby. I would have turned in the opposite direction, preserving my constraint, had it not been for the raised voices.

Their arguing echoed from the otherwise empty dining area, the heavy double doors failing to sufficiently conceal their disagreement. I had done everything in my power to keep them separate. They could have at least exerted some effort to help themselves. I crept closer, listening intently.

"You never escaped it, never let it go entirely. It will always be a part of you, so stop trying to convince yourself you're something you're not!" Aamon growled.

"Oh, I know it's still there. I don't need to be reminded. Maybe you're the one who needs to remember, Aamon." Griffin's voice was almost unrecognizable, his words so fueled by hatred.

"Is that supposed to be a threat?" Aamon spat.

"Alyssa, what the hell?" Noah's voice echoed through the empty hallway.

Shit! Not only had he found me, but he'd also just alerted both Griffin and Aamon to my presence. I tried to warn Noah. I waved my hands wildly at him, putting my finger over my lips in an effort to shut him up, but it was too late. He stormed through the lobby with Steven and Amelia in tow as the doorway I'd been eavesdropping outside was opened with such force, it was nearly ripped from its hinges.

Griffin was furious, his eyes angry and panicked darted between me and the oncoming trio.

"What's still there?" I demanded. Yet again, so much for honesty from Griffin!

Ignoring me, he yelled at Noah, "Jesus fucking Christ, Noah, you had one job!"

"Hey, don't fucking speak to him like that!" Steven

yelled back. It was the first time I'd heard him cuss, or yell, for that matter. Griffin was on fire today!

"Stop blaming other people, and for once be honest. It's your lies that are doing this, not Noah's ability to hide them from me," I snapped, pointing at Griffin.

"This is exactly what Kerwin wants, and you're all stupid enough to hand it to him," Amelia berated.

Seriously, of all the people to preach!

"Oh really, it was Kerwin's plan for you to stab me in the back with your fucking deception?" I snarled at Amelia. "You two really should consider hooking up. You're both such masters of betrayal, imagine what you could achieve together," I said as I gestured between Amelia and Griffin disdainfully.

"This isn't helping anything," Noah yelled over my voice.

"Maybe if they didn't lie…" Steven argued, siding with me.

"Maybe if you just did as you're told for once!" Griffin spat back at me.

Keep stoking that fire, Griffin!

"Who the fuck are you to tell me what to do?" I charged toward Griffin.

Amelia leaped in front of him, yelling, "You need to back off, Alyssa!"

"And what the fuck are you going to do about it?" I screamed, squaring up to her.

Noah and Steven jumped between us, Noah dragging me in one direction while Steven pulled Amelia in the opposite direction.

"Get your hands off her!" Aamon's voice bellowed from the doorway. Noah released me and held his palms up in defeat. I glanced up at Aamon, looking away immediately, my entire body shaking. I wanted nothing more than to run into his arms, but doing so in such a volatile situation would prove catastrophic. I hated that he seemed to possess the restraint that escaped me. That he could keep his stare fixed on me yet still maintain his distance. I did the only thing I could to prevent the situation from worsening. I left. I turned on my heels and bounded to the safety and solace of my room.

Chapter 18

I was awoken just past midnight by Zagan. I had no idea how long he had been there, sitting in the armchair opposite my bed, when I felt him close and realized I was not stuck in one of my twisted dreams. I sat bolt upright in bed and pulled the bedsheet up sharply, recovering my scantily dressed body, which Zagan eyed unabashed.

"What are you doing in here?" I croaked, horrified to discover him watching me sleep.

"We need a conversation, need to rally the masses. I fear an irreparable fracture may have occurred. This could be detrimental for all of us," he said in a hushed tone, moving from the chair to the bed. "Maybe you should dress?" His voice stayed low, and his eyes rested on my breasts. His sleazy stare made me feel exposed, almost violated, but before I could react, a growl from the doorway caused him to leap to his feet with panic.

"Get out, while you can still walk!" the deep voice from the doorway demanded, and without saying another word, Zagan rushed from the room with his head down.

Aamon closed the door quietly and leaned back against it. "We can't go into battle and expect to win like this."

"What do you want me to do?" I asked.

"Participate in a conversation," he suggested. "Keep me from ripping anyone's fucking head off."

"You want me to keep you calm?" I asked

incredulously, rising from my bed. I don't know what it was about Aamon that brought out the darker side of me. The feeling of power over someone so unbelievably powerful, maybe? I just couldn't stop myself from pushing his buttons. It was cruel and twisted, but having him lose control with me, on me, was such a turn-on.

I walked from my bed toward the closet, stretching like a cat arching backward, before pulling the oversized threadbare T-shirt I wore to bed up and over my head and dropping it to the floor. Wearing only panties, I sauntered into the closet. Aamon's heavy footsteps followed me but paused at the closet door. I was playing a dangerous game, but once I started it was hard to stop.

"This is your attempt at keeping me calm?" he growled.

I ignored him, enjoying the feeling of his eyes devouring me as I dressed. I walked toward him, stopping just about a safe distance away. That zone of safety was smaller now, merely inches. It burned being that close but not touching him.

"Are you trying to get me to lose my mind?" he whispered, keeping his eyes down, too close to make eye contact and retain control.

"I don't want you to lose your mind, Aamon, just your clothes," I teased breathlessly.

Too far!

I wanted to kiss him but knew that doing so would announce it to everyone else in the building. He read me like a book. He was back to being my dirty little secret. Even after everything that had happened with Amelia and Griffin, I still kept him hidden. He kept his eyes down as he skulked away.

I felt like shit.

He had assumed I kept our relationship hidden out of a sense of shame, that being with him was degrading. And I had let him. Allowed him to walk away believing that. The reality was I had to conceal the truth from him to maintain plausibility. I knew how much he hated Griffin and knew Aamon would not hesitate to play dirty if antagonized. It certainly had occurred numerous times before.

I gave Aamon time to leave before I headed down the stairs and outside onto the lodge's wide wooden deck. Griffin stood off to the right with Amelia and Steven close beside him. Noah stood just inside the doorway, and Aamon was to the left, leaning on the thick wooden handrail looking out across the darkness, flanked by Birsha and Seraphina. I needed every ounce of self-restraint not to run over to him, to tell him I was sorry, to show him he was the only thing I cared about. But the fear of where that would leave us, the danger that could and would put him in stopped me. I needed Griffin and his crew to side with us.

Zagan stood between the Sygans and my ex-family. Behind him, exactly between the divide, stood Magda. Like her I remained in the middle, opposite Zagan, pointedly not choosing a side. Trying desperately not to aggravate either party.

Upon my arrival, Griffin stepped forward. Aamon turned from the railings and stepped toward me also. Both wore the same expression, a pained longing. I felt it without even looking at either of them. Unfortunately, I was not the only one who noticed.

Zagan looked from Griffin to Aamon and back again, a bemused smirk danced across his lips. "She must be a phenomenal fuck," he sniggered.

Both Griffin and Aamon spun wildly toward him, chests puffed and fists clenched. Zagan, evidently not expecting such a volatile reaction, stumbled backward, his eyes wide in shock and fear. He really was dicing with his demise this evening.

"And meanwhile, on the savanna, we see two opposing prides square up against each other all for the affections of the lone lioness." Noah's voice sliced through the thick atmosphere.

"That's not funny," an ashen-faced Steven whispered.

It only occurred to me in that instant that neither party seemed surprised.

They each knew about the relationships I'd had with the other!

Zagan cleared his throat. "You both knew what she was."

"Suspected, never knew. No one knows for sure," Aamon corrected him.

Wait, what?

"I can protect her. All you can do is sully her, destroy her," Griffin snarled at Aamon.

"You can't protect her, and you can't protect yourself from her. Keeping her shackled isn't protecting her—it's enslaving her. She stays with me," Aamon snapped back.

I glanced nervously at Steven and Noah. I was so confused.

Aamon continued, "You think I wanted this, Griffin? Do you think I enjoy losing all control? Do you know how close to the fucking edge it sends me?"

Wait a second, exactly how much were we sharing here?

Griffin's eyes blazed. "So stay the fuck away then. I don't risk losing myself!"

"No, you just risk losing her. She isn't fucking collateral damage, you selfish little prick!" Aamon snarled, moving closer to Griffin.

"What, what am I?" I stammered.

Zagan attempted to intercept. "This isn't what we are here to discuss."

Both parties completely ignored him.

Aamon studied Griffin, reading every movement, every twitch as he glared at him. Griffin turned away, too little too late.

"Oh Christ, you haven't told her, have you? You son of a bitch, all this time I assumed she knew, but she's clueless." Aamon shook his head at Griffin.

Oh God, here we go again. It's like peeling an onion with the unending layers of lies they've created.

Griffin said nothing, his jawline clenched tightly, and his hands coiled into fists, whitening his knuckles.

Aamon pointed at Griffin, yelling, "You tell her about that day at the station, or I will!"

"What?" I pleaded, looking between them. "Griffin, please, I can't keep doing this with you. It's destroying me." My voice quivered.

"Take a breath, Alyssa. It's going to be okay." Steven's voice, gentle and calm, cut through my rising hysteria. Try as I might, I could not stop my body from shaking.

"You're a real piece of shit, you know that?" Noah hissed at Aamon. He turned to me and in a soft voice said, "It's who we were there for that day at the train station, who we were trying to save."

"I'd say it's a little more than that!" Birsha chimed

in.

"You weren't there to save me?" I hated how whiny and self-serving such a question made me sound. It wasn't that I had experienced any false sense of importance, then or now, but how that day's circumstances had transpired, it seemed reasonable to have assumed that I was the hapless victim in need of saving. Then it dawned on me, and a feeling of foolishness and humiliation washed over me. Noah was undoubtedly there to save the girl! The girl I had inadvertently placed in danger. "You were there to save the girl, obviously!" I said this like I had been aware all along. I wasn't fooling anyone.

As I looked at Noah, my stomach twisted. He blinked. Just once. The quickest, most singular of movements from the smallest area. Aside from that, he remained his composed genuine self.

But he blinked.

For anyone else that one blink would have seemed innocuous, barely noticeable at all. For me, it was a caveat that screamed in deafening tones. Sirens might have well been blasting. He didn't directly lie—that would involve speaking an untruth—but I knew with certainty there was something he was withholding, some falsehood or fabrication that he was specifically keeping from me.

My eyes met his. My confusion gave way to anger. I did not like playing games, least of all when I was the one being played for a fool, being publicly humiliated and left begging for deliverance, and all in front of an audience.

"You were there to save the girl, right?" I questioned. Again, a blink, my brain was reeling. Why was he so nervous? "Noah!" I snapped at him.

Noah sighed, just slightly; his right hand reached up to rub the back of his neck, and his left hand he shoved deep in his pocket, like a child trying to conceal something they shouldn't have.

"I was there to save both," he said, with a voice much quieter than his usual tone. Out of the corner of my eye, I saw Steven, shifting from one foot to the other. With each movement, he was edging toward Noah, attempting to make his travel seem casual and unintentional. I became a little perplexed. Acting in such a protective manner seemed unnecessarily dramatic and totally uncharacteristic of Steven. The calm resolve he had used to ground me moments earlier had dissipated.

There was a nervous energy on the deck, but I couldn't pinpoint where it was coming from or why. Dazed in a fog of confusion, I just could not make the puzzle pieces fit. Noah had saved me, of that I was sure, whether premeditated or not seemed so irrelevant. He'd stated clearly, he was there to save both, and he had. Jenny survived, albeit somewhat traumatized. I survived. Mission complete. Right? A job well done, so what was with the theatricals?

I closed my eyes, took a deep breath, and tried to clear my mind. What was I missing? I was sure it must be glaringly obvious. Was I struggling to see the forest for the trees? I opened my eyes and allowed them to sweep slowly around the open space. Amelia was rigid. She was practically pulsating with anxious energy. Her eyes darted between Noah, Steven, and Griffin.

Griffin was staring at the ground, arms tense as they hung at his sides, fingers twitching like he was battling to control impulses willing him to move. *Mr. Cool,*

Calm, and Collected about to lose his shit? Surely not! Each Sygan stood stiffly, eyes also darting, confused but receptive to the possibility of some impending threat, bodies poised for the unknown. And Aamon, Aamon was angry, fuming actually, but not anxious at least.

Only Magda remained composed.

Noah and Steven were now standing together. As my gaze swept over them, something I recognized flashed across Noah's features, something that increased the tone of the alarm bells that were already ringing relentlessly in my head, something that set my heartbeat racing—*fear!* I wanted to turn around. I was convinced that there must be something truly terrifying standing behind me, but I was too afraid to move.

Oh God, please don't let it be Kerwin!

I glanced nervously around to be greeted by the sight of nothing.

What is going on?

There to save us both, there to save us both was running on repeat in my head. No, wait, that was wrong. That wasn't exactly what he had said. *There to save both.* Not us, not you, no direct reference to me, but if not me, then who else was he there to save that day? There were only three beings facing off on the platform…Who else could he be referring to?

The molecules of truth that had been swirling like a swarm of gnats in the air between us finally took a nosedive, piercing me with the realization I had blinded myself to.

"What the actual *fuck*!" The words exploded from my mouth milliseconds before my brain had completely caught up. "*Kerwin, you were there to save fucking Kerwin!*" The piece of shit that tormented and terrorized me, who killed and harmed innocent victims for his own twisted gain, who freely chose to rain fear and pain—*Kerwin*. The realization sent shock waves reverberating throughout my body. I was hit with a wave of nausea as the floor tilted and spun, threatening to send me lurching to the ground.

But still there was something missing, still one damn piece refusing to fit, niggling in the back of my brain. *Save him from what, himself?*

I turned to Griffin. Evidently, he was in the loop. He and Amelia, both aware of something they had all conspired to conceal from me. "You think he deserved to be saved from himself?" I asked, my confusion evident.

Griffin looked up, his eyes meeting mine for the first time. What I saw broke me. His eyes were so full of pain for what was to come, they pierced me like jagged shards of shattered glass. I felt like a puppy about to be put down; the unknown was both agonizing and terrifying. I said a silent prayer to be put out of my misery swiftly. Tears, warm and desperate, tumbled down my red-hot cheeks. Again, I pleaded with him, "Griffin, I still don't understand."

"Say the words, Griffin." Aamon's voice was strained. "Stop torturing her and say it."

"We were saving them from you, Alyssa," Griffin whispered, his eyes locked on mine. He reached out for me. "Please, please just let me explain."

I was unraveling, and I wasn't the only one. The atmosphere around us pulsated, and nervous energy reverberated from entities on both sides, tipping me further over an already crumbling edge.

Magda was the only being who remained calm,

concerned but still serene and in control. Even in a state of hypervigilance, her calmness drew my attention. Wild and petrified as I searched desperately for a haven of safety, I found her. My eyes locked with hers. I mouthed the words, "What am I?" My chest was so constricted the words were no more than a hoarse whisper.

Regardless, she heard me. She understood. Her eyes held mine, and she responded accordingly as unwavering she replied, "The one."

The one.

Wait, what? Which one? Surely, she couldn't mean the evil "one," the one that everyone had been hunting for, the one they all wanted to kill? To rid the world of, to save the world from.

My question was answered by the frozen expressions of fear that greeted me whatever way I turned.

Oh!

I stumbled backward, my chest tight. I'd never felt a pain like it before. Like I was drowning on dry land.

And they knew, they all knew!

The realization cut deep. Like a trapped animal in a heightened state of panic, all I could think about in that instant was my escape. I had to get away from them. The thought of Kerwin terrified me, but this...this fear was immeasurable, this truth was incomprehensible. How could they keep this from me, and why were they telling me now?

How are they doing this to me again! How many times can I break before fixing me ceases to be an option?

I had never ever felt so forsaken, so devastated. The despair and humiliation were excruciating.

Over and over in my head, a voice chanted, *It's you, you're the bad one, it's you.*

I knew there was something wrong with me, something that made me unworthy of so many things, and that was it, I was always evil. And because of that, everything was fake. The friendships, the relationships, all fake, just a ploy to keep the enemy close, and I fell for it. God, I felt so stupid!

How desperate had I been for love and acceptance? Pathetic!

The lies from Amelia had hurt, made me question their trustworthiness, and sent me flying into Aamon's arms. The deceit from Griffin stung even more, but this was on another level. This left me injured, bleeding and raw, filled me with desperate sadness and forced me to question why I was so unworthy of any ounce of humanity, of love, of loyalty, of anything.

All the while the voice continued its mantra.

It's you, it's you, it's you.

Guess I am just a piece of shit then.

Steven had moved closer to Noah, and they both now stood between me and the doorway. The thought of physical contact with any of them repulsed me. As Griffin tried to move toward me, I darted around his outstretched arm, around the curved decking, and in through the door that led directly into the lounge.

As I went, Aamon and Griffin erupted into a furious argument. I sprinted up the staircase, pausing outside of Aamon's room. I gripped the handle tightly, squeezing it sharply to the left, snapping the locking mechanism with minimal effort. I knew exactly where to look. The energy from it was like a location beacon. I took what I had sought out and sprinted back down the corridor and into my room, slamming and locking the heavy door.

Aamon would know what I had done, but it didn't matter. By the time he realized, it would be too late. I bounded over to the window, ripped it open, and leaped through it without hesitation, landing three stories down onto a grassy verge. I jumped between rocky boulders and tree stumps, tall evergreens and mossy dirt patches, and raced far away from the lodge, from them, and from everything.

I stopped when I saw buildings and businesses that had closed hours earlier. I had reached the small mountain town I recognized from the journey in. I scaled one of the many dark and empty store units and jumped stealthily over the small brick wall surrounding its flat concrete roof.

I sat on the rooftop floor and pulled my legs to my chest, finally releasing the tears that had formed on the decking, sobbing uncontrollably as my heart imploded, a reaction to the loss of everything.

I hated them, hated what they had done to me, but more than that, I hated myself. Despised myself for allowing my desires to blind me to the truth. For being gullible enough to believe their fabrications, to believe I was part of something good and meaningful, to believe I was worthy of a family, to believe I was loved and accepted.

Why the fuck was I even still existing? Try as I might, I could not think of a single reason to continue. Kasey was happy. I was becoming a distant memory to him and probably for the best. I had been a shitty daughter and far less than my mom had deserved, but even that was irrelevant now. She had Kasey, a being of light and goodness to fill what had become her childless void during my absent years. The family I thought I was a part of had deceived me, abandoned me, and taken with them my reasons for existing, my friendships, my support, my job, my purpose. Oh, and not to forget, I was apparently fucking a demon who everyone wanted to kill.

It wasn't that I definitively wanted to die. I just couldn't exist anymore. There was nothing to live for, except an unending cycle of rejection, desperation, pain, and self-loathing. I merely needed to take the only option I had left and end it all. It was a simple solution; it was the only solution.

And just like that, the realization culled my panic. The anxiety that ravaged me internally like a trapped rabid animal paused and was pacified. The decision brought with it a calm resolve that settled over me like a weighted blanket.

Today would be my last. *This is how it ends.*

Chapter 19

The sun rose slowly, gifting the morning with a stunning display of orange and red, radiating what should have been a comforting warmth over the buildings and over me, but I felt nothing.

I had what I needed. I knew the instant I ran from them. The instant I realized there was no coming back from where I had been pushed to, that the breaking point had been breached, that the damage was just too great this time.

I couldn't explain why. I just knew it would suffice. If it was enough to kill Aamon, then it would absolutely be enough to kill me, and I wouldn't have to see another damn sunrise again.

Fuck them all.

With hands that felt like lead, I carefully retrieved the dagger from my jacket. The magnitude of the force it expelled was immense. It felt like Aamon, carrying a wisp of his essence with it. Thinking of him started to force me out of my bubble, the bubble that kept me devoid of feelings. I pushed the thought of him sharply from my head. When he crept in, my feelings stirred. I didn't need that. I liked the numbness. I needed it to see me through.

I uncoiled myself from the hunched-up ball I had become. Adopting a *sukhasana* position like I was about to meditate or participate in a yoga class, I straightened my back and raised my chin. I would do this with dignity.

I positioned the blade carefully over my wrist. I wasn't sure how it would work. Killing a dead person was probably different from killing a live person. The rationale for an incision to the wrist in a living human was not necessarily relevant to an entity without a beating heart and active circulatory system. But then my heart did beat; I felt it regularly. Either way, I felt sure any open wound caused by the dagger would have the required effect, and if this method failed me, I would simply plunge it into my chest. I guess a part of me just wanted to see if it would hurt, or how hard it would be.

It was easy. The blade sliced smoothly into my skin. My blood, crimson and warm, flowed steadily. I watched it expressionlessly as it ran in bright rivulets down my arm, warming my icy skin and dripping loudly to the ground, forming an ever-increasing circle of dark red on the concrete. My shaking fingers were the final thing to betray me that day, losing their grip and releasing the dagger clatteringly to the ground. One moment I was transfixed on the widening circle, the next I was viewing the world sideways on, my face against the cold concrete of the store roof, the red pond inches from my nose.

I was sure the voices around me must have been louder than I could hear. My ears felt like they were underwater. But I didn't care. I felt his hand on me. It burned against my freezing wet skin. Even as I became lost in the nothingness, his presence still managed to pierce my numbness and affect me. My heart ached for him, and a single tear fought its way out, hot and salty, scorching my cheek. I just wanted him to let me go, let me slip away, but I couldn't tell him. I was unable to speak. My eyes were beyond the ability to focus, and the light had started to fade. The ground tilted, and I slid silently into the darkness.

With it, the nothingness brought peace.

But like everything in any of my lives, it was short-lived.

Even the nothingness didn't want me.

Next came the ringing, rattling violently through my head, painfully deafening. Pain. Fuck. What happened to the beautiful numbness? As the insensateness faded, the volume and light increased rapidly, causing me to wince and cringe inward. I pushed myself away from it, wanting to return to the nothingness. And then Aamon, Aamon's breath, his flesh, his lips, his voice, pulled me sharply in the opposite direction. Without any conscious effort, I was drawn to him, like a fish hooked helplessly, dragged quickly through the murky frigid waters. For the second time, he pulled me from the darkness.

"Open your eyes," he pleaded.

I couldn't. I knew if I did there would be no escape, but when he begged again, when his voice cracked and his strong arms began to shake, a part of me I didn't even know existed started to break, and the pain it caused was far worse than the pain I experienced for myself. I turned into him, shivering and afraid.

"Open your eyes." His breath was warm against my cheek.

I opened my eyes. Aamon cradled me in his arms, my head supported in one of his palms, as his other hand stroked my face gently. I had never seen anyone or anything more beautiful than him at that moment. His lips met mine, and he kissed me softly.

"You don't get to do that. Do you hear me? You don't get to leave like that, not without me."

"What if I hurt everyone? What if I lose myself?" I murmured.

"I won't let that happen; I promise."

"We need to move her." Magda's voice carried gently through the air.

I could sense her but not see her.

Aamon swept me into his arms and carried me silently from the rooftop. He held me like a baby on the backseat of a large SUV as Zagan steered it away from the small town and back to the lodge.

I remained in Aamon's arms right up until he laid me gingerly on my bed, removed my shoes and covered me with a blanket.

"Don't leave me," I croaked as he turned to walk away.

Silently, he removed his shoes and slid carefully between the covers, wrapping me in his embrace.

"I don't want to hurt you," I stammered.

"You're my redeemer, not my damnation. The only way you can hurt me is to leave me."

I looked down at my arm, still bloody but dry. The wound had closed, leaving a silver line that ran from my wrist to midway up my forearm.

"It didn't work," I muttered.

"It would have. Magda sealed it," Aamon whispered.

"You made her."

"I persuaded her."

I looked up at Aamon. "Why did you save me?"

His eyes darted away from me, searching for anything but mine, a feeling I understood, fear of exposing vulnerability. But I needed transparency. I needed actual brutal unadulterated honesty like never before, and I didn't need to tell him. He knew.

He took a breath, and with furrowed brows, he lowered his eyes to meet mine. "I need you; my soul needs you; I don't have words for what it is. You'd probably call it love, but I've seen love. I've seen infatuation and obsession, and this is more than any of those things. Without you, there is nothing; without you, I don't exist. The thin line I walk between this world and the next would crumble without you. You're my darkness and my light. You opened a door I didn't know existed. You brought me back from a hell I didn't know I was in. I didn't even know I'd been waiting for you until the first moment I got close to you. Then I thought you'd been sent as my penance, to torture me. But you kept returning to me. Kept wanting me. Now I know you are my savior."

"You think I'm here to save you?" I asked him.

"No! I think it's my job to save you," he answered gruffly, turning his head away.

"No," I insisted, grabbing his face, pulling it toward me so that he couldn't look away. The fear dancing through my veins would not stop me. "You think I'm here to save you!"

"There's so little good left in me, Alyssa, sometimes I wonder if it still exists at all," he admitted with a sigh. "But then you did save me. You do save me, constantly. When I'm around you, I feel it. When you look at me, I feel it, and I can't let you go. Is the thought of being like me so appalling that you'd rather kill yourself?" he asked, his voice a haunted whisper.

I sat up sharply. "The thought of being lied to, of being denied the right to even know who I am is what made me want to do it. The feeling of complete abandonment, of having to deal with another betrayal. Of hurting people, of hurting you! But nothing about you makes me feel anything negative. Being with you is the only thing that has ever allowed me the freedom to be me, and to actually like me." The tears started without warning. "And I hate that I made you feel that way. No one else knows, no one else has seen you, and you're not fucking evil. You're beautiful, and I'm sorry," I hiccupped between sobs.

"Alyssa, I'm not good. I have killed, both on Earth and in Daeon. I live on a knife's edge. The consequences of killing in Daeon are far more extreme than those of killing on Earth. I gain no pleasure. I risk my last shred of humanity, but sometimes it's a necessity," he conceded.

"No," I insisted. "You are good, and what you do out of necessity doesn't take away from that. I see you, Aamon. I really see you."

Aamon's eyes glistened in the darkness. His lips found mine, and he wiped away my tears, taking me tenderly away, to a place that no one needed to understand, to a place where no one else existed, where fear and heartbreak became a distant memory, where we became one.

I didn't sleep but lay motionless in his arms, wishing all the worlds would just pass us by, leave us to dwell in each other's solitude.

"Alyssa." His voice, low and sultry, crept through the small space between us. "There are things about my past I want you to know. I don't want you to ever think I'm keeping anything from you."

"History with Griffin?" I murmured.

"Among other things, yes."

He sensed them before I did, muttering with a heavy sigh, "Another time, I guess."

I heard the footsteps as they approached. Willed them to think better and walk away, but they stopped outside of the door, patiently waiting to be acknowledged.

"I don't want to." I squirmed beneath the covers, like a child hiding from the monsters that came with nightfall.

"You need to. You deserve the whole truth. They had no right to deny you of that. You can't heal without it," Aamon insisted gently.

"When did you become so philosophical?" I muttered.

Aamon flashed me a rare smile and rolled gracefully from the bed, pulling on clothing with each step. I followed his lead, my nervous anticipation increasing with each layer I threw on. Aamon straightened the bed. I watched him, intrigued and momentarily confused. When the realization hit me, it brought with it a wave of shame. He was doing what he thought I wanted, making efforts to conceal our relationship.

I opened my mouth to say something, to reassure him, to correct him, but the knock at the door interrupted me.

Aamon opened the door and stepped backward, allowing Griffin and Magda to enter. His hospitality came at a price. He loathed Griffin, and it was clearly taking everything he had to refrain from acting upon his impulses. His jaw remained clenched, and his muscles tensed, but for now he maintained his composure.

I sat on the corner of the bed, Magda sat next to me, and Griffin stood awkwardly in front of me. I stared straight ahead, avoiding eye contact with him.

Griffin cleared his throat. "You deserve to know everything, and I should have been honest from the beginning, but the truth is, we didn't know what exactly we were dealing with." He crouched down in front of me, his eyes desperately searching for mine. "Alyssa, I'm sorry, so sorry. The last thing I wanted to do was to hurt you. All I wanted to do was to protect you."

Aamon leaned against the wall behind Griffin, his arms folded across his chest. He surveyed the kneeling Griffin with a look of disgust, only averting his stare when Magda glanced up at him.

"Kerwin was hunting you that day." Aamon stared dead ahead, like looking directly at me would prevent his candor. "You weren't supposed to die the day that you did. It happened too early. No one was prepared." Aamon wasn't pulling any punches. Griffin wasn't gifted the option to take his sweet time anymore. He would speak or be spoken for. For that, I loved Aamon even more.

He continued, "Griffin and Noah were there to help Kerwin. Even he realized your power, knew he was no match alone."

For once I didn't interrupt, didn't question, partially out of shock, partially afraid if Aamon stopped, he might never share these details with me in such a way again.

"A being with such a concentrated level of purity should have gone straight to either Laeon or Daeon. Remaining here was—is—unprecedented. Sygans believed the only option was to kill you." Aamon's jaw clenched tighter as he admitted, "Myself included. Your remaining on Earth was considered too dangerous. The power you have within you is immeasurable. One moment of lost control could be cataclysmic. The deal was, they would work together as long as no humans were killed and no souls stolen, but Kerwin broke the rules, endangered a human, so Noah had to intervene."

"It was more than that." Griffin's voice startled me. He stood up slowly, a pained look on his face. He kept a wide berth from Aamon and stepped back slightly to position himself on the opposite side of the room to him, ignoring his scowl. "I felt you slipping, felt the darkness growing. You were going to succumb to it. Kerwin was pushing you beyond your limits. Noah was saving him, but only to save you. Noah followed you, and I went to Aamon, told him he was wrong, that you couldn't be one of the sacred ones. As much as I felt your power, I also felt your soul. It's not just darkness. There's light within you."

I still had it? It wasn't consumed by the darkness?

"It was assumed the one we were waiting for would lose their soul when they passed. That they wouldn't have the ability to choose, that their power would be too strong and all consuming," Aamon explained.

"Maybe the rules changed. Maybe she refused to succumb to what was expected, and that's why she remained," Griffin said adamantly.

"I didn't believe him, so I started to track you myself," Aamon admitted, turning to me. "When you entered Daeon, it fed the dark element of your soul, started to engulf you. As much as I felt your power, I also felt your humanity, and something else, something so powerful between us. That's why I dragged you out of there."

My heart skipped a beat at the memory.

"Kerwin still wants me dead, though." I glanced

between them.

"Not dead. He wants you for different reasons." Aamon had both Griffin's and my attention now. For once, Griffin was as in the dark as I was about Kerwin.

"You nearly opened a door with the drunk driver. I think you felt it too," Aamon said. "That's why I intervened and killed him myself. I was afraid such an extreme act would send you spiraling uncontrollably, and you'd be lost in the darkness forever. I felt it happening."

"You would have done so with Kerwin if Noah hadn't intercepted," Griffin agreed. "He can sense what we can, your power becoming unleashed."

"Or harnessed. I think over time you will have the power to control it," Aamon said, staring defiantly at Griffin.

Griffin's fists clenched as he growled at Aamon, "And I think that's a risk no one has the right to take given the potential consequences."

"Either way, Kerwin is drawn to you. He wants to test you, break you, see if you can control your power when it's fully released. What he felt from you was more power than he had ever encountered from one entity before." Aamon stepped closer, continuing, "You have purity, to what degree we don't know, but Alyssa, being different and beyond explanation doesn't necessarily interpret as being bad."

"But what if I am? What if I do unleash something that I can't control?"

"And what if you don't? What if you're the only one strong enough to beat Kerwin's army?" Aamon gently took my hand. "There isn't a single thing you have to do alone. Kerwin will have to go through me to get to you."

"And me. Over my dead body will he get close to you," Griffin added.

Aamon's gaze lifted from me, and he stared intently at Griffin. "And that is the one thing we can finally both agree on."

Well, this is a whole new level of awkwardness!

"Gentlemen." Magda's voice broke through the uncomfortable silence. "May I have some time alone with Alyssa? This is a lot for her to digest."

Aamon nodded in agreement and moved to the door, opening it, and stepping back for Griffin to pass through. As soon as Griffin stepped into the hallway, Aamon slammed the door closed and strode back to me.

I turned away from Magda in an attempt to hide my amusement. Griffin would be furious. Aamon just couldn't help stoking the fire.

He pulled me to my feet and kissed me passionately. "I'll be close by if you need me," his deep voice assured me.

"Try not to kill anyone," I offered weakly.

"I make no promises," he muttered as he exited the room.

"So now you know. You are the one," Magda said softly with a smile.

"Where's the other one?" I asked hoarsely.

"There is no other one."

"Hold on. If I'm the dark soul, where is the light one, the sacred one, the *good* one?" The word *good* stuck in my throat. I suppressed a sob.

"That would be you, Alyssa."

"But the darkness…" I began.

"You are both. What we assumed would be two entities was always only one. Just you."

None of what she was saying made sense, so I decided to try a different angle. "Have you been to Laeon?" I asked.

"Oh yes, dear, I spend much time there. It's a place of great beauty. You will see for yourself one day."

I frowned at her, perplexed by her comment. "How could I ever…"

Magda nodded toward the door. "What they assume to be factual isn't always quite how it is."

"But if you know they are wrong, why wouldn't you tell them?"

"It isn't my place, dear. Besides, what makes you think they would believe me? What makes you think I haven't tried? They still struggle with the truth of what they are."

"Huh?"

"Griffin and Aamon are both pure. Their purity is stronger and more potent than any who have passed in centuries. When they join forces, their strength becomes synergistic, enhanced. But the ultimate power comes from the sacred trinity. The triad connecting the planes. Of the three, the two males are strong, but the most concentrated purity lies with the female. Together the three can travel between planes without consequence. Their purity is evil, but also good. Both qualities are necessary to align with all planes. They connect to each plane; they protect each plane without judgment." She reached out and grasped my hand. "For the longest time, I didn't believe it was real. I assumed it was just another myth. I placed no credence in such a notion until you arrived."

Finally, I understood. "I'm the female."

Magda nodded, squeezing my hand.

"With Griffin and Aamon, the humanity that lingers is the only obstruction they have to accessing their full potential. To a human, you can only be either good or evil. It's hard to accept that even the vilest beings still possess an element of good and vice versa."

"And the males you speak of are definitely Griffin and Aamon?" I asked.

Even in my wildest dreams I couldn't begin to imagine a world where they would work together in harmony.

Magda nodded with a small smile.

"Are they gods?"

"Define a god? Aamon was supposed to control Daeon, Griffin was supposed to control Laeon, and your purpose was to oversee both from the middle ground, Earth. Guardian to humans. It's in your nature. Look at your life as a human. Always compelled to help others, you chose to nurse, to be a mother, and ultimately you sacrificed yourself for your child. In death, your instinct was to try and save the girl on the platform rather than fleeing. That is what started to awaken your powers."

"But I'm evil." My voice was barely a whisper. My breath felt trapped in my lungs. "Doesn't that completely contradict what you're saying?"

"You are both. You are everything. You don't just complete the three. You unite it. Three is always the number of alignments," she said with a chuckle. "The three of you are connected. The light element of your soul connects to Griffin, but the dark side of your soul is the part that holds the real power. It's the foundation for your power. The connection you have with Aamon is far greater. The energy generated when you connect is beyond what has been before."

Again, I felt my face flush as I recalled my first physical encounter with Aamon. The energy between us superseded anything I had experienced with Griffin.

"It is possible to love two people at the same time, but not with the same intensity," Magda said, looking at me with a half smile and making my cheeks glow even more.

She continued, "Humanity is a funny thing. Its effect is like a disease that infects its host and lingers long after it is assumed to have been lost. Laeon is the place of light. Daeon is the place of darkness. But the human conjectures still leave you believing that light equals infinite goodness and dark equals infinite wickedness. Even though you know that Heaven and hell, God and the Devil are nothing more than a fallacy, still you assume each plane lives up to its stereotype."

She stood and paced back and forth, continuing in earnest, "Laeon and Daeon simply signify different elements of power. Each has an outer realm, providing the time and space for the dearly departed to grow, mature, and learn about their power. Daeon's energy is much more potent than Laeon's, and as such has a more dynamic effect on the entities in close proximity to it. The outer realms are like a preschool for transitioning between planes. The beings there have little control at first. These realms are full of power battles, conflict, and war. But this isn't a true representation of Daeon."

I turned to her. "I entered Daeon. Its energy was painfully oppressive."

"Only the outer realm. Once an entity matures and releases the last of their humanity, they pass beyond the outer realm into Daeon itself. The notion that they become devoid of emotions—narcissistic, soulless demons—is far from the truth. Daeon is actually a place of great beauty, not dissimilar to Laeon, just with a stronger energy derived from a dark source."

Magda paused for a moment before continuing, "Observing humans, the newly passed, even the Sygans and beings that have existed between the planes for years is surreal. Almost everyone aspires to end up in the place of light, to be revered as good. It's ironic that the real power lies within the darkness. The higher stratum of everything, reasoning, empathy, intelligence, strength, and love. It just takes longer to achieve self-awareness and control. The journey to Daeon's eternity is arduous in comparison to its 'lighter' alternative. The malevolence that emanates from Daeon is from its outer realm, its training ground, its holding cell for the neonates. New souls take time in both planes. They need to pass through infancy before they are ready to enter their eternity."

"Do Aamon and Griffin know that they're pure?" I asked.

"They do. Aamon for the most part has embraced his true self, but still struggles to accept that even the darkest of souls contain a degree of light. He has been to Daeon, traveled between the center plane and back again many times, a feat achieved by so very few. Griffin rebelled against his destiny, refusing to redeem himself. Griffin believes he needs to remain on Earth to make amends for his past…transgressions."

"And they know what I am?" I confirmed.

"They know you are pure; they know you possess great power, but they don't know your purpose or why they are so inexplicably drawn to you. And unfortunately, the time you should have had to learn, to come to terms with your metamorphosis, to understand your place, has been snatched from you. There isn't time for authentic truces, for forgiveness and conflict resolution. Opposing sides have been thrown together."

"I still think you should try to reason with them, give them the opportunity to learn from you."

How could either one of them not accept Magda's claims, after everything that had happened?

"For centuries, people like me have tried to educate the newly passed, but like humans, they learn at different rates. Some can let go of their human beliefs and preconceptions easier than others. It is something they must do independently, to evolve at their own rate. It isn't something they can be ushered into."

I could at least empathize with that.

"It's hard letting go of what you know, taking a blind leap of faith when you literally are completely blind to what you are releasing yourself to. How can the unknown not conjure a feeling of fear?" Magda said with a knowing smile.

"Nothing is coincidental. Kerwin was intentional in his actions." I recognized there was more to her words than I was able to comprehend.

Magda shared Aamon's mindset. There was more to Kerwin's plan than he had been credited with.

"You think we will fail?"

Magda turned to me, concern etched across her face. "I fear the divisions weaken all of you. Kerwin isn't your biggest threat. Unity is the key, and right now there is a war within a war taking place. Together you may be infallible, but divided you will fall."

Chapter 20

We were out of time. Out of time to mend the bridges separating and ostracizing us, out of time to form a sense of unity, out of time to build an efficient and competent team.

The resentment between Aamon and Griffin was deep rooted, but its origins would need to remain a mystery until a much later date. Having them in the same airspace created conditions that were volatile and unpredictable. Remaining neutral had failed me so far, and yet despite this, it was my only feasible option. My efforts were solely focused on preserving life for all of us, but it was hard to ignore the collateral damage that went with this. Aamon was left feeling unworthy. Griffin was left with a false sense of remediation. I was left feeling guilty and, above all else, repressed.

As the animosity between Aamon and Griffin grew, it generated a chain reaction that rippled through the ranks. The hostility between Noah, Amelia, Steven, and the Sygans worsened. More Sygans had joined our cause over the last twenty-four hours, bringing their total up to twelve, thirteen including Aamon. The increase in numbers only served to add to the contentious atmosphere.

As if we didn't have enough to contend with, a disagreement between Aamon and Zagan had generated a rift within the assembly of Sygans. Aamon was convinced that entering Laeon was not Kerwin's ultimate plan, that it was a diversionary tactic, and there was a real possibility that he would attempt to take control of Daeon. Aamon had insisted on deploying Sygans to guard Daeon's outer realm, leaving us with what Zagan deemed a skeleton crew.

The less familiar Sygans had little understanding of the collaboration with Griffin, Noah, Steven, Amelia, and I. Resentment that their hand was forced into consorting with those they deemed their enemy resulted in negativity seeping from every area and every person.

Despite the division in the ranks, for the greater good, I had to keep my distance from both Aamon and Griffin. I had no desire to be anywhere close to Noah, Amelia, or Zagan. Steven would remain by Noah's side, obviously, and the Sygans took their command from Aamon, meaning they would remain in close proximity to him at all times. The byproduct created was a state of total isolation for me. I would be completely alone walking a careful line between the two sides. Two sides masquerading as a cohesive team. And the worst thing was both Aamon and Griffin thought it was what I wanted, when in fact seclusion in battle was the very last thing I wanted.

Yet here I was. Here we all were.

This afternoon we would travel two-thirds of the way up the same mountain that housed the lodge, to a clearing surrounded by mountain conifers. Just beyond the clearing, nestled at the end of a path flanked by large rocky boulders sat the doorway to Laeon, the doorway Kerwin would attempt to infiltrate.

I couldn't leave things so undone with Aamon. And the distance I had forced between us had given me withdrawal. I had no hope of keeping my mind on the upcoming fight without my fix.

Battle prep was well underway. There was a flurry of activity throughout the lodge, in the midst of which I was able to beckon Aamon up to the third level. I entered his room without effort. The lock remained broken, damage done by my own hand.

As always, I felt him as he closed the distance between us. Coming up slowly behind me while I gazed out of the window. He stopped a few feet away, adjacent to the foot of the bed. The big Evil, so callous, so malevolent, and yet always so respectful of my boundaries. Such an attractive contradiction.

But there would be no safety zone today. I had other plans for him.

"I owe you an apology," I said quietly. I could hear the steady drumming of his heart. I turned and walked toward him, making it thud faster and louder. He stood stock still, hands shoved in his pockets, legs slightly apart, head bowed with dark and brooding eyes staring up at me.

"You owe me nothing. I understand," he replied gruffly.

"So, you don't want what I have for you?" I purred as I tiptoed toward him, brushing close enough to run my fingertips over his broad chest. I circled behind him as my fingers trailed lightly over his back. I stopped, still positioned against his back, and snaked my arms around his waist, flicking open the buttons on his pants. He inhaled sharply, breathing faster, as the energy between us became thick and heavy with sexual tension.

I stepped up onto the bed. I was still barely taller than him even with the elevation. With my hands on his shoulders, I tugged him around to face me. With my eyes locked on his, I stepped slightly backward and pulled my shirt up and over my head. I unsnapped each button of my jeans slowly and tugged them down, shimmying out of them to reveal tiny lace panties. I unhooked my bra and slid the straps down over my shoulders before tossing it to one side and stretching my arms up over my head, my eyes locked on him the entire time. Aamon's breathing became heavy and deep. His voice was husky as he murmured my name. I fell to my knees and crawled toward him, lifting his shirt, and kissing his stomach, pushing away his pants as he ripped his shirt off over his head.

I slipped him hard and throbbing into my warm mouth, aroused by his euphoric groans, stopping just before he climaxed. I rolled away and crawled seductively up to the head of the bed. Finally, his restraint broke, and he pounced, savage and out of control, ripping away the flimsy panties. He took me from behind as he pinned me against the headboard, which cracked and splintered under his ferocity.

He turned me around and pulled me sharply toward him, wrapping my legs around him and lifting my hips up before driving deep inside of me and holding me there. I arched my back as his tongue darted over my neck and his teeth grazed my breasts. Still, he plunged into me, making me scream in ecstasy as my body rolled in rhythm and a warm wet heat exploded deep inside of me. He tried to cover my mouth, to muffle the sounds, but I shook his hand away breathlessly, telling him that I didn't care who heard and demanding he fuck me harder.

And he did.

Exhausted and spent, we collapsed.

But sleep would not find us today; today we had other business to take care of.

I lay in his arms, savoring every moment. "Tell me about Daeon?"

"You've been there, you know."

"Not the outer realm, the real Daeon." My fingers trailed across his chest, following the lines and curves of his ink.

"I wish I could. There really aren't words," he said with a sigh. "It is beyond beauty. There's no weather, beyond the constant. No conflict. There are many lands within the plane, each different, each spectacular."

"But you came back. Why?"

"The unfathomable question, how I returned from the place of lost souls," Aamon said with a low throaty laugh. "Do you know how many times I've been asked that question? Not that I have ever given an answer."

He stroked my hair and kissed my head before he continued, "Magda says a soul isn't lost. It simply evolves. Eternal beings remember their humanity like an adult remembers their childhood, with fondness and nostalgia, and often with amusement at their innocence and preconceived notions. It is assumed the reason beings don't return from the inner realms of Laeon or Daeon is because they can't. They become trapped by either the light or the dark, like it's a bad thing, but it's the natural order of things. Its negative connotations are entirely man-made. When beings transcend fully, they release the ties that bind them to their human existence. They need to in order to pass into a higher level of existence."

"That's not an answer," I pointed out.

"I was afraid to let go. I had a feeling of

incompleteness, like there was something I had left behind. That's what drew me back each time. I wasn't seeking out a leadership role, but I became the strongest. Sometimes I was the only one who could maintain control, so that became my excuse, but deep down I knew there was something else. I just couldn't find it. I wasn't even sure it existed, until I found it, until it stumbled into Daeon."

"It?"

"You."

I held him, our bodies wrapped and twisted together. Again, I longed to remain there, happy for time to leave us behind, for life and existence to continue without us. Again, I was denied.

"You'll be keeping your distance now?" Aamon murmured into my hair.

I propped myself up on one elbow and ran my fingers lightly down the side of his face, promising, "For the last time."

We dressed, we kissed, we embraced, but no words passed between us. Each glance, each touch filled the silence with a hundred words. Thoughts of defeat on the battlefield may have caused some trepidation, but thoughts of losing each other invoked true terror. Words were unhelpful.

We left the solace of his room and headed toward the wide-open staircase, ready to rejoin our broken and bitter comrades. As I stepped forward to round the last corner at the top of the stairs, Aamon pulled me back, out of sight of everyone on the lower level. He pushed me gently against the wall, standing so close it made the air between us buzz and caused my skin to tingle. He bowed his head and rested his forehead against mine. With closed eyes and a pained face, he whispered, "I love you."

My breath caught in my throat. A thousand white-hot sparks erupted from deep inside of my chest, traveling at supersonic speeds throughout my body, leaving a shimmering wave of warm light in their path. I melted into a giddy euphoria. I melted into him, into a completed me. His kiss was still raw and untamed, but it hit differently. It was no longer a wanting; it was a needing that pulsed from within.

He had to break away. I didn't possess the control to unwrap myself from him. He kissed my hand and my fingertips before walking down the staircase. I followed a few steps behind, giving myself the space and time to gain composure.

The staircase led directly to the lobby, an open communal area filled with an array of lounge furnishings laid out in separate gathering areas within the one space. Aamon stopped at one of the social seating areas occupied by Birsha, another Sygan who looked vaguely familiar, and one I had never seen before. They exchanged brief greetings, and Aamon started to move away.

Birsha glanced in my direction, and nodded, a small smile played knowingly on his lips. "Looking a little tired, Alyssa. Hope you've been saving your energy for the battle."

The Sygan to his left snickered, and I felt a flush of heat creeping slowly across my face. I narrowed my eyes at him as I responded coolly, "I'm good. Thanks for your concern."

The vaguely familiar Sygan mumbled, "It wasn't you he was concerned about."

Aamon paused midstride but remained with his back to the group.

Swallowing a laugh, Birsha added, "Just out of interest, did any of the furniture survive, or should we bid farewell to whichever fool fronted the security deposit?"

Aamon took one step backward, and he turned toward me, eyes searching for a reaction, shoulders tense ready to leap to my defense if necessary. But I bit my bottom lip and smothered a giggle, warmed with confidence by the heat of his gaze. I playfully tossed one of the small sofa cushions at Birsha's head.

He responded with an appreciative nod and wink, and I realized for the first time that he was more than just one of the many, more than just the nuance that had been assigned to him. A way to simplify the complex. He was actually kind of an okay being. He was the most unSygan-like Sygan there was. In many ways, he reminded me of Noah.

Aamon, seeing I took no grievance with Birsha's remarks, simply shot him a look of disapproval and moved on across the room, stopping to assess and discuss the preparations being made by many of the Sygans who were occupying the space.

"You ready for this afternoon, Alyssa?" Birsha asked, ignoring the somewhat surprised looks from his companions.

"I guess. It's a little hard to prepare for the unknown," I replied with a sigh.

Birsha's smile widened. "And you're still playing Switzerland, I assume?" There it was, the reminder I didn't need, the reminder that I would be the only one going into this alone.

I simply gave a small nod.

"You'll be fine," Birsha responded with a level of confidence I longed for. "I've heard great things about you, and regardless of how neutral you want to play it, I've got your back."

I looked quickly at him, unable to conceal my surprise, and my gratitude. He gave me a final nod before resuming his conversation with his group. I turned away, for the first time in a long time comforted by the possibility of an ally.

Aamon crossed the lobby, taking long strides through the center of the wide-open space. As he passed an almost-empty seating area at the farthest point across the room, my gaze fell to the sole inhabitant, sitting quietly on the chair facing me. Aamon swept out of sight, and I was left snared by Griffin, his persistent stare holding me uncomfortably captive.

I was going to have to work really hard at not hating him.

His eyes were full of pain I didn't doubt was genuine. He was sorry. I believed that much at least. However, one lie would have been difficult enough to stomach, but the duplicity of Griffin's fabrications had left him feeling like a stranger to me. Each time he removed one mask, it was simply to reveal another one beneath. I couldn't trust him. I second-guessed and questioned every word, every look, every action. Always awaiting the next bombshell.

Being surrounded by strangers caused a feeling of unease. There were many unfamiliar faces in the lodge, many energies that stirred dread and put me in a state of constant hypervigilance. But with Griffin, my anxiety tripled. He masqueraded familiarity, carried with him memories of friendship and love and trust like a weapon of emotional manipulation.

I broke away, turning my head only to be met by a frosty glare from Amelia. She stood with crossed arms at the bottom of the staircase, her lips curled into a snarl, her brow creased with a frown. Whether it was my exchange with Birsha or my dismissal of Griffin's efforts, she was clearly disgusted by something I had done. Shocking!

I was over dealing with the drama that Amelia carried incessantly like an accessory. I stalked around the outer edge of the seating area, maintaining a wide berth from Griffin, and slipped outside onto the deck.

I chose a seat tucked away in a corner, obscured from the view of the bustling beings inside of the lodge.

The late summer air extended a comforting warmth. Wisps of cooler notes carried on gentle breezes hinted at the promise of a changing season as they danced amongst the sun's rays. Summer was passing, fall would grace us soon, another reminder of the brutality of time, charging forward without pause, without acknowledgement of its enormity as it pushes the dead further into the recesses of memories past, into the once upon a time.

The mountain views were beautiful. Peace and serenity flowed and swirled in every direction. I breathed deeply, willing my surroundings to impress upon me, to pull me into a tranquil state of mind. I understood the human reliance on gods. The most effective coping mechanism when it all gets too much is not to cope. To render yourself powerless, to hand over the control you were unable to retain to some sympathetic higher power, a higher power with answers and solutions, and infinite forgiveness for your screw-ups.

To have such faith was to never be alone or forsaken.

If only it was real.

And there it was, nipping at my heels like an annoying terrier. The sadness and remorse at the things that were lost. The yearning to retrieve what was, even though deep down I knew some bridges were unmendable. Inner thoughts confessed a bereavement I fought to deny. Images of Griffin and Amelia, of Noah and Steven danced across my mind.

I wish I still knew them.

Unfortunately, it isn't possible to remain focused on just one small element of the bigger picture, not once the full tapestry of betrayal has been revealed. My sorrow tumbled away, pursued by a tsunami of resentment and treachery, the sense of loss quickly consumed by tidal waves of anger, as the truth poked me sharply, bringing me back to my senses.

I never knew them, that's the problem. None of what we had was real.

I took a shaky breath, pushing them, specifically Griffin and Amelia, into the lightless recesses of my mind.

Familiar voices drew my attention to the ground beneath the balcony. I sank back into my seat, remaining unnoticed. Noah's voice was softer, quieter than normal as he pleaded with Steven.

"You're the only one I have ever loved. How can you even question that?"

"Because I'm just here, but you don't see me. I'm hanging on, Noah. I'm really trying, but I'm losing my grip."

Noah gave a heavy sigh. "I shouldn't have lied to you..."

"Which time?" Steven spat back.

"Come on, Steven. I'm admitting I was wrong. It wasn't my choice. I was following an order!" Noah protested.

"This isn't the army, Noah! This is not how people conduct themselves in a family. There shouldn't be orders to follow!"

"Do you want me to turn against him, now?"

"I'm not asking you to turn against anyone. I'm asking you to think about the consequences before you react. Think about your take on the situation, and make sure that you're doing what you'd do without Griffin commanding you. I'm asking you not to shut me out. I'm asking you to see me!"

"Baby, I do see you! I love you, Steven. You have to know that." Noah's voice cracked.

"I don't feel it. I don't feel anything from you anymore. You care more for Griffin's feelings, for Amelia's feelings, for everyone else's feelings, than you do for me." Steven drew a shaky breath before continuing, "I don't even need to be your first, Noah. I just need to be your something, 'cause right now you have a long list of loyalties and priorities, and I don't place anywhere."

Wow, I know that feeling!

Noah's footsteps were tentative and uncustomarily slow.

"Don't!" Steven snapped. "Don't think you can hug me and kiss me and think that makes everything better. It doesn't!"

"Tell me what you want me to do. Do you want me

to choose?"

"There's a choice?"

"For Christ's sake, Steven, if there was, I'd choose you! What more do you want from me?"

"The problem is that you feel like you have to choose, like either-or is an option for you. I guess that's the difference between us, Noah. To me there is no choice. To me there isn't another who could possibly even make me feel like there's the remotest possibility of a choice needing to be made. To me there's only you, but to you…there's a choice."

And where there was conflict, there was Griffin. I was beginning to think Magda had got it the wrong way around. Maybe Griffin was the actual harbinger of darkness.

I felt him step onto the balcony. Felt him scanning the area to locate me. Heard him softly padding over to me, stopping a step away, off to my side. I kept my stare forward, refusing to acknowledge him, hoping he would take the hint and leave. He did not.

He sank silently to the ground, sitting with his back to the wooden spindles and the majestic mountain views, opting to face me instead.

The hushed voices from Noah and Steven continued to carry faintly through the air.

"I can't do this anymore. Can't keep giving you everything I've got to get next to nothing in return." Steven's voice was barely a whisper. He walked away, and the door closed quietly behind him.

Noah started to break down. His soft sobs traveled through the air and poked at me with needle-like fingers, sharp and painful. I felt Noah's distress and despair, felt Steven's dejection and hopelessness. I hated all of it.

I looked at Griffin. "This"—I gestured below—"is all you."

I was careful to keep all emotion from my voice. It was surprisingly easy.

"I'll fix it," he replied. His lips formed a tight line and his jaw clenched.

I shook my head. "Your existence would be a lot easier if you stopped creating problems that needed to be fixed."

I looked away but could still feel the intensity of Griffin's stare.

"Just because I kept things from you doesn't mean that every aspect of our relationship was fake. I was honest about my feelings for you. I never had to pretend. I loved you, and I still do."

"That doesn't make me feel better. That makes it worse that you deemed deceiving me acceptable. And for the record, Griffin, no, you don't and never did. What you're experiencing isn't heartbreak at love lost. What you're experiencing is indignation at your failure to manipulate everyone, including me." I kept my eyes forward and my tone steady, continuing, "I don't know what twisted sense of accomplishment playing the puppet master gives you, and I don't care to know. This is where the games end for me."

"I get no satisfaction from any of this. I'd trade every one of my tomorrows for just a single yesterday if I could. The way we were, before Aamon, before Kerwin."

"Oh, I'm sure you would. That illustrates my point perfectly. Your ideal, your image of perfection is a time when you possessed complete control over me. When the mere prospect of me forming my own thoughts and making my own decisions unleashed your anger. Then you'd dangle the threat of losing control like a weapon, shutting me up and shackling me. All of it wrapped in a sexy little smile and concealed behind a mask of innocence and good. The fact that you can rationalize it means nothing. Just because it's explainable, doesn't mean it's excusable."

"Every day is a fight to maintain control. Do you think I enjoyed tracking you, worrying constantly about your well-being, about the well-being of our family? I begged you to listen to me. All I needed was for you to help me to help you!"

Our family! More emotional manipulation, tied together neatly with a bow labeled victim.

"What you did drove me to where I am." Griffin's tone had started to change. The dark energy I had witnessed so many times before ebbed and flowed, clawing at his features, causing his knuckles to clench involuntarily.

But today I would not allow it to silence me. My fear was long gone.

"Really? You stabbed me a thousand times, but now you're the one bleeding?" I almost laughed. "No, this is who you've always been. It's always somebody else's fault. And sharing your darkness with me doesn't suddenly disenable you, it doesn't suddenly make controlling it my responsibility. You choose to put yourself into situations that would potentially cause your mental health to deteriorate. An irrevocable decision from which you knew there would be no return, yet you still refuse to accept accountability for your actions, instead placing the onus on me."

"I was trying to protect you from your fate."

"The only thing I needed protection from was you."

"You don't understand, Alyssa. The darkness will consume you. You'll be lost to it forever."

"Why are you so afraid of it? Of yourself? It's a part of you and will always be. Have you lost control before?"

Griffin jolted, and his eyes flashed. I'd hit a nerve. It had controlled him at some point. Now it started to make a little more sense.

"Just because you were incapable of controlling it, don't assume I am."

"Aamon has infected you."

"Aamon freed me."

"I will not end up like him," Griffin vowed.

With a sigh, I stood and turned away, murmuring, "You already did, just a lesser version of him."

I entered the building via the side door that sat around the corner of the wraparound balcony, keen as always to avoid basically everyone. The only place that guaranteed solace was my temporary bedroom. I trudged up the stairs, painfully aware of the fast-approaching departure time.

I was more than a little irritated to be greeted by the sight of Magda sitting criss-crossed outside of my door. "Did you want me?" I asked wearily. My head really didn't feel like it could take in any more information, and Magda was incapable of sharing anything without depth.

"I wanted to check you were okay before I leave," she said gently with a smile.

"You're leaving? To go where?"

Had this been the plan all along? And who was supposed to mediate between Aamon and Griffin if Magda went AWOL?

"I'll be in Laeon."

"Oh!" I almost asked if she could take me with her. "And if Kerwin succeeds, if he makes it into Laeon, what will happen to you then?"

Magda didn't answer me. She simply smiled and patted my hand, rising gracefully from her spot on the floor.

What are you not telling me? What am I missing?

"Take care, Alyssa," she said as she glided down the hallway and out of sight.

I trudged into my room, crawled across the bed, closed my eyes, and curled up into a ball, rocking gently as I lovingly caressed my darkness. It crept gingerly out from its hiding place, scared by a shame it did not deserve. It soothed my anxiety and embraced me with love. I wouldn't be afraid of it. I would give it the love and respect it deserved, the love and respect every part of me deserved.

Nobody had the right to condemn any part of me, especially when their condemnation was spawned from ignorance and irrational assumptions. True perfection is imperfect, and my imperfections were stronger and kinder and possessed more beauty than my perfections. If the rest of the world failed to see it, that was okay. The only one who truly needed to see it was me, and finally I did.

Chapter 21

It was the worst way to go into battle. The most ununited front possible. Resentment and hatred coursing through what was supposed to be a collaboration. Had it not been so tragic, it would have been laughable.

We traveled together but clearly segregated. Aamon at the head, Griffin at the rear, and me somewhere in the middle, keeping as much distance as possible from either. The fact that my comfort zone was in the thick of unknown Sygans who were likely fantasizing about killing me, and who may well have hunted me in the past, illustrated how isolated I was.

When we reached the access point, Aamon ordered the Sygans to fan out, forming a perimeter around the clearing. There were three possible angles from which Kerwin could arrive. A Sygan was assigned lookout duty at each. We would have sufficient warning prior to his arrival.

I stood in the middle of the clearing, facing the pathway. Aamon stood off to one side, Gill, Seraphina, and Zagan close behind him, and Griffin stood off to the other side, Noah, Amelia, and Steven a step behind him. Birsha remained firmly within Aamon's boundaries but had edged as close to the middle as possible without actually crossing sides, placing him only a few feet from me. Sygan or not, he was a man of his word, and for that I was grateful.

I made the center of the clearing my focal point, avoiding eye contact with both sides. I focused my attention on reading each person's energy, quite easy for once with their movements being minimal.

The degree of conflict was far greater than I had realized. The newer Sygans were distracted by Griffin. Many were outraged at his involvement. Zagan remained indignant at Aamon's refusal to gather a larger army on the mountain, albeit leaving Daeon unprotected. Aamon was furious that Zagan continued to question his authority. Steven was resentful toward Noah, probably because, despite everything, Noah continued to conduct himself like he was Griffin's lapdog, and Amelia was a knot of contempt for seemingly everyone and everything around her. Although her loyalty to Griffin remained, all was not harmonious within their "family."

The awkward silence screamed volumes. Misleading some to form inaccurate assumptions.

Griffin assumed my distance from Aamon indicated a breakdown in our relationship. The pleasure he got from such a notion was evident, and I knew he would attempt to manipulate this to his own advantage, antagonizing Aamon at every opportunity. I prayed Aamon would rise above Griffin's childish attempts and focus on what really mattered.

One overarching sentiment shared by almost every being gathered was anxiety, riding somewhere between nervous anticipation and fear. All, that was, except for me. I realized that for the first time I was experiencing no anxiety. Quite the opposite, in fact. I was excited, I wanted this, I was made for this, and I could feel the desire within me, growing and further compelling me to fight, like some primeval predatory instinct had been somehow initiated. I was hungry not just for the fight, but for the kill.

A low whistle from the dense woodland to the left of the clearing informed us of Kerwin's passage and that he would be approaching from the right. The Sygans retreated into the densely wooded areas surrounding the clearing, camouflaged from the advancing troop. Aamon moved to the left of the pathway. Griffin took position to the right. Both standing with their backs to Laeon's gateway. I remained opposite and faced them, fighting fiercely with myself to abstain from direct eye contact with either party, particularly Aamon. Again, I detected smug pleasure from Griffin, my actions unintentionally corroborating his incorrect theory.

I felt Kerwin closing in. His energy, malicious and vile, caused me to wince and shudder. My fingers twitched at the thought of ripping his cold dead heart out. The thought shocked me. He brought out a part of me I'd never known existed. Maybe before him it didn't.

Remaining firmly on the middle divide, eyes focused forward, I walked into the space between Aamon and Griffin, turned when I was a clear step ahead of them, fixated my eyes on the center of the clearing, and pushed my view of them into the farthest corners of my field of vision.

Kerwin broke through the clearing cautiously, unperturbed by our presence. He stepped forward with an air of confidence, but contrary to everyone's expectations, his demeanor was passive and calm, causing a nervous confusion to ripple out amongst his opposition. He reveled in this. His pleasure was infuriating and made my fingers twitch even more.

I glanced around his group. It was fifteen to eighteen

beings. A cursory assessment of his "army" left me wondering where Kerwin's head had been when he made the decision to walk straight into war with such poor odds. My confidence and relief however were brief.

As they moved at a steady pace, closing in on the small clearing, and on us, I realized I had underestimated him. Technically he was outnumbered, but the beings were nothing like us. As powerful as we were, we were nothing compared to what he had managed to assemble. These creatures didn't even look human. They looked pure evil, the embodiment of what Magda had said resided in the outer realm of Daeon, unable to pass between planes.

Kerwin had outdone himself. I glanced at Aamon, rightly or wrongly judging him. How the hell had Kerwin managed to pull all of this together right under his nose? The second the thought was released the answer hit me, hard.

Me.

I was the reason all of this had gone undetected. I was the fucking jet wash.

Kerwin's steps were steady and measured. I realized quickly that he moved slowly for a reason. He was reading the group just as I had earlier, but where I had been reading it for insight, he was probing for weaknesses. We had been so preoccupied with bickering and altercations within the group, we had left ourselves wide open and defenseless to this tactic.

As Kerwin's gaze swept over us, his mouth contorted in a disapproving sneer, which was quickly replaced by a smile. He looked from Griffin to Aamon, his smile widening as he said, "How wonderful to see the two of you fighting shoulder to shoulder again, brothers in arms. I didn't realize my ex-comrades could be so forgiving to the traitor who abandoned them."

Kerwin turned to the Sygan on his right and, as he gestured between Griffin and Aamon, loudly proclaimed that, "Together they ruled Daeon with an indomitable force. That was until Griffin deserted his fellow Sygans." He smirked at Griffin, hissing, "All water under the bridge now, eh, Griffin?"

Griffin was a Sygan! And moreover, he'd stood with Aamon?

So many questions!

Griffin's jaw clenched slightly, but he upheld his composure. Noah and Steven's expressions remained indifferent, but Amelia's eyes darted between Kerwin, Aamon, and Griffin. This was clearly brand-new information for her too, and I recognized the shift in her emotional charge, recognized the look of pain in her eyes, and the disbelieving glances she threw toward her *family*. But I was devoid of sympathy. Instead I felt jubilation at witnessing karma in its full and long-awaited glory. It was about time one of them got to taste their own medicine.

Much to Amelia's indignation, I didn't even try to hide my amusement. She swung her attention toward me, yelling, "You think this is funny?"

"Yes!" I answered blankly and went back to staring impassively ahead, closing my emotions from Kerwin's lecherous prying attentions.

I needn't have bothered; Kerwin paid no heed to me at all. But the relief I should have felt was replaced with a gnawing apprehension. He'd spent too long making me his prime focus. Now all of a sudden, I wasn't even on his radar. Something wasn't right.

Griffin eyed him suspiciously, growling, "Go home, Kerwin. This isn't happening. Not here, not today."

Kerwin cocked his head to the side, surveying the trees that encompassed the clearing. He made a small gesture to the creature beside him, who in turn signaled to the remaining faction. They calmly spread out, creating a loose inner circle.

Now I was really confused. Kerwin must have been aware of the presence of the Sygans mere feet away from where he had positioned his soldiers, not just positioned them, but placed them with their backs to the Sygans, almost inviting them to attack. There was one within arm's reach of everyone, except that is, for me.

The atmosphere around us buzzed. Every soundless moment, every second without movement, increased the air of nervous anticipation exponentially.

I couldn't stand still any longer. I paced back and forth, crossing the line between the two sides. Passing by Aamon, eyes averted, composure retained, my movements remained fluid, but as I slipped by him, he moved his hand, just slightly, so that our fingers brushed, giving me the reassuring warmth I needed so desperately in that moment. No soul should have noticed. The inconspicuous role we played was award worthy, but it did not go entirely unnoticed.

It was the tiniest of occurrences that set in motion a devastating series of events.

I felt Griffin's eyes blazing. I turned defiantly toward him, but his venomous stare wasn't for me. All his anger and hatred was aimed toward Aamon. And I saw it, the wisp of darkness escaping from the fissure caused. It passed briefly over his features, leaving me with a fleeting splinter of fear.

The toxic cocktail of emotional overload felt ready to combust, when a movement behind Griffin drew my attention, and I finally had an opportunity for release. I was the only one not within reach of Kerwin's henchmen. Without hesitation, I shot across the clearing and into the trees. Griffin should have held his strongpoint, but instead he followed me.

The creature in the trees lurched forward as I rebounded from trunk to trunk and caught his chin swiftly midflight. My kick sent him barreling backward, but within seconds, he was back on his feet and without hesitation dove toward me. As I ran at him, Griffin's voice from somewhere behind me hissed, "Down."

With the creature millimeters from my face, I skidded across the ground, the momentum of my run pushing me clean beneath him as he flew over me and directly into Griffin. I scrambled to my feet and spun quickly, sprinting back to where the two of them were trading blows. Although Griffin was largely obscured by the creature, I could see it recoil as he swung for it. I was one step away when I caught sight of Griffin's right arm as he reached into his waistband mid-grapple and pulled out the dagger. He tossed it blindly toward me, and in one seamless motion, I snatched it out of midair and plunged it squarely between the creature's shoulder blades.

With a blood-curdling scream, it flailed backward, almost landing on top of me as Griffin sidestepped its swinging arms and wrapped one arm around my waist, pulling me to safety and holding me tightly against him.

"I'm good, Griffin. Let me go," I begged, knowing how badly this interaction would be received by the Sygans already dubious of my intent.

"Are you sure?" he asked, continuing his vise-like grip on my waist, his breath warm against my cheek.

I glared at him, my anger swelling like a burning wave of red-hot fury at the game he insisted on playing in the worst place, at the worst time. I might just have to kill him myself at this rate. I pushed against him as hard as I could, forcing him to release me.

We emerged from the tree line, snapped branches, and desecrated undergrowth, disclosing the full exchange to all.

The creature may have perished, but Kerwin had undoubtedly won that round. If his objective was to destroy us from the inside out, this would be an easy victory for him.

Griffin was a full step ahead of me, and so I didn't see exactly what he did, but I was aware of him gesturing smugly to Aamon. To my dismay, Aamon retaliated hissing, "Is that the best you've got?" as we stepped back into the open space.

Challenge extended!

Griffin stopped, turned to face me, and without warning pulled me roughly toward him. He kissed me passionately, holding me to him with an iron grip, rendering my shocked struggle to free myself futile. Without moving a muscle, Aamon glowered, fury contorting his face, and the large rocky boulders to the side of the clearing shifted and trembled.

I was shaking with anger and humiliation. Griffin had used me to take a cheap shot at Aamon. I could barely contain my rage, and with a roar, I shoved him fiercely. As his grip broke and he stumbled backward, I swung at him, hard, right hooking his face and splitting his lip. He laughed, the same twisted laugh as Kerwin, and muttered, "Totally worth it."

I recoiled from him, repulsed by his actions and his words. His head snapped up, realizing the severity of what he had done. He reached out to me, and I leaped farther back, shaking my head, fighting down the urge to vomit.

"Alyssa, wait, please," he pleaded desperately. "I didn't mean to do that. He brings out the worst in me. I swear I wasn't thinking straight."

Of all the people to make me feel violated, never could I ever have imagined this.

I held my shaking hands up to him, urging him to stop, willing words to form, but instead all I got were tears, making me hate myself almost as much as I hated him.

Again, he moved toward me, his words coming quicker, his panic increasing as the magnitude of the damage he had inflicted became apparent.

"Stay away from me," I croaked.

"Please, please, just wait," he begged me, his eyes wide and his face ashen. "Baby, please."

"Baby!" I balked. "*Fuck you, Griffin!*"

Had he banged his damn head or was this just another twisted attempt to further provoke Aamon?

A quick sweep of the clearing confirmed my worst fears. The entire exchange had been witnessed by all. The only saving grace was that every set of eyes was transfixed on Griffin, conveying a mixture of shock, disbelief, and above all else disgust. Even Noah glared angrily at him.

Aamon was livid. His muscles twitched and shook like he was embroiled in a struggle with an invisible entity. His eyes, red rimmed and coal black, flashed with sparks of fiery anger.

For all of our sakes, I had to pacify him. It left a bitter taste in my mouth as all I truly wanted to do was release him to attack.

I strode quickly, but kept my head high and my shoulders back. Never again would I be the victim. Never again would I scurry away in fear or push my gut feelings to one side to appease everyone else. I had remained neutral not for my own benefit, but for the sake of being the peacekeeper, for the sake of everyone except for me, and look where it had gotten me.

No physical line was drawn into the dirt, but it was there nonetheless, and without hesitation I crossed it, standing a few feet in front of Aamon. A side chosen. A choice made willingly.

"Are you satisfied?" Steven hissed to Griffin.

Kerwin's amused cackle reverberated around us. "I didn't expect such a degree of entertainment!" he squealed, drawing everyone's eyes to him before making a small flicking gesture with his wrists, initiating their assault. With flawless synchronicity, his soldiers attacked. Even in an adrenaline-fueled haze, it happened too quickly.

The explosion of chaos rendered me momentarily immobile. My brain slowed down time, enabling me to watch horrified as Kerwin's monsters pounced. All around me beings fought. Screams of anger and terror filled the air, along with the sounds of bones breaking and bodies crashing mercilessly into the ground.

And I remained, as though I was invisible, protected by the eye of the storm.

One of Aamon's Sygans flew through the air, landing feet away from me. His opponent leaped from the fray, skidding to a stop inches away as he struggled to stand. I ran at the creature as he raised one leg, preparing to cast a devastating blow to the Sygan's head. It felt like running into a brick wall. I don't know how the force of my run caused the creature to lose its balance, but it did, and we both flailed toward the ground.

My darkness was whining like a dog at the door, begging for me to let her out, and so I did, just a smidge. Like a bolt of electricity had passed through me, I shot up from on top of the creature as it crashed into the ground. I spun with great speed and the accuracy of a marksman, swinging my foot to land a deadly blow to the side of its head, killing it instantaneously.

I whirled around, desperate to locate Aamon. He was fighting alone.

Not for long.

With each step bringing me closer, my excitement increased. In some perverted sense, this was fun. The flash of anger I felt for the being fighting my man was snatched up by my darkness. She toyed and teased it like a cat with a mouse, twisting and cultivating it into a tool, a weapon of use. It gave me strength. It gave me power.

I approached my warrior and the beast from the side, skidding between the brawling two as Aamon swung heavily at the creature's head, causing it to lurch to the side. Before it was able to fully stabilize, I threw my fist up, smashing beneath its jaw with a brutal blow, forcing its head backward and snapping its neck. It collapsed to the floor with a thud at our feet. Aamon grasped my hand and pulled me into a standing position. He went to turn away, but I pulled him toward me, pressing against him hard but briefly, brushing my lips against his cheek, savoring his scent and his taste.

Instead of accepting what was lost, of admitting defeat and letting me go, the more evident my relationship with Aamon became, the more desperate and unhinged Griffin became.

The creature that fought against Griffin and Steven should have posed no threat. It was huge and ferocious but no match against the two of them. Furthermore, they had the upper hand. My gaze had swept over them many times as I continually scanned the clearing, assessing the battle.

The air was heavy with the thunderous sounds of battle, yet something about Griffin's voice alerted me, caused me to identify and isolate it from the pandemonium that surrounded me.

It could have been the interaction with Aamon, or it could have been the harnessing of my darkness that tipped him, but his actions defied sanity. He became illogically reactive, and with a blood-curdling scream, he abandoned Steven midbattle to rush at Aamon.

He left him!

My eyes widened as a deserted Steven struggled hopelessly against the beast. I swung my gaze wildly around the scene, desperate for someone close enough in proximity to notice, to help Steven, *to save him!*

There was no one.

As Griffin ran to Aamon, I ran to Steven. We passed each other like speeding locomotives.

Griffin's body impacted against Aamon's with a thud.

I skidded to an abrupt stop midway between Steven and Aamon.

Griffin had collided with Aamon with such force

that he had slammed him through the air and into the ground right at the feet of one of Kerwin's creatures. The opportunity did not go unmissed as the gigantic beast leaped on top of Aamon.

My breathing stopped.

The beating of my heart stopped.

It wasn't an impossible choice. It wasn't a choice.

Aamon would always be the one I'd run to. It was just a fucked-up and painful absolute that would result in Steven's demise.

I could not save both.

Aamon was my one.

And like an angel ascending from a heaven that was nonexistent, Birsha appeared, screaming at me to "Go!" as he ran to Steven's aid.

I turned.

I released.

I could hear each tiny piece of gravel as my footsteps caused them to shift and scrape against each other and the ground. Like a switch had been flipped, I gained tunnel vision in the literal sense; everything outside of my one shaft of focus became muted and dim. Aamon was all that there was. Aamon with the creature on top of him, pinning him powerlessly to the ground. Aamon struggling against the creature as it raised its arm in preparation for the final mortal blow.

Nothing that happened next was induced by conscious effort. I remember my eyes felt like they were on fire, burning yet icy at the same time, and my hunger for the hunt, for the kill, was intensified beyond anything I had experienced before.

As the feeling grew, I didn't feel like I was losing control as Griffin assumed I would, nor did I feel the need to rein it in like Aamon had assumed I would need to. It actually felt very controlled. It was the darkness inside of me that I had nurtured, cared for, loved even. And as it grew in size and strength, so did my power, hand in hand with my control.

The creature froze with its arm still outstretched. Its head snapped backward, forcing its eyes to the sky. Its back arched as its extended arm twisted violently three hundred and sixty degrees with a sickening snap. Its entire body became rigid, and an agonizing scream was cut short as it flew backward, landing in the decreasing space between Aamon and my approaching strides. I didn't have time to contemplate what had just happened. Without breaking my stride, I leaped over its contorted rigid corpse, its eyes black holes of lifelessness and its remains smoldering, pulling with me my leashed power.

Aamon stumbled to his feet. I reached him and extended my arm, pulling him to an upright position. He went to step away, resume the fight, my dark warrior, but I pulled him back, jumped on to him, wrapping my legs around his waist as my hands gripped his broad neck. One of his hands cupped my behind, and the other gently pushed away the wisps of hair that had fallen onto my face.

I had the most effective weapon of any arsenal. I had the truth, and the truth would hurt Griffin more than anything else I could possibly do to exact revenge upon him. I did what I should have done a long time ago. I pulled Aamon's head close, and I kissed him, a kiss that was real and wanted, that made my heart pound and was hard to break free of. A kiss that shot down any doubts from anyone else, that sent a clear and concise message. I was as much his as he was mine, and I would stand beside him come hell or high water. He was my man.

It was what Aamon deserved, and it was overdue.

It was also a massive fuck-you to Griffin. Exactly what he deserved. I dumped the whole damn canister of gas on the lit match and gave zero fucks about the consequences.

Out of nowhere Griffin rushed at him for a second time. Like hell was I letting this happen again. Aamon released me, and I stepped between them, my dark energy pulsating through every vein, every vessel, every last fiber of my being, willing me to let it play without restraint.

I turned to Griffin, my glare casting dark spirals of hostility and disgust. "Stay the fuck away from *us*!"

"This is what you wanted, isn't it? You bastard!" he spat venomously at Aamon.

"No, you sanctimonious prick, smothering her, denying what she is isn't going to save her. Take a look at yourself!" Aamon growled, stepping toward him.

"I will fucking end you, Aamon," Griffin screamed, his eyes flashing dark with rage.

"I'm done tolerating you, Griffin. You want to end it—let's end it right now."

I may have had control over myself, but everything else was descending into utter anarchy at dizzying speeds. All the while, the power within me pleaded for the door to be opened again, tugged at my heartstrings like an insistent toddler, begging for a second taste of freedom.

And grant its wish I did.

It swirled around me, shrouding me like a protective entity, awaiting my direction, my command.

"Stop!"

One word, one order directed at both of them. There was an abrupt intake of breath, then silence sliced through the air like a guillotine, brutal and sharp. The air around us tremored; maybe the ground did too. My dark shroud anesthetized me to anything beyond its embrace.

Wide-eyed and shaken, Griffin lurched backward. "Alyssa…" he stammered.

I reined it back in, needing to feel more control than was necessary, needing time to adjust to this completely new part of me, but also insanely needing to protect it.

"Leave her," Aamon demanded, but of course he had to twist the knife by adding, "What's wrong, Griffin? Is she looking too much like my girl now?"

Amelia was the first to notice Steven lying motionless on the floor as Birsha continued to struggle against the creature, desperately trying to prevent it from going in for the kill. Her scream alerted both Griffin and Noah, distracting Griffin from Aamon and giving Aamon the opportunity to help Birsha.

Through the fracas, I saw Noah scoop Steven into his arms, refusing Griffin's help as he carried him away from the clearing. Amelia and Griffin remained, preventing any of Kerwin's army from pursuing them.

I turned my focus to Kerwin. The simplest solution was to fix the problem at the source. Time to eradicate the queen bee.

And for the first time that day I felt his eyes searching for me.

Oh, now you see me!

He had made his way into the trees, hidden from the conflict. Retreating like a snake slithering back under its rock.

I picked my way through the mass of swinging limbs

and flying bodies, ducking and rolling to avoid the blows, but my steps never faltered. They continued steadfast and unwavering. As I stepped into the dense tree line, leaves rustled and branches snapped behind me as two of his henchmen closed my exit. I remained unconcerned. It would take more than two of them to stop me. His whole damn army could not restrain me.

Kerwin smiled, his crooked nefarious smirk. He spoke over me, addressing his guard dogs behind me like I had again become invisible to him.

"You see, we don't need to destroy them. Look at how proficiently they do our work for us," he sang gleefully.

I edged closer, just one more step and I would have been close enough to finally kill the bastard.

"And best of all we didn't even need to hunt our real objective. She delivered herself right into our hands, isn't that right, Alyssa?" he crowed.

I froze.

Kerwin turned to face me with sickening jubilation.

"Oh, I know you want to kill me, want to rip out my throat and tear me limb from limb. But I also know you won't."

I edged another inch farther forward.

I raised my eyebrows questioningly. Shifting my weight to disguise another inch closed.

"There are many you would forsake, but not dear sweet Kasey."

I stopped dead, paralyzed by his words.

He pulled something from the pocket of his jacket, clenched his fist tightly around it, then tossed it gently through the air between us. My hand snapped up, snatching it midflight. It was Kasey's name tag from his school backpack. His scent clung to it. The writing beneath the plastic was mine. It most definitely belonged to Kasey but proved nothing. Kerwin acquiring such a thing meant nothing. Kasey was nowhere near the vicinity; I'd have felt him if he was even remotely close by.

But Kerwin was just warming up.

He opened his hand to the creature on his left and was handed a cell phone with a video already in play mode. The image was grainy at first. A red circle with the words *live link* flashing beneath it blinked rhythmically in the top corner of the screen. It looked like security camera footage. The device displayed a panoramic view of the inside of a grocery store, a store I recognized, a store I had visited countless times before, a small mom-and-pop store that sat on a corner a few blocks from my mom's house.

Kerwin handed the cell phone to me, stepping back to create a small zone of safety between us before hissing, "Zoom in."

I really didn't need to. I could have spared myself the pain of picking out the pair huddled together against the shelves of dried pasta, my mom tenderly stroking Kasey's hair as he lay in her lap, the other hand shielding his eyes from the drama that played out around them, from the manic individual who scurried up and down the aisles waving the 9mm inches from the faces of the petrified shoppers and store clerks.

At first, I thought there were two of them. The one brandishing the gun and his accomplice who followed closely, never allowing more than a few inches to form between the two, working in tandem. But there was something about that second figure that drew my attention. His face, although distorted by the poor picture quality, was not familiar, but his mannerisms were. Oddly, the gunman acted oblivious to his presence. With a sinking feeling, the pieces fell into place; he was oblivious. His accomplice was not like him. His accomplice wasn't human, wasn't even alive. His accomplice was a Sygan.

It maintained close proximity to retain control, to fill a clearly broken mind with suggestive persuasions, enticing him into being a participant in their depraved game, treating him like a toy or a weapon just as Kerwin had done with the girl on the platform.

A gleeful Kerwin nodded to the beast-like foot soldier by his right side who, in response, pulled a cell phone from his pocket and tapped furiously at the screen. The Sygan in the store glanced down at the small device he held before whispering something into the ear of the deranged gunman. The man's head jerked up, and he paced fervently up and down the aisles, evidently seeking someone out. The knot that had started as a small ball of anxiety deep down in the pit of my stomach expanded quickly, pushing against my diaphragm and constricting my breathing.

I prayed he wasn't looking for Kasey or my mom. The image flickered, distorted by a bright flash. Even without sound, the panic in the room was apparent. He had shot someone at point-blank range. Bile rose in my throat, and my knees buckled as I pulled the phone closer with trembling hands, searching desperately for the image of the two huddled together, alive and unharmed.

I saw them.

My mom cradling a curled-up Kasey, rocking him gently as his shoulders heaved, probably from sobs or fear-induced hyperventilation. No doubt they were damaged, but they were not, at the very least, lying in a pool of blood.

I turned to Kerwin, my eyes blazing. My fingers curled involuntarily, and my voice became a growl. I had never wanted so much to kill anyone before. This exceeded even my desire to kill the drunk who had plowed into me. I took a step toward him, my shoulders hunched, ready to pounce.

Kerwin held his hand up in the space between us. "Ah, ah, ah, think about it, Alyssa. One word from me, and the next target will be your mother and child."

So this was his endgame all along. Bitterly I realized just how much I had underestimated Kerwin. As predicted, he had orchestrated a battle. We were just too stupid to see our opponent wasn't ever going to be Kerwin and his army. We were pitted against ourselves, the only true threat was from us, against us, and it had played out flawlessly.

I looked out across the chaotic scene with dismay. The purpose of Kerwin's creatures was not to fight against us, it was to distract us, and they did just that. Every being fueled by hatred and contempt, blinded to what was actually occurring.

Noah had carried an injured Steven to a place of safety, but it was hard to imagine them ever forgiving Griffin for leaving Steven mid-fight, forsaking him for such a stupid egotistical reason. Zagan, angry that he had to fight at all while so many of his soldiers remained redundantly in Daeon, had separated from the rest of the Sygans. Birsha was embroiled in an argument with what was supposed to be a fellow Sygan over his rescue of Steven, and Amelia fought alone, segregated by Griffin's betrayal and uncharacteristic actions.

With sickening dismay, I surveyed the fucked-up scene.

Amelia was not faring well. She lacked the size, the strength, and the inclination against the demonic creature battling her. As Kerwin turned to lead me away, I saw the knife, identical to the ones Aamon and Griffin possessed. Without warning, I grabbed the dagger, swiping it from its leather scabbard attached to Kerwin's waistband. He spun too late in my direction, his two comrades stumbling backward in fear. Without pause, I executed a fast spin throw in Amelia's direction, sending the dagger slicing through the air with force and impaling her opponent with deadly accuracy. Her eyes, confused and shocked, met mine for the briefest of moments before I turned and followed Kerwin, disappearing into the dense thicket.

Chapter 22

As soon as we had moved a distance from the battleground, I was blindfolded, my first indication that Kerwin had no clue as to who and what he was dealing with.

He could have taken away all my senses, and I still would have known exactly where I was. We made our way down from the mountain. I was bundled into a vehicle, a large one with a fresh new interior, and driven speedily away. I remained silent, focused on reading my captors, but more so on concealing my emotional energy from the intrusive curiosity of those around me.

We drove for a few hours, far enough away to prevent anyone from successfully tracking me. We were still within the preserve when we stopped, and I was led from the vehicle and into a building with similar features to the lodge, but on a much smaller scale. I could smell the scent of the timber beams, feel the warmth of the wood as it contrasted with the coolness of the polished rocks that created the structure.

I was taken into a room with what sounded like a fortified door. Multiple locking mechanisms clicked into place before the blindfold was removed. I could have removed it myself at any point. My hands were not bound. But I chose to participate in their game, maintaining their delusional belief that they were in control.

The room was empty except for a bed against the wall to the right and two chairs that sat beneath a window with iron bars directly adjacent to the door.

On the wall opposite the bed was a mounted television set. Although muted, the screen displayed a larger version of the security camera footage from inside of the store. Unable to zoom in, I could barely make out my mom and Kasey. They had been joined by a lady with a similar stature to my mom. The three remained huddled together on the edge of one of the food aisles.

My shackles.

I sat down on the bed and turned to Kerwin. He remained close to the door, the only exit should he need to make a hasty retreat. Just behind him stood one of his minions, eyeing me up and down like I was lunch. It was all I could do to refrain from gagging.

"Let them go." I was careful to mask my demand as a request, keeping a low and even tone.

"I don't think so," Kerwin sneered.

"I did exactly what you wanted. You have me. There's no one here to save me. You are free to kill me. There's no need to continue with that…" I gestured toward the screen.

"You really do catastrophize, don't you, Alyssa? My aim was never to kill you. Had I wanted you dead, I'd have killed you while you sat weeping like a baby on your mother's front porch during your very first days."

I flinched at the memory.

"I was merely the scientist, probing and investigating the specimen that just happened to appear before me. I had many theories about you, many that have been disproven, but your potential use to me thus far remains."

I wanted to ask him what it was that he wanted, what his plan for me was, what he hoped to achieve, but asking him directly was not an option. Asking him directly was like handing him power. Informing him explicitly of what I wanted would only encourage him to weaponize it. He would go out of his way to hold anything hostage, be it information, people, or a rationale. He was like a child with a defiance disorder. Instead, I would have to play his ridiculous and infuriating game.

"Whatever you want, you will fail," I stated with a certainty that aggravated him.

Whatever his goal was didn't matter. I would call his bluff, act like I already knew, like we had been two steps ahead instead of days behind.

"Are you really that arrogant to think you know better than Aamon," I spat, "than a god?"

"Tut tut, Alyssa, how quickly you forget your first lessons," Kerwin purred. "There is no god."

"There's no one absolute god," I corrected him.

"There are *no* gods, you imbecile," he screamed in my face. "Aamon is no different from me. Except for his purity, he's exactly the same as you and Griffin. The pure ones, the sacred trifecta," he sneered.

There it was!

He was so consumed with envy at what he lacked, what he was not, that he had failed to grasp the weight of the words he yielded.

"They chose the same side, don't you know? Aamon embraced it. Griffin was repelled and turned against it. Such a shame to lose raw talent such as his."

I fought hard to keep my composure, to sustain a neutral expression.

"You made quite the impression, you know, Alyssa.

You exceeded my expectations, burned it all to the ground from the inside out. You took a broken Aamon and fixed him and took a functional, albeit annoying, Griffin and broke him. In fact, you didn't just break him, you obliterated almost one hundred years of healing. You, young lady, are my fucking hero!"

Kerwin rocked on his heels, radiating in gleeful satisfaction as he summarized.

"Ahh, poor Griffin, he fights so valiantly to protect his precious light, to repudiate his darkness, but it is still there, tiptoeing softly beneath the surface, wanting, waiting. Poor fool doesn't realize that denying it simply makes it stronger. He will lose control. I thought learning how Aamon had fucked you six ways from Sunday may have done it. It certainly brought him close." He chuckled.

My cheeks may have burned with the humiliation of Kerwin knowing about my most intimate moments. However, the glow within me blazed even warmer at the mention of Aamon's name. But I kept it concealed, hidden behind an impenetrable screen.

Kerwin continued, "It's like ignoring a snake that exists bound to you. Aamon at least acknowledges his, feeds it, ensures its basic needs are met, and I'm sure has fucking fun with it sometimes! But Griffin, oh not Griffin. He tries to smother his, ignoring and denying it...torturing and starving it!" Kerwin's voice rose rapidly in volume and pitch until his words became a screech. He was practically delirious. Turning to me with eyes like saucers, he leaned in closely and whispered, "Then he wonders why it bites him." He clicked his teeth together loudly close to my ear.

Still, I remained emotionless, staring passively

ahead.

"I waited for what felt like a hundred lifetimes for that one missing piece. I had almost given up. There was no foreseeable way to ever coerce them into working together. Or so I thought," he mused, "until that is, you arrived."

Together?

My eyes lost their focus, blurring the scant images that surrounded me, but still I stared ahead.

Pride radiated from Kerwin as he announced, "You will be my bait. For you, they will do anything, risk anything, including themselves. To know one's strengths and acknowledge one's weaknesses—that is the way to succeed. I know my weaknesses; I know in a physical fight I could never win against either one of them." Again, he leaned uncomfortably close, his piercing eyes millimeters from my face, his rancid breath warm against my skin. "But up here"—he tapped the side of his head— "up here I annihilate them."

He was getting braver. Each time he moved toward me, he got closer, stayed longer. His fear was dwindling. Internally I smiled.

Still I stared ahead.

He studied me.

I played.

A small sigh, a swift blink, I dropped my eyes just slightly. I fed him the dismay he so desperately sought, the motivation he needed to continue.

"They will enter Laeon, they will find Magda and return her to this plane, or they will watch you. They will watch you as you witness the murder of your family. They will watch the vessel they worship as it is desecrated and defiled. They will watch you as you are taken apart piece by piece."

He's going to make them choose between me and an elder. No, something isn't right.

"And what do you think they will do to you then?"

"They'll do nothing."

"You really have lost your mind!"

"It's all up here," he repeated, tapping his temple.

"No, I'm pretty sure there's very little left *up there!*" I mimicked.

He laughed a low grumbling laugh, leaning closer than the last time. His lips brushed against my ear, making my skin crawl like a thousand insects had been released as he whispered, "There is no Magda. She never made it to Laeon. They will never see what happens to you. They will never return from Laeon. And if they do manage to crawl from there, I will be waiting to crush their fragile skulls with my boot heel. You're brand new, Alyssa." Kerwin's hand rested on my thigh as he sat next to me on the bed. He breathed in deeply, inhaling my scent. "You think you know so much, when in fact you know nothing. You didn't see what Laeon did to them last time. It sucked every shred of power from them. It was beautiful. They were like baby birds who had fallen from their nest. That's all I ever needed. They claim to hate each other, but once upon a time they were brothers. I could never risk rendering one powerless, educating the other to my plan, and trust there would be no retaliation."

I wanted to snap every one of his fingers slowly. My eyes fell to them as he continued to squeeze my thigh. I struggled to restrain myself. My eyes burned, and I think Kerwin felt it. He pulled his hand away quickly and stood, ready to retreat.

"Magda?" I whispered.

"She was their appetizer. They needed something."
He gestured to the doorway, to the creatures that stood
beyond it, the animals that did his bidding. "And you will
be their entrée."

"You killed her?" My voice was barely a whisper.

Kerwin crouched down next to me. "You're all such
hypocrites. How do you think Aamon got the power he
wastes? You think that desecrating a pure one is beneath
him?"

"I don't believe a word you say. Save your breath,"
I hissed.

"Yes, you do."

He smiled as he swept away.

The door banged shut, the multiple locks snapped
into place, and I started to shake.

Kerwin was gone. I felt his repulsive essence as it
vacated the area. He would be visiting Aamon and
Griffin, giving them an ultimatum. Aamon would either
kill him or succumb to his demands. Griffin, I had no
idea what Griffin would do. If it was Noah or Steven,
they would follow him in a heartbeat, but there had been
a darker side evolving within Griffin, and I had just
delivered the biggest fuck-you to him. There was a good
chance he hated me just as much as he hated Aamon right
now, more so even.

But right then I had a bigger problem to deal with. I
could hear and feel the creatures on the other side of the
door. They would not remain on the other side for long.
Kerwin was delusional to think they could be trusted
with me. It was like asking hungry hyenas to stand watch
over a carcass and expecting them not to eat.

I cradled my little flame, placed my hand on the door
of the cage holding her in, ready to release.

Heavy footsteps moved away from the door. Only one remained.

He entered quietly. He didn't want the others to know. This was one treat he wanted for himself.

He was triple my size and stature. When I looked at him, I felt the burning sensation of stomach acid seeping up my esophagus.

"Relax, little girl, you're not dying today. I just want a little taste is all. Who knows, you might like it."

He pushed the door closed but didn't bother to lock it. Why would he? To him, I was just a little girl.

His eyes stayed on me as he removed his belt.

I kept my composure in check, held my rage back, allowing it to build and expand, flowing freely just beneath the surface, undetected.

"And your name?" I murmured.

"Why would you want to know my name?" he asked, as intrigued as he was amused.

"So I know who I'm killing," I responded matter-of-factly, in a gentle voice.

"I'm Dietrich. I'll be sure to remind you of it when Kerwin is done with you and hands you over to me fully. I'll remind you again and again, each time I'm using you beyond what you ever thought any being could use you and that tight little body for. Each time I share you with my friends, and with every drop of blood that we take from you, I'll remind you."

I felt stripped beneath the intensity of his ravenous stare.

He walked with such confidence.

My heart pounded—adrenaline, fear, exhilaration, all swirled simultaneously.

With a start, he lunged forward. He gripped my hair,

jerking me viciously upward from my seated position on the bed. He dragged me across the room and slammed me against the wall with such force, it shuddered. His huge, calloused hand grabbed at my breasts as he pushed his body against mine, his stench filling my nasal passages.

The ringing in my ears became violent.

Deep inside of me, I flicked off the light. Now only darkness remained.

With a creak, the gate swung open.

And behold, your worst nightmare, fucker!

He realized too late.

My fingers danced. They were the only part of my body that moved, softly playing an imaginary piano. The darkness caressed me, enveloping me in a warm embrace as he perished in the most brutal and sadistic fashion.

His body contorted into unnatural positions like he was being electrocuted from the inside out. I stifled a laugh. His fingers became claws, leaving scratches on the hardwood floor. I waited patiently. Counting slowly in my head, minutes past his last movements, his last rasping breath, ensuring he was completely gone.

I wanted to kick his body under the bed, hiding it from view, but some sort of rigor mortis had frozen his corpse into a shape that would not allow it to fit, his arms rigid in an embrace with an invisible entity stuck out before him as his distorted remains lay on the floor. Huge eyes wide and deadened stared up at the ceiling. I stamped down on each arm crushing his bones like they were twigs, rendering his arms flaccid and resembling a rag doll.

As a human I couldn't step on a cockroach, the crunching sound made me nauseous. And yet here I was crushing the bones of Deputy Dead like a fairy-tale giant.

With a heave, I rolled his remains underneath the bed.

Without any effort at all, I left, creeping with feigned apprehension down the narrow hallway. The room, my holding cell, was on the ground floor. Directly across from the hallway was the doorway to the kitchen. To the right was an open-plan living space. Kerwin's soldiers paced the perimeter. There were at least two on the upper level but none on the ground floor.

They were probably ordered away to ensure some privacy for the bastard as he raped me.

Unfortunately, my energy called out to them, rendering any escape almost impossible. They knew I was on the move, and I felt their panic as they congregated quickly.

There was no surprise.

Escape had never been my intention, I merely wanted to guide them away from the mangled corpse shoved crudely beneath the bed and remove myself from its vicinity.

As I awaited their arrival, my eyes flickered to the flat-screen television set in the lounge area. A live news feed detailed the grocery store standoff. The image of a reporter who was at the scene filled the screen. He theorized about the gunman and the probable outcome for the hostages while standing two streets over. In the background, a bustle of activity, bright yellow tape cordoning off the area, uniformed officers, patrol cars with flashing lights and SWAT could be seen. Text-based graphics that overlaid the video content reminded viewers that the hostages were entering their fourteenth hour of captivity.

Fourteen hours! My poor baby.

Anger shot through me like a solar flare. I would enjoy paying him back for this.

They entered the living area through different doors and staircases, circling me like a wolf pack.

But Kerwin was right there, seconds from entering the building. I had felt his approach long before I left my cell, anticipating his arrival with impeccable timing. They would not attack in his presence.

Kerwin was euphoric. He didn't even question why I was no longer held under lock and key.

I didn't need the details of his encounter with Aamon and Griffin. His elation could only mean one thing. Both had surrendered to his demands. Both would do as they were commanded. Both would enter Laeon, undertaking what could well be a suicide mission.

He prattled on about the pleasure he derived from their pain. I chose to ignore him; his words bounced off me, providing no more than a background beat, the faint buzzing of a mosquito that had found its way inside but kept its distance.

That's the thing with words. You can't always shut another person up, but you can choose to listen…or not.

There was no planning, no assessment of danger. We left immediately. I was bundled back into the SUV, squeezed between two of Kerwin's creatures. Kerwin sat up front, and a third one of his soldiers drove. Thankfully no one questioned the whereabouts of Dietrich.

As the saying goes, only fools rush in.

We arrived back at Laeon's doorway less than seven hours after we'd left it. The sun had slipped away at some point during our journey. The air in the clearing was heavy with the remnants of the energy from those who had fought. Fear, pain, suffering. No bodies remained, but the stench of death clung to the carpet of pine needles. Even in the darkness, crushed boulders and bushes, snapped branches and logs were visible, illuminated by the bright moonlight.

And Aamon. His essence danced through the twilight, separating from the intermingled blend of energies, triggering my senses like only he could. I drifted with it, unwilling to allow its escape.

"There's been a development with the hostages. His negotiations have stopped. The police can't communicate with your human, so they're going in. Alaric is awaiting your command."

The words uttered by Kerwin's phone boy snatched me out of my trance-like state.

They were losing control; my time was running short.

"He can kill them all as far as I'm concerned. Just get someone down there with Vesks first. May as well make it a lucrative transaction."

"Even you aren't stupid enough to discard the only leverage you have," I spat, fighting hard to quell the panic that was rising quickly within me.

"Why would I need leverage? I only needed leverage to influence you, to force your surrender, and to get you right where you stand. The moment they enter Laeon, I give my order, and everyone dies."

I was almost out of time. But if there was one thing I was good at, it was working well under pressure.

Kerwin turned his attention to me.

I started to shake.

"Please, I'm begging you, don't hurt them." My voice was raspy and barely above a whisper.

With a gasp, I took a step backward. Kerwin responded by taking two steps toward me. I forced a look of fear upon my face, hoping it was enough to conceal the rage, to fool Kerwin into thinking I was afraid of not just the circumstances as they played out, but also of him.

"Please," I begged him. "Please don't do this."

Another step backward, stumbling slightly over the gnarled roots of a tree. The hapless victim trembling in fear as she is consumed by something that takes away her ability to even stand unsupported.

The hunter in him compelled him to continue his approach almost unaware of his actions. Another step, another stumble, another foot between Kerwin and his Sygans, another inch closer to me. Reeling him in, distancing him from his only form of protection.

I couldn't turn around. I had to keep my eyes, wide and doe-like, transfixed on him, entrancing him, feeding his misogynic impulses, using his best most effective weapon against him, maintaining his ignorance as I enticed him, leading him like a child to his death.

I didn't feel its power, certainly not in the way I had expected I would. I knew it was close but relied solely on my responses to alert me to a breach before it happened. My autonomic reaction failed me in spectacular fashion. I crossed between worlds like I had stepped from a curb. A transitional shift that was so minimal it was barely perceptible.

Too late, I realized the enormity of my action, what crossing the point of convergence without consequence signified. In truth, I didn't even realize it had happened. The sensation was no more than a momentary fleeting feeling of pins and needles on the heels of my feet. Whether the insensitivity was due to my heightened state, an overload of adrenaline, or a byproduct of the escalation of the power I had recently harnessed, I didn't know, but stepping, or rather stumbling, into Laeon resulted in a reaction that was barely a blip on my radar.

But to Kerwin, it was a revelation.

His eyes widened in shock and jubilation as his brain scrambled to do the math on what he had witnessed, what it meant, and above all else what such a divulgence now afforded him.

Luckily for me he was no mathematician. And even though the obvious appeared to profess its truth with deafening volume, Kerwin remained oblivious to what sat before him.

His was an elevator that did not reach the top floor.

"This is their essence. It clings to you like a parasitic leech." He giggled manically. "You fucked them both, didn't you? You will carry a little bit of them wherever you go, including into Laeon, you little whore!"

"You really do possess a greater power than we realized," Kerwin mused, a confused shadow inching its way across his face.

Uh-oh, now he was starting to catch on. I didn't have long until he finally understood what that meant.

"The ultimate power in infant form," he continued confidently. "It will be such a shame to clip those tiny wings."

There wasn't a man on Earth that had failed to underestimate me, that had avoided tumbling into the pit of assumption. There were clear-cut gender-specific roles I must aspire to fulfill or desires I would be naturally compelled to seek. What had seemed to some as major advancements in equality on Earth had in actuality been a steady crawl at best. I don't know why I had ever thought that the men in the alternative plane could or would be any different. Of course, Kerwin would see an infant before him. Of course he would measure my growth by his. If it took him one hundred years to attain a commendable level of power and control, it would take a woman one hundred and fifty years.

I suppressed an eye roll and moved into action.

He didn't get to finish his demented rant. Fueled by fascination, he had moved close enough. Before another word could pass his moronic lips, I reached out and grabbed him, snatching him backward as I simultaneously leaped farther into Laeon.

Chapter 23

It was a stupid idea, one with so many possible outcomes and none of them good. Magda had said that the three of us together were impervious to harm. I had started to hope she meant that in literal terms.

As stupid as my idea was, it had seemed like the only option. Desperate times called for desperate measures. I had to get into Laeon before they arrived, before they went rushing in on some falsified grand mission, before Laeon stripped them of their power and rendered them defenseless, before Kerwin could figure out what bringing the three of us together meant.

The opening was right there, but to make a dash for it would only have sped up Kerwin's limited cognitive functioning. I had to convince him I had no intention of crossing the planes. I had to use another tactic to get us both close enough to Laeon's doorway.

And so, I used the one weapon every female has ever had since the beginning of time. The egotistical assumption that the female is always the weaker one, in physical strength, in mental capability, and above all else, in bravery. I played the victim flawlessly. Maybe once upon a time it wouldn't have been a performance. Maybe once upon a time I would have acted with genuine fear. But I'd made a promise to myself to never be a victim again, and besides, I wasn't the same person I once was.

I had to break first, and what is broken is never fully restored to its original version, but that's not always a bad thing.

There was no stark difference between Laeon and Earth, nothing that was noticeable immediately, at least. Beyond the line that joined the two planes was a wooded area, almost an extension of what lay on Earth, but it was so very quiet. No breeze, no sounds of nature, just silence. The air felt different, crisp and fresh as a winter's day but without the chill. There were no shifting weather patterns; there was no weather. The colors of everything were a shade darker, the bark of the trees, the green of the leaves, the lilac of the bluebells that sat in clumps between the tall evergreens. The night sky was dark blue, but the muted light from the moon touched everything, even the shadows radiated a dim light. Everything was constant, everything was still, everything felt new and untainted. Until our arrival at least, until the moment that I desecrated that peace and tranquility by holding hostage a creature composed of everything that Laeon was not.

I held Kerwin in a neck lock, one arm across his throat, my hand gripping the triceps of my other arm, securing his restraint. The hand of that arm clenched a fistful of his hair as I dragged him backward, farther into Laeon, decreasing the chances of him successfully escaping back to Earth's plane.

Laeon made him weak. He stumbled backward, shaking and gasping for air. When the thud of his heart slowed down and his breathing became raspy, I stopped.

We remained still, facing the entry. Waiting.

Even from a different plane I could feel them getting closer. I prayed they would experience far less of an effect than Kerwin had.

"It doesn't matter," Kerwin croaked through the silence. "I still win."

Time for some payback!

"How quickly you forget your first lessons," I whispered into Kerwin's ear.

"There is no god," he insisted.

"No one god," I corrected.

"You are not a god," he growled.

"The sacred trifecta. What is it to be pure, if not to be godlike," I murmured, enjoying the experience of antagonizing him. I was being unnecessarily cruel, a cat playing with a mouse, but I felt no guilt—an eye for an eye.

"Did you even bother to contemplate what that meant? The ramifications for bringing the three pure ones together. I underestimated you, Kerwin. You managed to do what I could not, what Magda could not, what Zagan could not. You got Aamon and Griffin to work together. You hotwired the engine, then stood in front of the fucking car, you imbecile."

"No," he stammered.

"Oh yes," I purred. "Even they don't know it yet. Unison was all it took to unlock our real power. How does it feel to know you hammered the nails into your own coffin?"

"You won't get away with this...My father will avenge me. My fathe—"

I cut him off, smothering a laugh at the feeble and pitiful depths of his desperation. "Really, you're relying on Daddy to fix your problems? I'm sorry, my mistake. I thought I was talking to a grown-ass man monster, not a child who has to run to Daddy for assistance."

"What's wrong, Alyssa? Jealous that I have a father, that I wasn't abandoned?" he retorted.

I laughed. "Really? You think I'm the one with daddy issues? I'm more of a man than you'll ever be. Instead of focusing on growing a pair of balls, maybe you should have tried to grow a pair of tits. Then you'd have had the courage to fight your own battles instead of scurrying off to Daddy dearest like an impotent fuckwit," I snarled.

"Maybe if your father had stuck around long enough to parent you, you would have kept your legs closed, maintained a relationship beyond an evening," he spluttered as my arm tightened around his neck.

"Ahh, what a poetic way of saying that you don't have consensual sex...ever." I glowered.

"There's a reason no man ever stayed with you," he choked, enraged and incapacitated almost beyond the ability to speak.

"You think I sought relationships? What am I, a character from *Little Women*? I got exactly what I sought. And besides, your theory is flawed. One stayed. Isn't that right, baby?" I spoke toward the doorway.

Aamon always did have impeccable timing.

I'm not sure what exactly he and Griffin were expecting as they leaped superhero-style into Laeon, but I'd wager me holding Kerwin hostage while trading catty insults definitely would not have made their predicted top ten.

They screeched to a halt, momentarily frozen in shock, both wearing bewildered and dumbfounded expressions as they surveyed the scene before them.

They both came, even believing it was a suicide mission, they still both came!

311

My heart skipped a beat.

Aamon was the first to speak, exclaiming, "Jesus fucking Christ!"

His eyes locked securely on mine, searching for reassurance that I was okay. I longed to wrap my arms around him, to kiss away his concerns. Kerwin gagged, fighting for breath as my muscles tensed involuntarily. I dragged my eyes away from Aamon's, fighting against every impulse in order to maintain control.

I was experiencing minimum physical and mental repercussions of crossing into Laeon. My thought processes felt a little sluggish, my darkness retained its force but remained contained deep within me, and there was a dull throbbing pain that radiated from the base of my skull down into my neck, but I was fully functional.

The effects on Aamon and Griffin, however, were much more severe.

They stumbled, disoriented, shocked at what was playing out before them. Their features darkened with anger as their eyes fell upon Kerwin. Each emitted an aura of confusion, relief, and vengeance intermingled with an obvious physical pain that this plane inflicted upon them. Although weakened, for now, they stood strong. I recognized immediately that standing literally shoulder to shoulder allowed their energies to support each other. But it would not last for long. With each passing moment, they were deteriorating.

I could feel their force, the combined strength and the power it generated. But it was the power of two, not the power of three. They were close enough that my presence could extend to them a degree of protection but far enough away that it would not last.

"Move closer," I hissed.

Griffin remained rooted to the spot. I understood his apprehension. When you're drowning, you don't dive deeper beneath the surface to search for air. But Aamon followed my request without hesitation. Blindly placing his absolute trust in me, he darted forward, yanking Griffin along with him.

"Kasey?" I rasped, wincing at the thought of what could have come to pass.

"He's safe." Aamon's voice was strong and resolute.

"They all are," Griffin added, his eyes flashing darker than I'd seen before.

That was all I needed to hear. Relief flooded through me, and with it came a force. As powerful as a hurricane-heated wind sweeping through a derelict house, blowing open every door as it departed, enabling every element to seep out, light and dark power emerging in unison, unrestrained, free.

I don't know what it was that shifted. Maybe it was the first time neither Aamon nor Griffin had been at each other's throats, maybe it was being in Laeon, maybe they had finally accepted what was and their final walls had fallen, but what started as a small glow, a ball of warm energy deep down somewhere beneath my heart, grew. The energy was scorching and strong, and they felt it too.

Kerwin fell silent.

The energy wafted between each of us, twisting and winding, amalgamating as each person's force came into contact with the next. The power was heavy but comforting, like a weighted blanket. At least, it was for me.

Aamon's eyes flashed dark and hot. He was controlling the proliferating surge of power but not without effort. He was in pain; I could feel it radiating from him like a white-hot flow of magma, thick, steady, and unrelenting.

Griffin was not experiencing physical pain, adding further credence to Magda's claims, but he was struggling in other ways. He was unraveling at an alarming rate. His eyes burned black, and his apprehension and fear were replaced with an inordinate amount of rage. He was drowning in an ocean of overwhelming emotions. Hostility and aggression bounced off him, and the grasp of his self-control lessened as his energy grew darker, intensifying with each passing moment.

A wisp of fear blew through me. I was afraid to remain, and afraid to leave, fearful of what awaited our exit from Laeon, afraid of the repercussions of snatching Kerwin from Earth.

But one thing was clear: Aamon and Griffin could not stay here. Kerwin had assumed their weakness would lead to their demise, but at this rate, it would be their power that would kill them.

"We need to leave," I said, my voice barely a whisper.

Aamon said nothing, but a glimmer of relief passed across his features. I wasn't the only one to notice.

"Maybe not." Griffin's voice was a low growl.

"He isn't leaving here alive," I said, pulling their attention back to Kerwin as my arm tightened across his neck.

"*No!*"

I jumped, startled by their tone and volume as they both screamed in unison.

"Don't." Aamon held his hands out toward me, imploring me to stop. "I'll take him. I'll do it in Daeon.

You can't do that here."

"You will not!" I snapped. Aamon was already walking a thin line with his humanity, like hell would I leave him to do my dirty work and risk losing him to Daeon completely.

"Then I'll kill him on Earth, or you can," Aamon bargained. His voice was quieter, his shoulders sagged, he was becoming weaker.

"You're not leaving here to do that," Griffin's voice boomed. He stood in front of me, folding his arms across his broad chest defiantly. Laeon's energy was now feeding him, not draining him. He had succumbed. Clearly, this was not such a great time for him to have opened the door to his power. The rational Griffin, the one of sound mind, was becoming a distant memory. Handing infinite power to an angry, slightly deranged being would probably not bode well for any of us.

"You all need to leave."

The unfamiliar voice came from somewhere behind us, belonging to someone who had managed to approach without being detected. We all jumped, turning quickly in the direction from where the words drifted.

The man stepped toward us, repeating, "You all need to leave." His gaze fell on Aamon and narrowed slightly. "You're stronger than last time," he mused.

He was as tall and broad as Aamon and Griffin but older. His eyes shone silver and bright. His energy was fearless, his words calm and spoken as a matter of fact.

I didn't know him; I didn't need to. I knew immediately who or rather what he was. He may have been unfamiliar, but his essence was overwhelmingly powerful, pure and identical to Magda's.

An Elder.

Griffin's face twisted in pain; did he know about Magda's death?

He stared intently at the man but didn't refuse his demand. Aamon swayed, fighting to stay on his feet. That was enough for me. I nodded humbly and grabbed Aamon's arm, pulling him and a barely conscious Kerwin roughly back toward Earth.

Griffin remained rooted to the spot. "I belong here." Like the elder, his voice remained calm, and his words were spoken passively.

The elder shook his head. "Not like this you don't. Come back without them, and we will help you to heal."

"I don't need to heal," he insisted.

"You need to heal more this time than you did last time," the elder responded.

Last time?

I turned from Griffin, pausing at the point of crossing. "Aamon, stay behind me," I begged. "They're waiting for you on the other side."

Despite his obvious pain and his inability to stand up straight, Aamon turned to me, flashing me a rare but breathtaking smile. "You're not the only one with a few surprises up your sleeve."

Before he could elaborate, two sets of arms reached across the space separating the planes and dragged him swiftly out of Laeon. Their image was distorted, but their energies I knew.

Birsha and Steven.

I crossed shakily, maintaining a vise-like grip on Kerwin.

The clearing was not as I had left it. The Sygans, all of Aamon's Sygans, had assembled, wiping out Kerwin's soldiers with ease, the remnants of which lay scattered around in the moonlight like a grotesque post-apocalyptic war scene.

Standing next to Birsha was Steven. Off to the side, looking somewhat out of place, stood Amelia and Noah. Amelia's eyes searched beyond us, no doubt looking for Griffin. I breathed a sigh of relief.

Only one thing left to do.

"I'll take him back to Daeon. I'll end him there," Aamon wheezed from his seated position on one of the large boulders; his eyes bore into mine, dark and intense like he could read my thoughts.

I shook my head.

My left arm was still clamped across Kerwin's throat. I pulled it back slightly, readjusting it so that my hand gripped the side of his head. I placed my other hand firmly on the other side of his head ready to break his neck; once his lifeless body hit the ground, I would run him through with the dagger. At least that was my intention.

But before I could snap anything, my feet left the ground. My momentary confusion was quickly replaced with terror as two huge hands snatched me abruptly back into Laeon.

Aamon roared, Kerwin's body hit the ground with a thud, shouts rang as I disappeared back across the opening.

"What the fuck are you doing, Griffin?" I gasped.

He held me tightly, my back against his chest, something cold and powerful pressed against my neck. I'd felt that power before, felt its pressure against my skin, felt it slice into me like a warm knife into butter.

"Really! You're going to kill me now? Here!" My panicked voice became a shriek.

"You're not leaving. I know what you want to do. I won't fucking let you become him," he hissed as he stepped backward, farther and farther into Laeon.

"Let her go!" Aamon's screams were thunderous, bouncing off every surface that surrounded us, causing the dense air to shudder and the ground to shift. He stumbled, disabled by Laeon's energy, but his darkness roared unrelenting.

Of course he had followed me!

This was not what nature intended—the forces turning on each other, energies flowing against the tide, the conflicted power churning wildly, edging beyond control, like a tsunami crossing paths with the ultimate riptide. Myself I could control, when it was just me, but when my power combined with theirs, that leash on my control started to slip from my grasp. I grabbed frantically at it, anxiously trying to pull it back to me, trying desperately to find my feet as I was dragged hopelessly along with the swell.

I had to make it stop. Someone had to break away, and Griffin had made damn sure it wouldn't be me.

"Aamon, go back!" I yelled, screaming to the beings on the other side, "Get him out of here!"

Aamon dropped to one knee, his burning eyes holding Griffin in an enraged glare.

"I'll do it. I'll kill her right now," Griffin insisted, pushing the dagger into my neck.

"No, you won't," Aamon rasped.

"I'll kill her, then I'll kill myself. I'd rather we both die than see her destroyed by you, damned by you, turned into some demonic whore by you," Griffin snarled.

I held my hands up in surrender. "Okay, Griffin, Aamon's leaving now. It's just us, and I'll do what you say."

The force from the dagger was making it hard to breathe, hard to speak, and even hard to think.

"No." Aamon lurched forward.

I stared at him, wide-eyed and unblinking, as I slowly reminded him, "You're not him. You don't control me—remember that."

He blinked, fighting against his urges and the oppressive weight of Laeon.

"For fuck's sake, Aamon, go! I'm choosing to stay. It's my choice, my free will."

He struggled to stand, staggering sideways as Noah and Steven crossed over.

"Get him out of here," I begged.

Noah stared open-mouthed at Griffin. "What are you doing?" he yelled, his voice breaking in disbelief.

"Leave," Griffin bellowed.

"Please, please, please, just go," I pleaded, fighting back tears.

"Alyssa…" Noah began.

"Go!"

Noah stumbled backward, failing to contain his tears as he, with Steven, heaved Aamon back across the opening, back to the Earthly plane.

For the longest time, I said nothing. I fought to catch my breath, fought to control the waves of nausea, and fought to quell my heart rate, the speed and ferocity of which was causing me physical pain.

"I know you must hate me," Griffin whispered.

"I'm not talking to you as long as you are holding a dagger to my fucking throat," I replied.

He loosened his grip, pulling the weapon from my neck and dropping his arms to his sides. I gingerly stepped away, just a little, and turned to face him.

His shoulders were slumped, but his eyes remained steadfast on mine. He believed he was doing the right thing; he had found some way of justifying his actions to align with the greater good, he was beyond reasoning with.

"Why can't you accept who I am, the real me?" I asked, my voice low.

"Why do you think that's who you are? Alyssa, I've seen the real you, the light and the good and the beautiful you, not this dark and twisted version he has turned you into."

"Do you know how long it took for me to accept me, the real me? For me to stop trying desperately to mold myself into something I am not, just to fulfill the unrealistic expectations of others?"

"You weren't always like this!" he argued.

"No, I wasn't, not entirely at least," I agreed. "But here's the thing, Griffin. You don't get through any existence without scars, not this life nor the last. There is no such thing as perfection. It isn't real. It doesn't exist. You choose to look at me with disgust. Well, fuck you. I carry every damaged little piece of me with pride. I won't try to hide any of it anymore. They are my scars, and it's my damage, and it maps my journey and my survival. I'm not shunning those parts of me anymore, and it isn't your place to shame me because of that. When did survival become something not to be celebrated? And for the record, you don't need to be okay with it. The only person who needs to be okay with it is me, and for the first time in any of my lives, I am!"

With furrowed brows, he watched me carefully but said nothing.

I continued, my voice remaining low and calm, "The real irony, Griffin, is that some of those scars that are too ugly for you are scars you gave me."

He flinched, tears welling in his eyes.

"You have scars too. You have damage, and I don't hate you because of it. It pains me to see you hate yourself because of it."

"I hated what I was," he whispered hoarsely.

"So you changed to become a better version of you, but you can still do that and accept every part of who you are. You aren't defined by one element, by one era. No one stays the same. Don't you think a part of me grieves for the person I was?" I asked, brushing away tears with the back of my hand. "Those parts of you don't make you evil. They make you strong."

"I'm broken," he mumbled, using the words I'd used to Aamon what seemed like a long time ago.

"We're all broken, but broken isn't always ugly. Broken can be beautiful," I murmured softly.

I felt Amelia's pain as she entered Laeon, felt the huge life force that was Noah, and, in sharp comparison, felt the tightly wound angst of Seraphina, who remained firmly at the opening. Such contradicting energies working together was bizarre.

"It's time to go, Griff." Noah placed one hand on Griffin's shoulder, squeezing it slightly.

"This is all just too much. You need time. We all just need to go home," Amelia agreed, her voice trembling. She gently slipped the dagger from Griffin's palm, handing it behind him toward me. My confused gaze met hers, and she nodded just once. Without further hesitation, I grabbed the dagger, stuffing it down the back of my jeans. Its smooth metal pressed cold against my skin. I moved toward the doorway as they tenderly led Griffin out of Laeon.

I was feet away from the opening when my step faltered, when the wisp of what would be drifted through the air, dissipating quickly into the ethos of Laeon. An invisible finger traced the outline of my spine, leaving an icy trail of dread in its wake. I could see it in Seraphina's eyes. Her purpose was not to guide them out but to prevent them from reentering once they passed over the threshold. I could feel it in the energy emanating from Aamon, so powerful it traversed across planes. He would not let Griffin return home; he would kill him as soon as he stepped back onto Earth's plane.

And it would destroy him. And Noah, and Amelia, and Steven.

Collateral damage for Griffin's breakdown.

I spun quickly. "Leave now. Tell them he is staying here under the care of the elders. Go!" I hissed to a baffled Noah and Amelia.

I ran at Griffin hard, sending him and me flying through the air, ripping him from the supporting arms of Noah and Amelia.

We landed hard on the ground, me on top of him.

"What are you…" Griffin stammered, confused at what could have brought about my sudden freak-out.

"Run, into Laeon now," I begged, scrambling to my feet and pulling him up with me. I could feel Seraphina's movements. She had stepped farther into Laeon, ready to pursue him, but she would not make it to us quickly, and when she did, she would be too weak to pose any real threat.

An angry expression flashed across Griffin's face. "You think I'm going to run away from him?" he spat.

"No, I think you're going to take action to save me, to save a man you once considered a brother, and to protect your family. If you don't want to heal for you, then do it for them."

I stood in front of him, anxiety coursing through my veins. "This is me, begging you, Griffin. Tell me what I need to do. What do you need me to do to get you to save yourself?" I yelled at him.

"Like fuck will I let him win!" he bellowed.

"Win what? Take a look around, Griffin. There's no one winning here!"

He glanced at me, raised one eyebrow, and started to speak, when I hissed, "I swear if you even think about implying that I'm something to be fucking won, I will punch your damn face!"

He closed his mouth and stubbornly folded his arms across his chest.

We were running out of time.

I saw the movement behind him. The man from before stood patiently waiting. But it had to be Griffin's choice, free will even when he was on the cusp of losing all rational functioning.

I grabbed his shirt with both hands and yanked the stubborn idiot roughly toward me, pressing my lips against his, and it worked, igniting his passion and extinguishing his anger and his defiance. He kissed me hard, his tongue caressed my mouth, and his arms pulled my body into his, and I let him.

I let him until his heartbeat steadied, and the heat of his fury ran cold, until there was nothing else there but us.

Then I pulled gently away.

His eyes locked on mine, heated by something other

than anger, warmed with his interpretation of victory. Maintaining his gaze, he backed slowly away.

Chapter 24

The walk out was slow. My head was in turmoil, and the thoughts that bounced around it were conflicting. That serpent of self-loathing had slithered its way back in. I'd done what I had to do, what felt right in that moment, but it left a bitter aftertaste. The only lips I wanted to taste were Aamon's, and I couldn't shake the notion of betrayal. It wasn't even the kiss. It was the actions that protected Griffin from Aamon that stabbed at my conscience, although in truth at the time, I had been just as concerned about saving Aamon from doing something I knew in my heart he would regret, maybe not now, but certainly at some point in the future.

As I stepped back across the line of convergence, all activity ceased. I felt like a stranger walking into a locals-only bar. Tumbleweeds could have drifted past, it felt that uncomfortable. Aamon stood in the center of the clearing. His dark gaze, brooding and intense, sought me out.

We walked to each other, meeting somewhere in the middle. I opened my mouth to speak, and he placed a finger upon my lips, silencing me. He tilted my chin upward and kissed me. Oh God, the feeling of his lips on mine, like that first sip of wine after detox. I craved him more than I had ever craved anything before in my life. He awakened an energy deep within me. Powerful warm waves lifted me above the ground, carrying me high, then dropping me low, and my stomach lurched like I was riding a coaster. He pulled away gently and nodded to Zagan, who signaled the mass of Sygans to retreat. Only his core people hung back, a respectful distance along the tree line, looking in any direction but ours.

"You saved him," he said, a half smile playing on his lips.

"I don't know enough to know if it was the right choice. I do know there's a history between the two of you, and to hate someone as much as you despise him, there must have been a strong relationship there at some point. I don't want you to do anything you'll regret. I don't want to do anything I will regret either," I admitted.

"Maybe you made the right choice. I can't see beyond blind fury for what he did to you, and I'm not sure I would ever want to."

"He stayed?" Amelia's voice carried across the clearing. Her eyes darted between me and the entrance to Laeon.

"Well, I didn't kill him if that's what you're worried about!" I retorted, the words coming out harsher than I had intended.

"I wasn't saying that!" Amelia protested, her voice barely a whisper.

"It's the right place for him," Steven agreed, approaching me tentatively. He glanced at Aamon before grasping my hand. "Alyssa, I just need to know that you're okay?"

I flung my arms around his neck. "I promise you I am. But, Steven, are you?" I whispered into his ear.

He squeezed me tightly. "I think so, but I guess time will tell."

Kerwin was bound and restrained by Birsha at the

end of the trail that led down to the lodge. I had paid no attention to him. I knew Aamon's intentions were to kill him. I was surprised to see him still alive. There was no reason, aside from the potential of using him as leverage should the need have arisen. But whether Aamon intended to kill him on Earth or in Daeon was irrelevant. It would still be another step toward the demise of his humanity, one step closer to severing the delicate strand he retained to pass freely between planes. Eventually, his body count would leave him bound to Daeon. Come hell or high water, I would not allow that to happen.

Dawn was approaching; the sky had shifted from shades of black to inky blue. We started to file out from the clearing, making our way back down the mountainside, back to whatever our new normality may be. I hung back slightly, waiting until only Birsha, Aamon, and Kerwin remained.

I passed by Birsha and Kerwin without extending either a second glance. As my foot landed directly in front of Kerwin, I pulled the dagger from my waistband and drove it swiftly into his gut, pulling it sharply upward in one fluid movement. The entire time my eyes remained forward, my pace did not falter, and my feet passed by before his guts could soil my shoes.

I wiped the blood from the dagger off on my jeans and with a flick of my wrist spun the blade upward, grasping the handle in my palm as the flat side of the dagger rested flush against my forearm. The scar beneath the metal surface tingled upon contact with it. The sensation of a million tiny pins pushed from within my arm, like a piece of it had been left behind, trapped below skin that healed too quickly.

Kerwin made no sound as he crumpled to the ground

with a soft thud.

Birsha flinched and stepped back in shock, turning to Aamon with a questioning look.

Ahead of us, Amelia, Steven, and Noah paused midstride. Their muscles tensed, but they did not turn around. They didn't need their eyes to see. They knew the instant it happened what had occurred and at whose hand. Their pause was brief, then they continued silently on with slumped shoulders and downcast eyes.

Aamon remained half a step behind me. His warm dark energy encased me, eradicating the last residues of my Laeon-inflicted numbness, bringing me back to life, or whatever the hell this existence was.

We arrived back at the lodge.

Many had departed immediately after winning the battle. Only a few remained as we entered, and even they were on their way out of the door. They bundled into dark SUVs and with screeching tires sped away from the remote structure, leaving one car and us.

Just us.

I walked up the wide staircase, my mind reliving the past twenty-four hours in fast-forward mode. With each step that I took, the enormity of what had happened, of what I had done, blossomed and grew inside of me, twisting and creeping like a dog-strangling vine, suffocating me and making my legs feel as heavy as lead. Aamon's gaze followed my every step.

I reached the top of the stairs and made my way through the first room, dragging myself into the bathroom and over to the bathtub. I turned the shower on and set the temperature to hot. I peeled away my clothes, dropping them to the floor, and stepped sluggishly beneath the stream of water.

Then I broke.

Despite the scalding temperature, I shivered uncontrollably. My diaphragm heaved and rattled as sobs burst from me, uncontrolled and painful.

I felt him as he entered the room, surveying the scene briefly before stepping quickly into the shower. He stood behind me and pulled me toward him, his drenched clothing sticking to his body, and without saying a word he held me, tightly. His huge hands, warm against my wet skin, reduced my shivers and comforted my shakes.

His body took my weight when my legs failed me. His energy soothed my hysteria and absorbed my pain. He didn't try to silence me, patiently riding alongside me till my breathing steadied and my sobs subsided.

He turned off the water and wrapped me in one of the oversized towels, scooping me up effortlessly and carrying me from the bathroom, through the bedroom, and up the next flight of stairs to his room. He placed me gently on the bed. I attempted to sit up, expecting him to tend to himself, to leave to change into dry clothing, but instead he pushed me down, not allowing me to do anything for myself.

He took the towel and used it to gently stroke my skin, drying every inch of my body with meticulous attention, rubbing lotion into my skin and massaging my muscles, each action carried out with affection and care.

And then he dressed me, showering me with a thousand tiny kisses as he did.

When he was done, he pulled me gently into a seated position, undressing and redressing brazenly in front of me. I watched him, studied each curve, the contour of each muscle, each dark patch of hair, each scar, and the pattern of each tattoo, every element that went into the artwork that was him.

With a small smile, he tugged me to my feet and led me downstairs. He pushed aside the array of chairs surrounding the large stone fireplace on the first floor and tossed blankets and cushions down, creating a nest of comfort. He lit the fire and disappeared briefly, returning with a bottle of wine and glasses. The doors to the deck were open, allowing a cool breeze to carry the scent of conifers and spruce through the air into the room.

And before the roaring fire, between sips of a velvety rich cabernet, he shared with me his past.

Part of it I knew. Whispered confessions through the darkness from Griffin. I had just failed to realize the "us" Griffin had referred to related to him and Aamon.

They were the friends in London so many years ago that Griffin had spoken of. A relationship that transcended friendship, that became a brotherhood. They worked together, they ran together, they survived together, they died together. They remained on this plane together, their drive for vengeance identical and deep seated.

Their passing was not peaceful. They entered their next existence with anger and hatred. Too preoccupied to comprehend the power their passing had bestowed upon them and the significance of such dominance.

Aamon refused to enter Daeon, raging that he wanted revenge for what had been done to both of them. Griffin refused to enter Laeon, as he didn't think that he could be redeemed for his transgressions. In addition, he would not abandon Aamon to what he believed was purgatory. They both remained on Earth but walked between Earth and Daeon, slowly losing their humanity.

They ruled the gateways and Daeon. Aamon excelled as a leader, but the stronger one was Griffin, until he started to reject his power. His mental health spiraled, and he broke down, rebelling in his own twisted and berserk way against what he had become. He killed Sygans, repulsed by them and more so by himself. When his actions came to light, Aamon was forced to intervene to prevent Griffin from being killed by his former followers as retribution for the murder of his own kind.

They argued and they fought. Aamon did the only thing he could to keep him alive. He took him to Laeon, knowing this was where he was meant to be, knowing that turning against it was what was damaging him, and knowing it was the only place of safety from the Sygans that hunted him.

Aamon almost died crossing over. Griffin was unconscious and saw none of Aamon's sacrifice. All he knew was that they had fought and argued, and he woke up in Laeon. He viewed Aamon's actions as betrayal. Magda nursed him back to health, guided him down a different path, and helped him to embrace an alternative way of life.

When Griffin finally left Laeon, Aamon commissioned round-the-clock security, unbeknownst to Griffin, to protect him from the Sygans that still hunted him. Knowing they would persevere until their objective was met, Aamon had little option but to kill them, with each death condemning him further into the darkness.

Magda remained in close contact with Griffin. She warned him of the coming of one with a soul even purer than his. She also warned Aamon. At that time, Magda believed there would be two souls. She didn't realize one person could possess both purities. No one did.

331

Griffin and Aamon met with Magda and reluctantly agreed to work together for the greater good. But I had passed earlier than expected, and my purity was so potent it was initially unrecognizable, which kept it concealed and protected me. Plus, the mixture of both light and dark energies within me had conflicted with what was expected.

"You were quite the paradox," he murmured softly, his lips brushing against my hair as my head rested against his chest.

"What now?" I asked, pulling myself up to a seated position next to Aamon.

"We exist. We fulfill what fate intended. We do it together. You stay my forever."

"And Griffin? Do you know what will happen to him?"

Aamon's jaw clenched. "Oh, I'm sure he'll resume his role of being the biggest pain in my ass at some point. We are two very different people. I stopped knowing him a long time ago and that suits me. As long as I can restrain myself from killing him, I'm sure he'll be just fine."

I tried unsuccessfully to smother a laugh at Aamon's reaction.

He raised one brow. "Are you laughing at me?" His eyes flashed like black glowing embers, and his deep voice growled, making me laugh even more. In a flash Aamon twisted his body, pushing me down and pinning me to the ground with his torso. "You laughed at me?" he baited.

I squirmed against him, making him inhale abruptly. The moment his guard dropped, I pushed sharply against one shoulder, freeing enough space to roll from under him. In one swift motion, I swung one leg over him as he rolled onto his back, straddling him and holding him beneath me.

He gave a deep and throaty laugh, pushed himself up to a seated position, and pulled me even closer, raining light kisses down my neck, pulling me into ecstasy.

Tomorrow could wait for the time being. The uncertainty of what it would bring did not matter, not on this night. This night was ours. Because that was all you ever really got, regardless of what life you were living, what existence you were granted. The past might shape you. The future might compel you. But the only one true absolute is the here and now, and what you make of it is the only thing you can ever really control.

So for now, this is how it ends, for today at least.

From the other side, with love.

A word about the author…

Julia Harrison was born in London and grew up in the Northwest of England. She is a graduate of Liverpool John Moores University and mother to three sons and one daughter. She moved to the USA in 2016 and currently resides in Florida with her husband, their younger children, and a variety of rescue pets.

Learn more about Julia Harrison at
https://juliaharrisonauthor.com/
https://www.facebook.com/people/Julia-Harrison-Author/61574650037279/
https://www.instagram.com/authorjulia.harrison/
https://bsky.app/profile/juliasharrison.bsky.social